P9-DIW-810
B 11-15

RANDOM
HOUSE
LARGE
PRINT

Precious Gifts

Also by Danielle Steel
Available from Random House Large Print

Betrayal
Country
First Sight
Friends Forever
A Good Woman
Happy Birthday
Hotel Vendome
One Day at a Time
Pegasus
A Perfect Life
Power Play
Prodigal Son
The Sins of the Mother
Undercover
Until the End of Time
Winners

DANIELLE STEEL

Precious Gifts

A Novel

RANDOM HOUSE
LARGE PRINT

Precious Gifts is a work of fiction. Names, characters, places, and incidents are the products of the author's imagination or are used fictitiously. Any resemblance to actual events, locales, or persons, living or dead, is entirely coincidental.

Published in the United States of America by Random House Large Print in association with Delacorte Press, an imprint of Random House, a division of Penguin Random House LLC, New York.

Cover design by Lynn Andreozzi
Cover photograph by © Ben Anderson Photography

The Library of Congress has established a cataloging-in-publication record for this title.

ISBN: 978-0-8041-9497-6

www.randomhouse.com/largeprint

FIRST LARGE PRINT EDITION

Printed in the United States of America

10 9 8 7 6 5 4 3 2 1

is Large Print Edition published in
d with the standards of the N.A.V.H.

To my wonderful, loving children,
Beatie, Trevor, Todd, Nick,
Sam, Victoria, Vanessa, Maxx, and Zara,
you are the brightest stars in my heavens,
you are my hope, my dreams,
my most cherished memories,
my source of love and laughter,
you are my joy . . . my life.

With all my heart and love,
Mommy/d.s.

To John,
For our wonderful children, the happy years, the best years of my life, and the memories I will treasure forever, and so many gifts.

With all my love,
Olive

And in loving memory
of Sammy Ewing,
beloved friend, special boy,
you will be so greatly missed!
Forever in our hearts,
dance on among the stars!

With my love always,
"Black Mom"

Precious Gifts

Chapter 1

Timmie Parker sat with one leg tucked under her at her desk. As the stress of the morning increased, she had shoved her long blond hair into a rubber band, and by noon there were four pencils and a pen stuck through it. She wore a clean but wrinkled plaid shirt with the sleeves rolled up, over a tank top, torn jeans, and high-top Converse, and no makeup. She had the tall, lean, elegant frame of her father. She was six feet tall in bare feet, twenty-nine years old, and had a master's in social work from Columbia. She was currently working for a foundation whose mission was to find free or low-cost housing for eligible members of the homeless population of New York, and she'd been at her desk since six o'clock that morning trying to catch up on work. There was a mountain of files on her desk. And she would have liked to find a place to live for every single one, and knew that if she was lucky and continued pounding on government agencies and other resources they used, she'd find a home for one or two who were eligible. The word "eligible" was used as a catch-all phrase to filter out all those who needed it most.

It was a sweltering July day, and as usual her air conditioner wasn't working. She could already tell it was going to be one of those days where nothing worked quite the way she wanted it to, and she'd be delivering bad news to some of her most desperate clients. Heartbreak was her stock in trade. She lived in a permanent state of outrage over the injustices in the system, and how ineffective it was to help her clients. Helping the homeless had been her passion since her teens. She was a dedicated and deeply caring though often angry person. Her tirades over social issues at the dinner table in her youth had been frequent. And she had spent all the years since trying to do something about it. Above all, Timmie Parker wasn't a quitter—she worked tirelessly for those she served. And once she found them housing, she stuck with them. Once they were isolated in tiny government-owned efficiency apartments, without the support system they had come to rely on in the streets, loneliness, despair, and suicide became serious risks.

Timmie had a hundred great ideas about how to make things work better, but there was never enough money or support teams. Poverty programs had been slashed in the economic crisis, private foundation funds were dwindling, too, and no one in government would listen. Timmie felt like she was emptying the ocean with a thimble, as she watched her clients slip through the cracks, waiting a year or more to enter free detox programs or qualify for a place to live. The women fared worse than the men on the streets and were often victims of violent crimes in shelters. She faced miles of red tape every day, trying to help people fill out forms for disability benefits or ID cards. Her soft spot was always teens, but it was easier to refer them to youth programs around the city, and they were more resourceful about surviving on the streets. Timmie had already seen six clients by noon that day and had a dozen more to see that afternoon. She rarely left the office before eight or nine p.m. and sometimes stayed till midnight, and came in long before office hours began every day. Her work was her life, and for now it was all she wanted.

She'd lived with a man in grad school, who had cheated on her with her best friend. And she had been engaged to another man after that, who cheated on her, too, though at least not with someone she knew. She'd broken up with him and since then had poured all her love, passion, and energy into her work, and hadn't dated anyone for the past two years. She often said that the women in her family were unlucky. Her younger sister Juliette had an unfailing weakness for losers. They sponged off her for as long as they could, took advantage of her gentleness and kindness, and eventually, after getting everything they could out of her, dumped her for someone else. And the only one surprised by it was her sister, who would cry over it for months, and then find another one just as bad.

Her mother, Véronique, had spent the twenty years after her divorce being loving and supportive of their charming, handsome father, who had been a cheater, too. She had discovered that he had been unfaithful to her during their entire marriage, which ended over a twenty-three-year-old supermodel. He had had a trail of beautiful girls ever since, while Véronique made excuses for him, and said things like "you know how your father is." Timmie knew all too well how their father was, and she had finally come to the conclusion that all men were the same. Charming, often handsome, and rarely honest, they cheated and lied and used women. She had never been close to her father because of it, and was horrified to discover that the men she got involved with were no different, although never as charming and handsome as her father, who was a master at the seduction game. Few women could resist him. He could charm the proverbial birds off the trees, a characteristic she had come to hate. She hated charming men, and her mother and sisters accused her of hating all men. She didn't, she insisted, just the liars and cheaters, and the men who seemed to fall for her. She instantly assumed there was something wrong with them if they wanted to be with her.

Only their youngest sister, Joy, had avoided the same fate. She had always been their father's favorite, because she was so beautiful, and looked just like their mother, who was still beautiful at fifty-two. Both Véronique and Joy had thick dark hair, porcelain-white skin, and violet eyes, although Joy was taller than their mother and had modeled in college. Since she was old enough to talk, she had always managed to wrap their father around her little finger and get anything she wanted from him, but she kept her distance from them all. Joy was the most independent, and stayed aloof from the men in her life, too. It was easy to see that she was afraid to get hurt. She was always getting involved with men who lived on the opposite coast, or who were as focused on their careers as she was, so she could keep them at arm's length. They all seemed to adore her but were never around.

Timmie liked to point out that none of them had decent relationships, which she attributed to what she called "the family curse." In her opinion, their father had condemned them to a fatal attraction to the wrong men. It was a part of her that she hadn't been able to change so far and now no longer tried. She had too much else on her plate, and finding housing for her clients was a lot more important to her than meeting the right guy. At this point, she didn't really care.

The phone rang on her desk, between clients, and she was in a rush to see the people waiting for her. She thought of letting it go to voice mail but didn't want to miss a call from a client in distress, or any of the housing agencies she had contacted that morning by phone and e-mail, so sounding stressed, she picked it up.

"Timmie Parker," she said tersely, in an official voice. She wasn't a warm, fuzzy person, although she had a good heart, as witnessed by her job.

"Hi, Timmie. Arnold," the caller announced himself, and a chill ran down her spine. The voice at the other end was instantly familiar. It was Arnold Sands, her father's attorney and closest friend. She had known him since she was a child. Her father had been very ill for the past year, after a stroke left him incapacitated and in a nursing home. She had seen him two weeks before, and he had drifted in and out of consciousness, while she sat there silently, watching him and holding his hand. His left side was paralyzed, and it was painful to see him so diminished. He had always been vital and looked years younger than he was, until the stroke. He had been slowly slipping away for the past year, at eighty. And despite her disapproval of his lifestyle for most of her life, it was still comforting to know she had a father, and there was always the secret, unspoken, magical belief that one day they could turn things around and have an honest relationship, and he would magically become someone she could admire and count on. She knew that was never going to happen, but as long as he was alive, she clung to that hope. He had never been there for anyone, not for her, her mother, or her sisters. Her mother had forgiven him for it. Timmie never had.

"I'm sorry to call you at work," Arnold said, sounding serious, and Timmie sensed instantly what was coming.

"Dad?"

"He slipped away quietly last night." They all knew it had been inevitable, and it had taken longer than they thought. Juliette had gone to see him several times a week, Joy hadn't visited him in two months—she lived in L.A. and was busy and seemed to have the hardest time facing him in that condition. She did everything she could to avoid it. Timmie had gone to see him every few weeks, although she hated doing it. And their mother had seen him a month before, in June, before she left for the summer in the South of France. Véronique had rented a house near St. Tropez for two months, and she had spent a day with Paul before she left, and had confessed to Timmie that she was afraid it might be the last time she'd see him, but she said that they'd said everything they needed to say. She didn't tell her daughter, but Paul had apologized to her for his many failings as a husband, and even as a friend, and she had been at peace when she left. She had come to terms with all of it many years before. Twenty years since they'd been married was a long time, and Véronique was a forgiving person. She wasn't bitter about the end of their marriage, or the reasons it had ended, or even the enormous settlement she had given him, which he had been squandering on other women and his comfortable lifestyle and excessive luxuries ever since. The settlement hadn't hurt Véronique financially, nor the girls. They had depended on their mother when they were younger and never on him.

"Have you told my mother yet?" Timmie asked quietly. She had expected this news sooner or later, though not precisely on that day. When it would happen had been hard to predict.

"I wanted to call you first. I didn't know if you'd want to tell your mother and the girls. She'll probably want to make the arrangements," he said accurately. There had been no serious woman in their father's life since Véronique, who had remained close to him. There had been a never-ending parade of girls since the divorce, younger than his daughters in recent years, all of whom had disappeared in the months since he'd been sick. He didn't date the kind of women who would stick around when things got rough, and he could no longer write them checks. Even at eighty, he had had a heavy dating life, with women who were still dazzled by him, just as Véronique had been at twenty-one, when he was forty-nine. His looks, charm, and elegance were almost impossible to resist. Even the nurses at the nursing home talked about what a handsome man he was. Timmie had inherited his looks, but she was nothing like him in any other way. She was solid, dependable, hard-working, and trustworthy.

"I'll call Mom in a couple of hours," Timmie said practically. "I have to see two clients first. Can you call the girls? They're expecting it, it won't come as a surprise." But even she had to admit she was sad. It was finally done, the game was over. The father who had never really been a father to them was gone. And she found she had mixed feelings about it, and felt the impact of the loss, and she was sure her sisters would, too. It would be hard for their mother. He had been an empty figurehead, but Véronique had loved him, in one form or another, as husband, brother, friend, for thirty-one years. He had become almost a father to her in recent years, and was certainly old enough to be. And she had mothered him, particularly once he was sick. It was a relationship Timmie had never fully understood. It seemed painfully inadequate to her, especially for her mother, but it seemed to work for them.

There had been a bad phase when his blatant affair with the famous model had ended their marriage. And a worse phase after that when Véronique discovered that the model was not his first affair. But somehow after the divorce, she had forgiven him enough for them to become friends, and maintain a bond that had lasted for twenty years, and proved to be more durable than their marriage. Véronique said she did it for the children. But Timmie always felt that they did it for them, out of their own need for each other.

"I'll tell the girls not to call your mother, until

they hear from you," Arnold said with a sigh. He was going to miss his old friend, and already had for the past year, since the stroke that had left him so impaired and suddenly seeming old, which was so unlike the man he had known.

"Thank you, Arnold," Timmie said quietly. "I'll be in touch." She thanked him again and hung up. She sat in her chair for a moment, looking out at the grim street of lower Harlem, where her office was located. There were children playing in a fire hydrant outside. Her mind drifted backward in time for a moment, remembering what a hero she had thought him as a child, until the divorce, when he had all but disappeared from their lives.

She had been nine when her parents divorced. There had been sweet moments after that, during holidays, cameo appearances at birthdays or on Christmas, when he would sweep in like the glamorous figure he was. He was like a beautiful bird in flight, with splendid plumage. You could never quite catch up to him, but only admire him in the sky, as he disappeared once again, and you never knew when he'd reappear, and even then only when it suited him. He defined narcissism. He wasn't a bad man, just a totally self-centered one, and a lousy father. His children had paid a price for it till the day he died—she, in her deep distrust of men like him, and all of them in their unconscious attraction to men who were similar to him. Juliette, who collected losers and users. And Joy in her fear of abandonment and disappointment, which kept her from getting too attached to any man. She was still young, she might still get it right. But Timmie was convinced by now that she and her sister Juliette never would. The die had been cast, and their habits and belief patterns had taken hold. It was hard to change.

She stood up and went around her desk to open her office door. There were two people sitting in the waiting room, expecting to see her. She smiled at both of them, asked the man to wait for a few minutes, and ushered the woman in. She was younger than Timmie, had matted hair and no teeth. She had been on the streets for three years and had a long history of drugs. She had three children in foster care and was carrying all her belongings with her, a filthy sleeping bag and two garbage bags full of clothes. She was waiting to get into a detox program. Timmie had bad news for her. They were shutting the facility down, and she'd have to start at the bottom of the list somewhere else, which could take another two years. Their situation seemed so hopeless.

Timmie sat down across the desk from her, to tell her the news. And as she did, she thought of her father, and how ridiculous, self-centered, and wasted his life had been compared to her clients. He had never done anything for anyone, except himself and, briefly, the women he went out with. His had been a life of total self-indulgence, which was part of why Timmie worked as hard as she did. The one thing she had always known growing up was that she never wanted to be anything like him. She wasn't, and now he was gone. She focused on her client then, and tried to forget her father, for an hour or two at least, until she had to call her mother and tell her that Paul had died. As the oldest of Véronique's three daughters, the hard jobs always fell to her. Juliette was never up to them. And Joy had abdicated with her very separate life in L.A.

When Arnold called Juliette at her tiny sandwich shop and bakery in the Park Slope area of Brooklyn, she was right in the middle of the lunch rush that happened every day. Her shop, Juliette's Kitchen, had been a hit since she opened it three years before. At her mother's urging, she had majored in art history, and had gotten a master's degree at the Sorbonne, only to discover, when she took classes at the Cordon Bleu in Paris "just for fun" when she finished, that baking was her passion. She made sandwiches on the irresistible croissants she baked fresh every day, and she also sold cookies, cakes, and pastries from recipes she had found in France. And her plans to become a curator at a museum, or to teach, went out the window after the Cordon Bleu. She was never happier than in the kitchen, peering into an oven, serving a mug of steaming coffee to an elderly customer, or pouring a cup of hot chocolate smothered in whipped cream for a child. It satisfied all her needs to nurture people, and her little sandwich shop had done very well. After a lot of discussion and some serious thought, her mother had lent her the money to start it, although she'd been very disappointed at Juliette's abandoning her career in art. Véronique was still hoping Juliette would get over her baking passion one day. At twenty-eight, she was still young. Véronique wanted a more interesting and intellectual career for her than a sandwich shop, and Véronique had always loved the idea that Juliette had inherited her own passion for art, and Véronique's father's. It was in their blood. But Juliette had given up art for her croissants. And in the end, her mother helped her with the loan.

Juliette was the softer, smaller version of her older sister Timmie. They were only a year apart and had been like twins growing up. But they were as different in character as night and day. Timmie and Juliette were green-eyed like their father, and Juliette had always been slightly overweight, but pretty anyway. Timmie was taller and thinner, Juliette shorter and rounder, with a womanly figure that had gotten bigger as she sampled her baking to test the recipes, and she had a spectacular bosom that Timmie always teased her about. She had long blond hair like Timmie, but hers had hung in a mass of ringlets as a child and was wavy now. Her hair was fair and natural and she looked beautiful when she wore it down, which she couldn't do when she worked. She wore it in a braid down her back, with a haze of soft curls that always sprang loose around her face. Everything about Juliette was welcoming and warm, and she'd had a motherly quality even as a young girl. She wanted to take care of everyone. Timmie always said she collected all the lame ducks in the world, particularly if they were men.

All of Juliette's romances had begun because the men she got involved with needed a place to stay, money, or a job. They slept on her couch initially, wound up in her bedroom, and eventually wended their way into her bank account, where they indulged themselves for a while with Juliette's help, and then after she had spoiled them liberally, they dumped her for someone else. According to Timmie, it had happened too often by now to be an accident—it was a pattern, and a bad habit. Juliette always managed to find handsome men like their father, who took advantage of her. There hadn't been a good one in the lot so far, and they usually stuck around for about six months until they moved on. Juliette would cry for a while, take solace in her work, invent a few new recipes, and gain a few more pounds. Then some other guy in need with a broken wing would come along. She was a beautiful, appealing girl and never alone for very long, unlike Timmie, who had been alone by choice now for two years, angry at the mistakes she'd made.

Juliette was willing to forgive everyone, including herself, and never seemed to learn. But the only one she ever hurt was herself. The strongest facet of her personality was how kind she was to everyone, her customers, her family, and her men.

She had just finished serving one of her regular customers when Arnold called. Unlike Timmie, who was unfailingly practical and seemed to take everything in stride, he knew Juliette would be deeply upset and he hated telling her. And predictably, as soon as he told her that her father had died the night before, she burst into sobs. The last customer of the rush at lunch had just left, and she was alone for a few minutes, as she dissolved in tears.

She had considered herself the closest to her father, because she was willing to do anything to win his love. According to Juliette, he could do no wrong. Even before he got sick, she called him every day to tell him what she was doing and ask how he was. He had been to her sandwich shop/bakery only once, and she acted as though he came all the time. It never dawned on her that her daily phone calls with her father were always placed by her. He never called any of his daughters and stayed out of contact with them for weeks or months until they called him. Every relationship he had was one-sided, with the effort being made by the other person. Neither Timmie nor Joy expended much energy on it, but Juliette did. She even dropped off her best baked goods at his house, so he could taste her new recipes. She was desperate for him to approve of her.

Paul Parker didn't disapprove of any of them and was proud of his beautiful daughters. He just didn't want to play the role of a father and all it entailed. And as they grew older, he preferred to be their friend. They never had that confusion of roles with their mother, who always made it clear that she was their mother, not their friend, although she loved spending time with them. It was Véronique who had had full responsibility for them growing up, but Juliette still insisted that she was close to her father. As Arnold had expected, she took the news of her father's death hard, almost as though she hadn't realized for the past year that he was going to die. For the others, it came as no surprise. For Juliette, it did.

"I thought he'd pull out of it," she said as she wiped her eyes on her apron, and Arnold sighed. There had been no hope of it for the past many months, while Paul went steadily downhill. And even in the last weeks, when he had been so seldom awake, she had talked to him when she visited him, convinced that he could hear her and would rally again. He never did, and Arnold thought it was a mercy that he had died. The Paul he knew and had been friends with for thirty years wouldn't have wanted to live in the condition he was in. Paul had been so vital and alive that to see him that way saddened Arnold as his friend. It was better for Paul this way, and in their many conversations over the past year, Arnold knew that Paul was ready to die and had no regrets about his life. But Juliette was clearly not ready to let go of her father, or her illusions about him. She was still crying after twenty minutes when he tried to get off the phone.

"Timmie said she'd call your mother in a couple of hours, so don't call her yet," Arnold warned her.

"I won't," Juliette said obediently, and after she hung up, she went to the door of the shop and turned the "open" sign around to "closed." She went to make a sign then, and taped it to the door: "Closed due to death in the family." And then she walked home to her one-bedroom apartment four blocks away. She never paid much attention to decorating it—all she did was sleep there, and the rest of the time she was at work. She arrived at the bakery at four o'clock every morning, to bake all her breakfast goods for her first customers, who arrived at six, and she was usually there until seven p.m., when she went home and fell asleep in front of the television for several hours, exhausted from the long day. Like Timmie's, her life centered entirely on work.

By the time Juliette got home that afternoon, Arnold was calling Joy, the youngest sister. She was harder to reach, as he had expected her to be, and had a very different life. Joy lived in L.A., where she had been pursuing an acting career. She had a real musical talent, and her mother had wanted her to go to Juilliard to develop it. Instead, Joy had dropped out of college at the first opportunity and headed for L.A. She took voice lessons that she paid for herself, worked as a waitress, and after six months of singing with bands that were going nowhere, she switched to acting lessons, and had been struggling to make it ever since. She had done a few minor commercials and bit parts on TV. She was hoping to get a part in a series, and had a knack for comedy. At twenty-six, she was still working as a waitress and had been in L.A. for five years. Her big break hadn't come yet, but she still believed it would. And her father had believed it, too, and always encouraged her.

She was a spectacularly beautiful girl with long, dark hair, huge violet eyes, an incredible figure, and a great singing voice she rarely used. She took every acting job she could get. She went to every audition and was willing to endure all the hardships of a budding acting career. She still insisted she would make it one day. She had told her sisters that if nothing major happened in L.A. by the time she was thirty, she would try Off Broadway in New York instead. But she wasn't willing to give up on landing a part in a hit series in L.A. yet. She was determined to make it in Hollywood. She'd been on several daytime soaps, but never as a regular. Véronique watched her on TV, but lamented the small parts she got.

Joy had a boyfriend who was an actor, too. He

was in the road company of second-rate shows, and rarely at home in L.A. They hardly ever saw each other, which was typical of the men in Joy's life. She always seemed to pick someone emotionally unavailable or physically far away. And in the past five years, she had drifted away from her family, while pursuing her career in L.A. Their lives were so different from hers, she had less and less in common with her sisters, and didn't even look like them. Sometimes she felt as though she had been switched at birth and wasn't even related to them. And although her father had always made a fuss over her, mostly because of how beautiful she was even as a child, she had even less in common with him. Her looks had fed his narcissism, but she always felt that he didn't really know her, and had never tried.

And she and her mother had had problems for years. Véronique was still upset at her for dropping out of college, and the life she lived, working as a waitress more than she got acting jobs. It wasn't the life her mother wanted for her. She was capablc of so much more, and it seemed like a dead end to her, and she hoped she'd get over it and come back to New York. It was a subject Joy's parents never agreed on, and always argued about. Her father's conclusion was always "oh, let her have her fun," unconcerned about her. Her mother worried about her, and her sisters never took Joy seriously either. Making it as an actress in Hollywood seemed like a long shot to them, and they acted like it was a hobby, not a career.

But whatever their arguments about it, Joy had been doing what she wanted, with no help from them, and eking enough of a living out of the bit parts and waitressing to get by. She wanted to find a decent manager and a better agent, but hadn't found the right ones yet. It all took time. She loved what she was doing, and the years she had spent on it didn't seem long to her. The time had flown by. She had an apartment in West Hollywood that she loved and could afford. She was at a casting call for a commercial when Arnold phoned. She knew how sick her father had been, and that the end would come one day. She just hadn't expected it then. She went out into the hallway to talk to him, while she waited her turn.

"Oh," she said after Arnold told her, and there was silence on the line. She didn't know what else to say. Like the others, she had a long history of disappointment with her father, although she'd had no arguments with him. It had always made her feel strange when he said she was his favorite, openly in front of her sisters, since she'd never had a real conversation with him. Her father didn't have real conversations with anyone. So her being his favorite never felt genuine to her, but just something he said. But she was still sad to hear the news from Arnold. He was her father, after all, and the only one she had, however inadequate he had been.

"Are you all right?" Arnold asked her when she didn't say anything.

"Yeah, just surprised, I guess. I didn't think it would happen so soon." She hadn't seen him in two months, and hadn't seen him deteriorating rapidly, as the others had. "Do you know when the funeral is?"

"Timmie's taking care of it. She's going to call your mother in a couple of hours. I'm sure they'll get in touch with you," Arnold said simply. "I'm sorry, Joy. We all know how crazy he was about you. You were always his baby, right up to the end."

She nodded, with tears in her eyes. "I know," she said, in a choked voice, suddenly overwhelmed by the realization that her father was dead. If nothing else, he had always approved of her acting career and dreams of becoming a star, which was more than the rest of the family did. They all acted like it was something she'd get over, and had to get out of her system. He had been her biggest fan. She had sent him DVDs of all her performances. And whether it was true or not, he had said he watched them all and loved what she did. He was the only one who praised her work.

"I'll see you at the funeral," Arnold said in a sympathetic tone, and she went back to the casting call after talking to him. She didn't get the part, and returned to her apartment afterward, feeling numb and thinking about her father. Suddenly it seemed like a huge loss. She hadn't expected it to hit her so hard.

Joy texted both Juliette and Timmie that afternoon, and she asked Timmie if she could stay with her. She had just decided to take the red-eye to New York that night. She wanted to go home. Timmie answered her immediately that she could. She lived in the West Village, which was inconvenient for work, but she loved her neighborhood in the old meat-packing district, and she had a rent-stabilized apartment that was a third-floor walk-up, but it was sunny with charm. Joy always liked being at Timmie's better than at Juliette's tiny apartment in Brooklyn, and she wanted to be in the city. She could have gone to her mother's, but it was more relaxed at Timmie's, who made no comments about her life, unlike their mother, whose disappointed look was worse than words. Véronique hated Joy working as a waitress even more than her acting, and the subject always came up. As the youngest in the family, she felt as though they still treated her as though she were fourteen, not twenty-six. She would have to face them all now, and it was strange to think that her father would no longer be there singing her praises and calling her "baby." Suddenly, she could no longer imagine a world without her father in it, and tears were streaming down her cheeks when she called the airline and booked her seat.

* * *

Timmie waited until after she saw her last client to call her mother. It was four in the afternoon by then, but she hadn't wanted to be rushed when she called her, knowing that someone with bigger problems was waiting for her. As she glanced at her watch, she knew that it was ten o'clock at night in France. She hated giving her bad news at night, there was always something more depressing about that, when you had the whole night to lie there and dwell on it, unable to sleep. But she had no choice—she knew she couldn't wait until the next day to tell her. And if Véronique happened to call the nursing home to check on him, as she sometimes did, Timmie didn't want her to learn of his death from a stranger. So she called her at the rented house near St. Tropez. Véronique answered on the second ring on her French cell phone, seeing that the call was from Timmie. They hadn't spoken in several days, and she wasn't surprised to hear from her.

"Hi, darling." Véronique's voice sounded almost like a young girl's. Both Timmie's parents had always looked younger than their age. Timmie hoped it was an inherited trait. She felt every bit her age, and sometimes older, and as though she were carrying the weight of the world on her shoulders, especially now, delivering bad news to her mother.

Despite the divorce, Timmie knew how sad her mother would be. Véronique had no family except Paul and her children. Her own mother had died when she was fifteen, and her father when she was twenty-one, which was why she had married Paul so young. It had been a year after she lost her father, and she had been alone in the world then, vulnerable and scared, despite having inherited a very large fortune from both her parents. Her fortune had drawn Paul to her like a beacon when they met, and she had been a beautiful and innocent young girl.

"Hi, Mom," Timmie said, sounding serious. "I don't have good news." She wanted to give her some warning of what was coming.

"Your father?" Véronique asked, holding her breath, although she had expected it to happen, and had had the feeling when she saw him in June that it would be the last time, and he had felt it, too. They had been particularly loving to each other that day.

"Arnold called me. He died last night. Arnold said he went peacefully in his sleep." There was silence at the other end, and then she could hear that her mother was crying. It wasn't a surprise, but it was a huge loss to her anyway. He had never really left her life—he had just stepped into a different role with her, as older brother, father, and friend.

"I'm sorry for you," her mother said kindly. She remembered how she had felt when she lost her father. He had been heartbroken after her mother's death from leukemia, and had never recovered. He had been an important financier on Wall Street, American, and her mother had been thirty-five years younger and French. He had never expected to lose her, she was the love of his life and so young when she died. It had happened very quickly, three months after she got sick. Véronique's mother, Marie-Laure de Bovay, had been nearly as young when she married Phillip Whitman as Véronique was herself when she married Paul Parker.

Véronique had lived in several places with her parents—Hong Kong, London, Paris. She had learned to speak Chinese as a child and was fluent in French, because of her French mother and their frequent stays in Paris. Her roots in France had pulled at her more strongly in recent years. She was spending more time in Paris and had rented a house in the South of France in the summer, hoping to lure her daughters there for a few weeks, although this year all three had been too busy to come. And she had bought an apartment on the Île St. Louis, on the Quai de Béthune, overlooking the Seine, a few years before. She still owned her parents' home in the seventh arrondissement, on the rue de Varenne, but it had been unoccupied for years, with a caretaker to keep it running and in good repair. It was an exquisite eighteenth-century **hôtel particulier.** She didn't want to give it up, but it made her too sad to go there. The house held too many memories for her. She and Paul had stayed there frequently early in their marriage, but she hadn't spent a night in the Paris house in twenty years, since the divorce. And she didn't need to sell it, so she was keeping it, for the girls.

Véronique's maternal grandfather had been the most respected art dealer in Paris, and her father, Phillip Whitman, had bought most of his Impressionist paintings from him, and then married his daughter. Véronique's parents' marriage had been unusual due to the thirty-five-year age difference between them, but they had adored each other, and Véronique had countless memories of her loving parents, whose deep love affair had included her.

When her father died, Véronique had inherited her mother's sizable, important art collection—some spectacular paintings—and she had her father's enormous fortune, wisely invested, which had grown over the years. At twenty-one, young and alone, Véronique was living between their apartment in New York and the house in Paris that Marie-Laure had inherited from her father and never sold.

Véronique met Paul Parker a few months after her father's death, at a wedding. It had been a whirlwind romance, and they were married a year later, when she was twenty-two. She had followed in her mother's footsteps, marrying a much older man, which seemed right in the circumstances. She needed a father even more than a husband. And marrying her had changed Paul Parker's life forever. Born of aristocratic parents with no money, distant cousins of the Astors, Paul had adapted quickly to her lifestyle, although Véronique was a much simpler, more discreet person than he. Paul was outgoing and flamboyant, elegant and charming. He had lived lavishly on her means—he gave up the small job he had never liked and became a gentleman of leisure as her husband. They had been happy, particularly when the children were born, although it all ended with his affair and her discovery that his dalliances were legion. He could never resist a pretty woman. After ten years the marriage was over, although Véronique still loved him when she divorced him. And Timmie always suspected that she still did, even though she said they were just friends, and Timmie hated being the one to tell her now that he was dead.

"Have you done anything about the funeral?" her mother asked her, and Timmie admitted that she hadn't had time that day. His body was still at the nursing home.

"I wanted to talk to you first." She knew that her mother would want to make the arrangements, since Paul had no family other than Véronique and his children. Both of them were only children, so there were no cousins or distant relatives to deal with.

"I'll take care of it," Véronique said quietly. "I'll come home tomorrow. I'll call Frank Campbell's from here." It was the funeral home on upper Madison Avenue in New York that most people they knew used. She mentioned that she could even call her florist in the morning before she flew home. And they had to write an obituary for **The New York Times.** It occurred to Timmie that there was little to say about her father other than that he'd had a wonderful life, in great part thanks to her mother, who had provided for him well. He'd had a thirty-year vacation because of her.

"I'm sorry, Mom," Timmie said sincerely. Whatever her feelings about her father, she knew how much her mother loved him.

"It's all right, darling. He wouldn't have wanted to stay the way he was. It was time."

They talked for a few more minutes then, and Véronique called both her other daughters after she and Timmie hung up. Juliette was crying in her apartment when Véronique called her.

"I'm coming home tomorrow," Véronique told Juliette. It was nearly midnight in France by then, and they talked for a long time. She was inconsolable, talking about the wonderful father he had been. Véronique didn't contradict her—she knew that Juliette had harbored that fantasy for years. It was Timmie who always called her on it, not her mother. Véronique knew his failings as a father and a husband but had never criticized him to the girls.

She reached Joy while she was packing for the trip. She sounded distracted and numb.

"I'm taking the red-eye tonight," Joy said to her mother. She was still trying to absorb the fact that she no longer had a father. The news had been a shock. She'd been in denial until then.

And after that Véronique called Timmie again. She was still in her office, completing a dozen different forms for SSI.

"I forgot to ask you if anyone called Bertie," Véronique said, sounding distressed. He was Paul's son by his first marriage, and he had been eight years old when Paul and Véronique married. His mother had died in a drowning accident when he was four. Véronique had treated him like her own son from the moment they married, but he had always been a challenging child. Bertie looked exactly like his father, but had none of his charm, even as a boy.

It had been no secret, over time, that Paul had married her for her money, although it took Véronique years to understand that, but he had been loving to her as well. Bertie was **only** interested in money, however he could get it, even as a child. Paul had done everything in his life with grace, elegance, and style. But whatever Bertie did came across as conniving. He had been thrown out of some of the best schools in New York for bad behavior, and for stealing. He had been kicked out of Dartmouth for cheating. And after college, he had been involved in dozens of get-rich-quick schemes that were always slightly shady and had never panned out. Now at thirty-eight, he was always broke, "on the verge of making a killing," according to him, borrowing someone's office or living on someone's couch. He had gone through every penny Véronique had lent him to finance his schemes, and even Paul had given him some money to get on his feet. Bertie always managed to blow it and wind up in the midst of a lawsuit or get fired. He lived his life close to the edge and hand to mouth.

Véronique always explained his bad behavior by saying that he acted that way because he'd lost his mother as a very small child. And she had made every effort to support and help him when he was young and treated him as her own son, even after the divorce. But even she had finally stopped giving him money several years before. He was a bottomless pit. Véronique hadn't seen Bertie in two years, although she felt bad about it. And she rarely heard from him, unless he wanted something.

Bertie was fiercely jealous of his sisters, and had been since they were born. He had taken their allowances when they were children and had grown up to be a profoundly greedy, dishonest person, with no integrity. If there was a choice, he took the low road every time. But no matter how unpleasant he was, he was still Paul's son and had to be informed of his father's death. He had never married, had no children that he knew of, and always had some sleazy woman on his arm. And he hated Timmie even more than the others, so she didn't want to call him. He had tried unsuccessfully to bilk her out of money several times, saying he only needed to borrow it for a few weeks, but she knew him better and wouldn't give him a dime.

He never wanted to believe that his sisters lived on what they earned and had no money to spare. It was a lesson their mother had wanted them to learn. Véronique had been far more generous with Bertie, to try to help him get on his feet, which he never did. But she hadn't wanted the girls to be indolent or behave like heiresses, no matter how much they would inherit from her one day. They would be very rich women once she died, but for now they lived on their salaries, with only occasional help from her, like the loan for Juliette's sandwich shop. Véronique had been far more rigid with them than with her wayward stepson, but she had finally given up on him. He had become an extremely unpleasant person as an adult, and was someone to avoid. But she couldn't avoid him now, and didn't want to. Although he and Paul didn't see eye to eye, he had lost his father, too. And Véronique had always been more compassionate with him even than his father, who had lost patience with him years before. He had burned his father for money, too.

After she hung up with Timmie, Véronique called Bertie on the cell phone number she had for him. She hadn't spoken to him in nearly a year, since his father's stroke. And Bertie had hardly come to see him while he was sick. He always had some excuse and said he was too busy.

Bertie answered immediately and was surprised to hear his stepmother's voice. She told him gently that his father had died, and how sorry she was to give him such bad news.

"I'm not surprised," he said coolly. "Are you coming back for the funeral?"

She sounded shocked by the question. "Of course." He had correctly assumed that since it was summer, she was in France.

"I'm in Chicago, but I should be back by tomorrow night."

"I'll call you as soon as I've organized everything," she promised, "and of course you're welcome to come to the funeral with us."

"Thanks, but I'll get my own car." It would have been crowded with him riding with them, but she still felt an obligation to ask. She was the only mother he had had growing up, even if he hadn't been an endearing child. He had lied at every opportunity and been nasty to his sisters. He was always making one of them cry. And there was no love lost between them now. They had all written Bertie off. Only Véronique was still pleasant to him, although she wouldn't give him money, which was all he cared about.

Knowing how upset Paul had been about him, she couldn't help wondering what his father had left him in his will. He had never told her. Paul didn't have much left, and was always short of money himself, but he still had some of the settlement she'd given him, although it had been dwindling fast. He had always lived beyond his means, making grand gestures, and he had spent too much on women. He had never changed. And Paul still had the château in France that she had bought for them and given him in the divorce. He had wanted it desperately as part of the settlement, and then had lost interest in it, as he did with everything. He still owned it, it was boarded up now, and she knew he hadn't been there in a dozen years. She assumed he'd left it to his four children, and now the girls would have to share it with Bertie, or dispose of it together, which seemed more likely. None of them needed the headache of a crumbling château in France and all would benefit more from the proceeds of a sale, particularly Bertie. It was reasonable to believe that Bertie would receive a quarter of his father's estate, even if all of what Paul had had come from her. Bertie was still his son, whether an admirable person or not, and the money Véronique had given Paul was his to bequeath as he chose.

She ended the conversation with Bertie and went to bed that night thinking of all she had to do, and the funeral she had to arrange. Timmie had promised to help her. It was a strange feeling knowing that Paul was gone now. She knew she would miss him. He had been good to talk to and sometimes fun to be with even after their divorce. She was no longer in love with him, and hadn't been for years, which was a relief. But she loved him as someone who had been important in her life. It would be hard to lose that now. She fell asleep thinking about the ten happy years of their marriage, which had been the best years of her life. No one had ever been as dazzling as Paul Parker. There would never be anyone like him. And whatever his failings, it was what his daughters were thinking that night, too. He was unique.

Chapter 2

Joy arrived at Timmie's apartment, from the red-eye flight from L.A., before Timmie left for work. Joy was due at the apartment at seven, so Timmie had agreed to wait, and she had texted as soon as she landed, to confirm that she'd be on time. Joy was as organized and reliable as her older sister, while Juliette had always been vaguer and more fey, and was the most emotional of the three. Timmie had talked to Juliette the night before, and Juliette was distraught over their father, who from hero had become saint, which had irritated Timmie, although she tried not to say it.

Timmie had written a draft of the obituary when she got home from work the night before. There wasn't much to say about him, and she had never been charitable about her father. "Successful fortune hunter dies after a year of illness following stroke, in New York," didn't seem appropriate. She didn't say that, but she thought it, as she wrote that he had graduated from Princeton, been married twice, and had four surviving children, and listed them by name. His career had been undignified and brief, and had consisted of small, unimportant jobs on the fringes of banking, and then in real estate, until he met her mother, which had been a windfall for him. Véronique never made an issue of it, but it was no secret to their children. The only fortune he had made was from his marriage to their mother. Timmie hated the fact that he had cheated on her and destroyed her mother's illusions about him, and theirs.

Paul had been beautiful and impressive when he walked into a room, and an asset at any dinner table, but he had accomplished nothing, and his penchant for vapid, pretty young women had added little to his life and nothing to his CV. He had lived only in the moment, wanting to have fun, and never thinking of the future, or the consequences of his actions, right to the end. His last female companion had been a beautiful young Russian girl, who had disappeared the moment he got sick. At least they wouldn't have her to contend with, Timmie thought. It would be bad enough dealing with Bertie, who would scramble for every penny. Timmie had no illusions about him, none of them did, and most of the time she forgot about him completely. They'd hardly seen him in recent years, which was a blessing. And he avoided them, too, since staying in touch with them was of no benefit to him. He seemed to have only their father's worst traits, multiplied by a thousand, with none of his good ones to mitigate them. Their father had said as much himself.

Joy looked sleepy when she got to Timmie's apartment, and more beautiful than ever when Timmie opened the door to her. She was wearing a short white skirt and a T-shirt, and even in flat sandals she was almost as tall as Timmie, although they had entirely different styles and appearances. Timmie had the blond aristocratic good looks of her father, while Joy was absolutely dazzling with her dark hair, violet eyes, and creamy skin. She had their mother's looks and father's height. Timmie hadn't seen her in a while, although they talked from time to time. Joy was never great at returning calls or staying in touch. Timmie and Juliette spoke far more often. Joy was too busy with her auditions, go-sees, cattle calls, acting jobs, and waitressing in between.

The two sisters embraced the minute they saw each other, and for a long moment, Joy clung to her, as they both thought of their father.

"I can't believe he's gone," Joy said in a hoarse voice as she walked in. "I kind of thought he'd go on forever."

"We all did," Timmie said, as she poured her a mug of coffee in the kitchen and handed it to her. She was wearing a different plaid shirt, clean jeans, and the same Converse she'd had on the day before.

It was a rag-bag unisex look, similar to what everyone wore at the foundation, hardly different from their homeless clients, whereas Joy looked sexy, young, and very L.A. in her miniskirt. Her older sister smiled at her. Joy was unarguably the family beauty, as her father always said. She looked like a taller version of their mother, with a huge dose of sex appeal added to the mix. Their mother looked more demure, but their features and coloring were the same. And with their father's height, they were very striking women.

"Mom's coming in the afternoon," Timmie filled her in. "She texted me when she got on the plane in Nice three hours ago. I told her you were staying here." It wouldn't surprise her, since Joy almost always did when she came to New York, which was as seldom as she could. The two sisters liked being together downtown, and it gave them a chance to catch up. Timmie seemed older and more mature, even though they were only three years apart, which had made a bigger difference when they were kids. "I think the funeral will be in three days. Mom will figure it out when she gets here."

"Is she going back to St. Tropez afterward?" Joy asked her, feeling guilty that she hadn't made time to go there this summer, but neither had Timmie. And Juliette couldn't get away either, since she had no one to relieve her at the sandwich shop, except her bakery assistant, who didn't speak English and wasn't up to it. Juliette had hardly taken a day off in three years, until her father's death the day before. And now she wanted to take the rest of the summer off to mourn and honor him, and take some time for herself. Even though it had been expected, her father's death was a shock to her.

"She didn't say," Timmie answered. "I think she only has the house till the end of the month, and I get the feeling she's been lonely there." But she had nothing to do in New York either. Véronique had relied heavily on them to fill her life while they were growing up, and in the past few years, she had been at loose ends.

Véronique was talking about starting to paint again, but had done nothing about it. She had been a very talented portrait artist and had gone to the Beaux-Arts in Paris, but she had only dabbled at her art while the girls were young, and said she didn't have time. Now she did, but had been away from it for too long. She hadn't figured out what to do to fill her days. She read a lot and went back and forth to Paris, had done some charity work, but hadn't found a real focus for her time. She had dated a few men since the divorce, but hadn't had anyone serious in her life since Paul. And she spent just enough time with him to curb her appetite for companionship and keep her from being too interested in finding someone else. Timmie had been wondering the night before if his being gone now would make a difference, and she'd be more open to other men, but Véronique always said that at fifty-two, she was too old, which Timmie couldn't argue with, since she felt too old to try again at twenty-nine, or in her case too disheartened. Timmie was sick and tired of cheating men, but Véronique had never had the bitterness that had tainted Timmie. For now at least, Timmie had no desire to try again, unlike Juliette, who had a revolving door in her life for losers, and Joy, who always had a boyfriend, even if he was never around.

"I'll try to come home early," Timmie promised, "after Mom gets in. I told her I'd go to Frank Campbell with her. Knowing Mom, she'll have everything worked out and planned before she lands." They both smiled at the truth in that. Their mother was flawlessly organized and ran a tight ship. She had been a perfect mother and wife, which made it even harder for her now, with nothing to run except her own life.

Timmie gave Joy a quick kiss and left. She was at work later than usual, at eight a.m., and as she walked to the foundation from the subway, she thought about her father again. In many ways, he had been a no-show in their lives, and at the same time, he had been a strangely unifying bond. It was still hard to believe that he was gone.

She had just enough time in the office to sort through the files on her desk, and by nine o'clock there were three people waiting to see her, and they were a welcome distraction from her own confusing feelings about her father's death.

* * *

By the time the plane landed at Kennedy Airport, Véronique had already made several lists during the flight. She had to call the caterer, the priest, and the florist, pick a casket with Timmie at Campbell's, make arrangements at the cemetery, submit the obit to the **Times,** and ask several of Paul's acquaintances to be pallbearers at the church. She thought Bertie should be one, and Arnold Sands another, but they needed six more. Paul hadn't had close friends. He preferred the company of women, and most of the people he knew were superficial socialites he saw socially but wasn't close to, and the people he ran into at parties who weren't really friends. Moments like this pointed out what she already knew, that there had been no depth or substance to Paul's life. He was all about having fun, with as few responsibilities as possible. It made it difficult to come up with people who truly cared about him—other than Arnold Sands, his attorney, who had been his best friend, and his only confidant. It already felt strange, knowing Paul was no longer there. And Véronique was grateful to have the funeral to arrange so she didn't have time to think, but her sadness over his death kept creeping in anyway.

A representative of Air France came to escort her off the plane, and whisked her through immigration and customs, since she had nothing to declare.

She had worn a simple black cotton dress, which seemed suitable, given the reason for her return. She wasn't his widow, but it almost felt like it. She had to remind herself, as Timmie had when they spoke, that she and Paul were no longer married. But she had just lost a big piece of the history of her life. And it reminded her of the agonizing sadness of losing her parents when she was young. She had had only Paul to rely on after that, after they met. And now she had only herself. Especially in recent years, and since the divorce, she had never relied on Paul to make any decisions, but rather the reverse. Particularly as he got older, she was the one he turned to when he needed something, had a problem, or wanted advice. She was by far the wiser of the two once she grew up, and he knew it well. He expected her to decide everything about their children and didn't want to know about their problems, only their victories and joys. He was the original good-time guy. And she was the rock, the foundation that their lives were built on, the person everyone knew they could count on. He was a figurehead and nothing more.

Her housekeeper was waiting at the apartment when Véronique arrived. Carmina told her how sorry she was about Mr. Paul. "He was a good man," she said, making the sign of the cross. She hadn't known Paul when he had been misbehaving during their marriage, but as he was to everyone,

Paul had been sweet to her. He was an easy man to like, if you expected nothing from him.

Véronique went to her study and made all her calls, while Carmina unpacked for her. And then she texted Timmie to tell her she was home. She sat back at her desk then, and had the cup of tea Carmina had left there. She only worked for her in the daytime. Véronique didn't need anyone there at night, and preferred to be alone. She made herself something to eat when she was hungry, and didn't want the pressure of someone preparing meals for her. She had the same arrangement in Paris, with a maid who came in during the day. Once the girls had grown up, she had simplified her life and had very little staff. During Paul's tenure and when the girls were young, he had insisted on many employees. Her current setup suited Véronique much better. She didn't like being waited on, although she was grateful to have Carmina now, and her apartment on Fifth Avenue was large.

Véronique had two guest rooms, and her own suite, and a beautiful view of Central Park, and the perfect walls for her art. She still had a remarkable collection of her grandfather's Impressionist paintings, and had sent a few to Paris. In the New York apartment, there were several Renoirs, two Degas, a Pissarro, a Mary Cassatt she loved in her bedroom, a Chagall she was crazy about, and a Picasso in her dining room, and countless smaller paintings by Corot and other artists, and a series of Renoir drawings. The apartment was elegantly decorated in soothing tones. She preferred simple things of great quality, and had always had a passion for art.

And in the hallway leading to the bedrooms, she had hung several of the portraits she'd painted, including one of her father. She had done large impressive oils, and women in a John Singer Sargent style. There was no question that she had talent, although she had done nothing with it for years. She sketched occasionally, but that was all. And she had done lovely portraits of her children, which were in her dressing room. One of her great fascinations had been studying and researching forgeries, which she knew her grandfather had been intrigued by, too. But she had never pursued that path either, although she had an eye for great fakes. And her mother had painted watercolors, which Véronique had hung in the guest rooms. They were peaceful and pretty. Art was in their genes, although none of Véronique's daughters had ever wanted to draw or paint. The passion for it seemed to end with Véronique.

Timmie called her at four o'clock and said she'd meet her at Frank Campbell, and Joy had decided to join them. They met in the lobby, after Véronique walked over from the apartment. Timmie was still wearing her work clothes, and Joy had changed into an even shorter black skirt and high heels. She looked like she'd just stepped off the cover of

Vogue. Her mother was pleased to see them, kissed both girls, and thanked them for meeting her.

They were three very beautiful women as they met with the director to organize Paul's funeral, and a rosary the night before. He hadn't been religious, but Véronique was, although she wasn't planning to do anything excessive. And she had spoken to the priest at St. Ignatius that afternoon, and they had set a date and time for the funeral mass in two days. She had all the information ready when they sat down in the director's office, and neither of the girls was surprised. Véronique already had Paul's funeral planned.

They dealt with all the unpleasant tasks at Campbell, and the director kept addressing Véronique as the widow—it was pointless to explain that they had been divorced for twenty years. And afterward they all went back to Véronique's apartment, and Juliette joined them. She had been too upset to meet them at the funeral home. She looked disheveled and distraught when she arrived at the apartment, immediately burst into tears, and sat sobbing in her older sister's arms. Timmie refrained from making acerbic comments about her father, but Joy could see in her eyes what she was thinking. It was no secret among them how critical Timmie had always been about him. It took an hour for Juliette to calm down, and then they went to the kitchen to have something to eat. Carmina had already left for the day. Véronique suggested they order in takeout food, but no one was hungry, and Juliette had brought a box of pastries with her, but no one wanted to eat them. Her slightly rounded figure was testimony that she sampled her own wares, whereas her sisters and mother were far more careful about what they ate and it showed. The pastries went untouched, except by Juliette, who nibbled at a chocolate croissant.

"I can't believe he's gone," Juliette said for what seemed like the hundredth time, and Joy admitted she couldn't either. Véronique was thinking the same thing, but was distracted by the details of the funeral she was organizing as a final tribute to the father of her children, and man she had loved so passionately long ago. The flowers were going to be spectacular, and she had selected music he loved. This was her final gift to him, and she wanted it to be as dignified and elegant as he would have wanted. Just as he had lived, Paul Parker was going out in style.

The four women sat in her kitchen for two hours, talking and drinking tea. Timmie actually dared to suggest at the end that Juliette was mourning the father he hadn't been as much as the one he was.

"That's a terrible thing to say," Juliette said immediately in his defense. "He was a wonderful father." Timmie clenched her teeth and didn't speak, and Véronique distracted them with more of the details, which were a mercy for her. She didn't want the girls arguing now, of all times, although she knew that what Timmie had said was true. Juliette had had illusions about her father all her life, and although she said they spoke almost every day, no one pointed out that she had called him. Then finally Timmie and Joy went downtown to Timmie's apartment, and Juliette went back to Brooklyn, to be alone.

They were all going to the rosary together the following night, and the funeral the day after. Notice of it would be printed in the **Times** the next morning, and Véronique had arranged for two cars to pick the girls up, and for the funeral the next day as well. She wanted to make it all as easy for them as she could. She knew what it was like to lose a father, and no one had made it easier for her. She felt as though it was the least she could do for them. It was typical of her, to think of everything she could to make their lives easier, although they didn't notice it and were used to their mother doing for everyone, in her quiet methodical way. She had done it all their lives.

Véronique sat lost in thought after they left the apartment, dreading the formalities of the next two days. She couldn't help thinking that once again, he had left her to comfort their children, take care of everything, and pay all the bills. It had been an assumption he had always made, even when he was alive. In death, it was no different. But she suddenly missed being able to call him. There were no friends she wanted to share this with, and most of them wouldn't have understood. Their relationship was too unusual among divorced people, particularly as he'd never been much of a father or husband, but he was her friend, and had been for more than half of her adult life. It was a lot to lose, and he had the elegance, panache, and style of another time.

The rosary the next day was simple and formal. Long lines of people she didn't know came to sign the leather book she had set out. There were pretty young women, younger than his daughters, who didn't introduce themselves, well-dressed couples, and a number of men close to his age, who had been his acquaintances or friends. A few of them shook Véronique's hand and extended their condolences, and several of them eyed Timmie, Juliette, and Joy, all of whom had worn simple black dresses, and looked serious as they stood with their mother. And afterward they all went home exhausted, and feeling drained.

The next day was more of the same, though on a larger scale. And much to Véronique's surprise, the mourners nearly filled the church. The smell of the fragrant white flowers was heavy in the air. There were huge urns of them throughout the church, and a blanket of tiny white orchids over the dark mahogany coffin they had chosen, and she had managed to find two of his friends to act as pallbearers with Bertie and Arnold, the other four were provided by Frank Campbell's, and the casket was moved on wheels.

Bertie hadn't come to the rosary the night before, but he showed up at the church before the service to meet Véronique and the girls. They were startled that he had a young woman with him. She was wearing a short black skirt, a low-cut black silk blouse, stiletto heels, and too much makeup, and seemed bored. She never said a word to them, and Bertie didn't introduce her. They had no idea if she was his girlfriend, or just a woman he had brought along. He didn't bother to explain, and no one asked.

He appeared faintly annoyed to be there, although he had worn an appropriate black suit, white shirt, and black Hermès tie, with expensive well-shined shoes, and he was as handsome as his father. He had the look, but not the heart. Paul had been self-centered and narcissistic, but there had been a warm side to him as well. The stare Bertie gave his stepmother and sisters was calculating and ice cold. Véronique invited him to sit in the front pew with them—he was Paul's son, after all. After the casket was in place, he slid onto the front bench with the young woman, and whispered to her as they waited for the funeral to start.

They all agreed afterward that it was a beautiful service, worthy of their father. People shook their hands outside the church, and the family disappeared to Woodlawn Cemetery in the Bronx, where the priest said a few brief words, and they left the casket at Véronique's family plot. She didn't know where else to bury him, hadn't wanted to buy a single lonely grave, and she thought the girls would like him with the rest of the family. Véronique's parents were buried there as well.

Bertie had a separate car to take him and the young woman back to the city, and they had figured out by then that her name was Debbie. They joined everyone at Véronique's apartment, where the caterer had set out a full buffet in the dining room, there were white flowers everywhere, and more than a hundred people were eating, talking, and waiting for them. The only person Véronique recognized in the crowd was Arnold, whose face lit up when he saw her, and he approached Véronique and the girls.

"It looks like a wedding," Timmie said under her breath with obvious disapproval to Joy, who nodded. It did. Their mother had done a beautiful job, honoring him, which came as no surprise. "Did she do this for him, herself, or us?" Timmie asked out loud.

"Probably all three," Joy answered, as Arnold embraced their mother. It had been obvious to everyone for years that he had a major soft spot for her, and would have loved to pursue it with her, but Véronique wasn't open to the idea, and although she was kind to him, she had always made that clear. He was somewhere in his sixties, a very successful lawyer, an attractive man, and had been divorced for many years. Véronique had no interest in him other than as an attorney and Paul's closest friend. Whatever his aspirations, it went no further than that for her.

"You did a beautiful job," Arnold complimented her, and Véronique smiled and thanked him, as Juliette helped herself at the buffet, still looking ravaged by the funeral service. The "Ave Maria" had nearly destroyed her, and she still seemed shaken, as she filled her plate. Joy and Timmie stood talking quietly. None of them knew anyone in the room, among Paul's friends. They looked like what they were, café society and jet set, people who had known him in a superficial way but had come anyway and were enjoying the party atmosphere at his ex-wife's home.

"Your mother must have spent a fortune on this," Bertie commented unpleasantly to Timmie, as she gave him an ugly look.

"Apparently she thought Dad was worth it," she said sternly. Joy stood there wondering if fireworks were going to erupt, just as Arnold walked up to them. All three sisters were together with Bertie, while Véronique said something to one of the waiters, who was pouring white wine and champagne for the guests.

"I'd like to make a suggestion, since you're all here," Arnold said blandly. "There's no longer a formal reading of the will. But since Joy's in town, why don't we get together tomorrow in my office and go over it? That way we can discuss it, and I can answer any questions you might have." It seemed like a sensible idea, and he didn't make it sound ominous. None of them expected their father to have left a fortune, and the only property they were aware of was the château in France, unless he'd mortgaged it to the hilt, which no one knew. He had never been very responsible about money.

"Sounds like a good idea to me," Bertie said, interested, and the girls nodded and seemed surprised. None of them had even thought about the will.

"Do you all have time?" Arnold asked, as Véronique joined them.

"For what?" she asked.

"I thought we could all go over the will together tomorrow and get it out of the way," Arnold said calmly. "I think it would be nice if you came, too," he said to Véronique. She looked surprised. She didn't expect Paul to leave her anything, since everything he had he had gotten from her, and she assumed he would leave it to the girls, and something to Bertie, but surely nothing to her.

"How do you feel about my being there?" she asked the girls, and they all said they would prefer it, and Bertie said he didn't care. It was easy to see that all he was interested in was what had been left to him.

"Does nine o'clock tomorrow morning work for all of you?" Arnold asked the assembled group of heirs and their mother, and everyone nodded and agreed.

"See you then." He smiled and left shortly afterward. Bertie exited right after Arnold, and Timmie told him not to bring Debbie to the meeting the next day.

"Obviously," he said, with a look of disdain. Timmie always managed to enrage him. She did it on purpose. She couldn't stand him, and it was entirely mutual. Debbie said nothing to Véronique or the girls when they walked away, she only spoke to Bertie.

The rest of the guests were gone two hours later, after finishing off the buffet and an astonishing amount of champagne. Timmie made a comment that they had shown up for the free food and champagne more than for their father, and Véronique gave her a look of disapproval. And by the time the girls departed, everyone was exhausted.

When the apartment was cleared of people, Véronique felt as though she had been run over by a bus. She was sorry she had agreed to go to the meeting in Arnold's office the next day. She had no reason to be there, and it seemed unnecessary to her. She was so emotionally drained that all she wanted to do was sleep in the morning, but she had agreed to go, and she didn't want to cancel and upset the girls. She took off her clothes, lay down on her bed, and fell asleep without even turning off the light. She was relieved to know she had done her job well, and that Paul had been laid to rest just as he would have wished, with all the pomp and circumstance he would have felt he deserved.

Chapter 3

Véronique went to Arnold's office the next morning, for the last chapter of the ordeal. Yesterday's funeral had been hard enough. Once they heard the details of his will, they would be able to go on with their lives. Timmie and Joy were ready to do so. Juliette was planning on closing her sandwich shop for August, until Labor Day. And on her way to his office, Véronique was thinking about when she should go back to France. She had until the end of the month in the rental house in St. Tropez, but she wasn't in the mood to go back now. Paris was dead in the summer, so she didn't want to be there, and New York was too hot. She hadn't made up her mind. She hadn't bothered to make plans for August, and wasn't sure what to do next. She got to Arnold's office before she came to any conclusions and discovered she was the first to arrive. Traffic had been lighter than she thought.

"You did a beautiful job yesterday, no surprise,"

Arnold said warmly after he kissed her on both cheeks French style, and then hugged her, a little too close. He was always friendlier than she liked. They talked about the girls for a few minutes, and then everyone arrived almost at once. Bertie was wearing another good-looking suit, a pale blue shirt, and a businesslike dark blue tie. He looked like a prosperous banker, not the hustler that he was.

Arnold led them into a conference room, where a secretary offered them coffee or tea, and all of them declined. They wanted to get the meeting over with, and the business side of their father's death behind them. Joy had already booked a flight to L.A. that afternoon, and said she had an audition the next day for a small part on a soap, and the restaurant where she worked five nights a week needed her back. It was a busy place, and the tips were great and paid her rent, so she didn't want them to get mad or fill her spot.

Arnold began the meeting with a serious expression. "Your father and I discussed his will extensively in the last year, while he was still well enough to do so, and I want to preface what I explain to you by saying that the provisions he made are somewhat unorthodox, which was his intention. We had very different views of how these things should be handled, but I'll admit his were more creative than mine. And he was heavily influenced by knowing that you all stand to inherit a great deal from your mother one day, and that your future is secure because of her, which your father felt allowed him some leeway to view things differently. He wanted to address your immediate needs, not your long-term ones, which are covered." Arnold was aware, as Paul had been, that Véronique's philosophy was that the girls should make a living and support themselves, no matter what they would inherit later. She wanted to be the safety net under them for special cases and emergencies, not the source of money they lived on. She expected them to earn that, and they did, with energy in all three cases. Paul hadn't agreed with her and thought she should be more generous, but she adamantly didn't want to ruin them and encourage them to live like spoiled rich girls, or like their father, spending too much of someone else's money, which he had done with her. She thought it was a bad example to set their daughters, and not the role model she wanted for them. And Arnold was impressed at the lessons she was trying to teach them, even if Paul didn't like it. She had made them self-sufficient in spite of what she had and what they would inherit from her one day. And they were definitely neither lazy nor spoiled, whether she approved of their career choices or not.

"So his will," he went on, "reflects that philosophy, of wanting to make a difference for you now, since your long-term future is covered by your mother. And to that end, he has left you disparate amounts, which is unorthodox as well, but reflects, he believed, what each of you might need in the context of what you're doing presently with your lives. It does not reflect, as he expressed in his will himself, any disparity in his love for each of you." He looked around at each of them then, and Véronique noticed that Bertie had a hopeful, somewhat impatient look. He didn't care about his father's reasoning—he just wanted to know what he would get. "Your father wanted you each to have what would benefit you most, and he was very specific about it," he explained, and the three girls nodded. Arnold then picked up Paul's last will and testament and read directly from it. He had copies to hand to each of them, but he hadn't distributed them yet. He preferred to explain it first.

"'To my daughter Timmie, whom I love and admire greatly, I leave the following amount.'" Arnold stated it, and Timmie's eyes opened in surprise. It seemed like a very large bequest to her, and to the others. "'And my wish is that she purchase a house with it, in a neighborhood that seems reasonable to her, in order to open a facility of her own, to assist the kind of indigent people she works with, and start a foundation of her own, in the way she can do the most good, with the freedom she needs to do so exactly as she wants. I have every confidence that she will do a wonderful job of it, on her own. And through her, I am able to help people I have never assisted in my lifetime. I hope that this bequest will somewhat improve her poor opinion of me as a very selfish man. I have indeed been one, but my wish is to help her, and through her these needy people, now.' " Timmie's eyes were swimming with tears as she listened. She had never expected this from her father, and her sisters and mother were smiling with approval through tears as well.

"I don't know what to say," she said in a whisper, deeply moved by his bequest.

"Your father and I did some research, and the amount he bequeathed you seems as though it would adequately cover the purchase of a house as he described, and what you'd need to get a project like this off the ground." And then to qualify it to the others, "Yours is the largest bequest he made." Everyone nodded, and the girls didn't seem upset, although Bertie looked tense. It sounded like too much money to him, and he doubted that his father had four times that amount to leave to all of them, not even close.

" 'And to Juliette, my beloved daughter,' " Arnold went on, " 'I want to leave her the gift of time, so that she can hire people to work at her bakery, a manager so that she can get away, travel, and live more extensively than she has for several years. I am leaving her enough to pay for some staff, to make improvements to the sandwich shop, and enlarge it if she wishes. But my darling Juliette, I want you to go out and live. You're a wonderful woman, and you need to see more of the world than you do now.' " He had left her a handsome amount, though much less than what he'd left Timmie, and she sobbed in gratitude. Juliette had never needed or wanted a lot of money, and his bequest seemed more than generous to her. She smiled through her tears as she looked at her sisters and squeezed Timmie's hand, sitting next to her. She had no jealousy for what he had left her older sister—she wouldn't have known what to do with that amount. And if Timmie opened a homeless shelter of some kind, even on a small scale, she would need far more money than Juliette needed to improve and staff her bakery so she could get away from time to time. He had calculated well and tailored his bequests to meet their needs, just as Arnold had said. And he had clearly put careful thought into it.

" 'And to my very beautiful youngest daughter, Joy,' " Arnold continued, " 'although I know her mother does not approve of her acting career, I believe she has real talent and I would like to be the angel who helps her to fulfill her dream. My bequest to her is to hire a decent manager, hopefully the best in L.A., to help get her career off the ground, and attract a better agent. I am giving her enough to take acting lessons from the best teacher in L.A., and enough to live on for two years, so she can stop working as a waitress and concentrate fully on furthering her acting career, so she can have the success she deserves.' " He and Arnold had figured out an amount that would allow her to pursue some avenues that hadn't been open to her before because she didn't have the money, and stop working as a waitress because Véronique would not fund a career she didn't approve of. Joy sat beaming as she listened, looked apologetically at her mother, and was relieved to see that she was smiling, too. They all were. And she knew that what he'd left her was more than enough to give her a big push professionally. It was exactly what she needed and sounded perfect to her.

By then Bertie was squirming in his seat and looking impatient. He was tired of hearing about the girls and their dreams. All he wanted was to hear about him.

"'In addition,'" Arnold said, as Bertie looked relieved, they were finally getting to the part of the will that concerned him, "'I am bequeathing my château near St. Paul de Vence, in four equal shares, one each to my three daughters Timmie, Juliette, and Joy, and'"—Arnold seemed to hesitate before he went on as they listened—"'the fourth equal share to my daughter Sophie Agnès Marnier, daughter of Elisabeth Marnier, with whom I had a tender union for several years. I realize that Sophie's existence, and that of her mother, will come as a shock to my children, and to Véronique, and for that I apologize. Sophie's existence and her mother's in no way diminish my love for my three older daughters, nor for Véronique, while I was married to her. It is something that happened a long time ago, and I wish to acknowledge my youngest daughter now at my death, and do for her what I didn't do during my lifetime. I wish her to own an equal share of the château with her sisters, with each getting one quarter of it, and I bequeath the remaining funds in my estate to Sophie, after my bequests to the three older girls. It will be a far smaller share than what they receive, but it will help her and her mother, and it will be useful to Sophie and take some of the burden from her mother, which is the least I can do for them now.' "

There was dead silence in the room after Arnold spoke. No one moved, no one said a word, no one even breathed. Not even Véronique, who looked as if she had turned to stone in her chair. Joy looked the most shocked. She had always thought she was his baby and favored child until two minutes ago, and now she realized he had another younger daughter, and she hadn't been his baby at all. Everyone was stunned.

"How old is she?" Véronique finally asked in a choked voice, and he knew how painful the answer would be to her.

"Sophie is twenty-three years old, three years younger than Joy." They both knew what that meant. Paul had still been very much married to Véronique when he'd been involved with the girl's mother. Sophie had been born three years before the divorce, when all was supposedly well with them, and Véronique hadn't yet known about his affairs. She had learned of them after they separated, and it had been a shock as their marriage unraveled, but Elisabeth Marnier was not a name she recognized. He had managed to keep that a secret till now. And clearly it had been serious, since they had a child. Véronique knew it shouldn't have surprised her of Paul, after what she'd learned, but it did, and he had kept it hidden from her for all these years.

The girls were speechless as Arnold went on. And Bertie's face was bright red. He had listened carefully and could do the math. The four girls had become owners of the château, with no share for him, and whatever funds remained in the estate were going to his father's illegitimate daughter Sophie, which left nothing for Bertie.

" 'And to my son Bertrand,' " Arnold continued, " 'for whom I have funded a dozen business ventures, all of which failed for lack of good judgment, good practices, and solid business plans—and whose stepmother helped him far more generously than I when he was younger, with just as little success for fifteen years—I feel you have had far more advantages than your sisters, and more money than I am leaving them, after never giving them a penny until now. In my estimation, you've already had far more than your fair share of my estate, and your stepmother's help, and I am afraid that anything I would leave you would be wasted like the rest. I know this is a hard lesson for you, son, and I love you, but you now have to do the work yourself, earn your living fairly and honestly, and learn what Véronique and I have tried to teach you with no success. You need to build your career and your fortune on your own, without help, without shortcuts, to achieve the results you want. It's the only way it will ever have any meaning for you. I hope that you will work hard and act wisely in the future, exercising good judgment. I gave you all the help I could when I was alive. Now you have my strong hope that you will do well on your own. And although this may appear to be a harsh decision to you, rest assured, I love you, son.' " As Arnold finished reading, Bertie exploded from his seat with a look of rage, glancing at the girls and Véronique in fury.

"You bitches! All of you! You bilked him out of everything, kissing his ass when you visited him, and whining to him, and bad-mouthing me! And you!" he said, turning to Véronique viciously. "You with your holier-than-thou ways about making it on your own, and making everyone crawl to you for money, and pretending that you're poor—you did this, you talked him into screwing me over, just so the girls would get it all." They all knew that none of what he said was true. They had never complained to their father or expected anything from him. And Véronique had never pretended to be poor or expected her children to crawl for money. She had wanted them to have honest jobs and work for a living. And as Paul said in his will, she had been far more generous and tolerant of Bertie than she ever had been with the girls. She had wanted to make up to him for the mother he didn't have. She had always felt sorry for him because of it and made excuses for him that he didn't appreciate or deserve. But Bertie was blind with fury over what he didn't get in his father's will.

"Is that it for me?" he said, turning to Arnold, who nodded.

"Yes, Bertie, it is. I'm sorry. He thought he was helping you." And Arnold had agreed, which he didn't say now. Bertie was a wastrel of the worst kind, and it would have been pointless to give him anything. The girls would put Paul's money to better use, constructively. Bertie would waste it on schemes and throw it away, which Paul understood. He was realistic about his son.

"You'll hear from me about this!" he said menacingly to Véronique and the girls. "This isn't the end of it, not by a long shot." Then he strode out of the conference room and slammed the door, as the girls sat silently.

It had been a day of shocks and surprises at their father's hands, for Véronique as much as the rest of them. The announcement of his illegitimate daughter was far more astounding and upsetting to them than anything Bertie could have said, or his being left out of the will, which had amazed them, too. They had assumed that Bertie would get part of whatever their father had. But they had never expected him to be left nothing, and a new sister to appear. Véronique still looked pale and was shaken to her core, as the girls began speaking all at once and asked Arnold about Sophie.

And then Arnold called them to order again. There was more. "'And to my ex-wife Véronique, whom I love deeply and who is the most extraordinary woman I know, I leave my love, my heart, our memories, and a request. The request is that she begin painting again. You have enormous talent, and should go back to your artwork. In addition, I bequeath to you the painting that we bought on our honeymoon in Venice, thought to be by Bellini, but never authenticated, which you thought was a fraud. We both loved the painting whatever its value or lack of it. You promised to pursue its provenance and never did. If it is worthless, I hope that it will bring back happy memories for you, as it does for me. I have enjoyed it for all these years.'" She had relinquished it to him somewhat reluctantly in the divorce, because of its sentimental value to her. But Paul had wanted it even more, so she had let him keep it. "'And if it proves to be a true Bellini, I leave it to you with joy as a valuable gift, which is far less than you deserve for all you've done for me over these many years. In addition, I apologize to you from my heart for the revelation of a child you knew nothing about. Please believe me when I say that I never loved her mother as I did you. You were always my only true love. I am sorry I was such a fool in my lifetime. I love you although I was never the husband you deserved.' "

Arnold looked at them, and saw that Véronique was in tears. "And then he signed it," he said quietly, as Véronique discreetly blew her nose. Paul had shown far greater insights in death, about his children, and even about her, than he had shown in his lifetime. And Véronique thought he would do the girls some good with his bequests, and Bertie, too. She wondered if Bertie would try to overturn the will, although Paul was under no obligation to leave him anything. Unlike French law, in America he didn't have to leave his children any part of his estate, and he had eloquently explained why he hadn't left anything to Bertie. It touched her, too, that he had left her the Bellini, a reminder of their good times together, and their passionate beginning, although she still didn't believe it was real. That had never really mattered to either of them—they just loved it, and had fallen in love with it when they first saw it. And she was touched that he thought she should paint again. She had considered it many times herself since the girls had grown up, but never got around to it. And she didn't know if she would now or not. It was so many years since she'd painted and it was hard to start again. And they had far more important issues to discuss and think about now, like Sophie Agnès Marnier. The girls wanted to know everything about her from Arnold, and were extremely upset, understandably, not about her share of the estate, but about the very fact that she existed, and that their father had never told them about his love child. It was shocking news to them now, and they couldn't question him about it, only Arnold.

Arnold said that she lived near St. Paul de Vence, near the château, which was how Paul had met her mother, and that, as far as he knew, Paul had not seen Sophie or her mother in thirteen or fourteen years. He had done little to help her, which was why he wanted to do so now. And he had pushed her from his mind, until he began examining his conscience closer to his death. His adding her to his will had been an afterthought. Arnold said he knew nothing else about her except an address, which they had verified for the purposes of the will. Paul had not contacted her or her mother before his death, and Véronique found herself thinking that he had walked away from his obligations and responsibilities to her, too, just as he had done with everything else, although he had tried to repair some of the damage posthumously.

As they left Arnold's office, Timmie suggested they have dinner together, and Joy volunteered to postpone her flight until the next day. Getting back to the restaurant was no longer crucial since the reading of the will. She was going to be able to quit when she went back and focus only on her career for the first time in five years. And they had much to discuss and think about, and decide what to do about the château. They each had a project that their father had funded with his bequests. And they wanted to discuss what to do about Sophie. They owned a château with her now. Arnold said he would be sending her a copy of the will, and her share of the bequests.

They all agreed to dinner that night, and Véronique as well. They arranged to meet at Da Silvano, near Timmie's apartment, at eight o'clock. And as Véronique rode back to her apartment alone in a cab after the meeting, she was still devastated about the discovery of Sophie and her mother. She couldn't help thinking that even after he died, Paul had managed to hurt her again, deeply, by revealing an affair that had happened during their marriage, and a child whom she had never known about. It was a good reminder of who he had really been, and the sort of man he was. Selfish and narcissistic, he had done whatever he wanted, no matter who it hurt, or the damage it did later. And the only person he had really cared about during his entire life was himself.

Chapter 4

Véronique took a cab downtown to Da Silvano, and arrived on time, at eight o'clock. Joy and Timmie arrived right before her, and Juliette shortly after. They took a table outside in the warm July night, and Timmie ordered wine as soon as they sat down. It had been a long, shocking, emotional day, and the discoveries of the morning had unnerved them all. Along with the thoughtfulness and insights of their father's bequests to them, and the freedom it would give each of them to pursue their dreams, he had decked them with the revelation of his illegitimate child. Not to mention Bertie's menacing outburst and accusation that his being left out of the will was somehow due to them and not to his own behavior for the past twenty years. They had lost a brother and gained a sister in a matter of minutes, and they were pleased at neither one, although the existence of Sophie Marnier upset them far more. They had all given up on Bertie years before.

"Well, girls, so how's everyone feeling about our new baby sister tonight?" Timmie said sarcastically after her first sip of wine. It had haunted her all day, and she was worried about their mother, who still looked deathly pale. The thought of it had tormented her since their meeting in Arnold's office that morning.

"I guess I'm not the baby anymore, and never was, or not for long," Joy said, looking glum. She knew it was stupid, but it bothered her. Her father's dishonesty about it had upset them all. "Her mother must be some kind of gold digger, and now they luck out and wind up with a quarter of the château. What if Sophie stops us from selling it?" Joy said, looking seriously worried.

Véronique shook her head. "She can't do that," she said sensibly. "You girls outnumber her three to one. The majority will rule in any decision to sell. There was nothing in your father's will about needing a unanimous vote to dispose of the château. Her ownership is technical and fiduciary. It just means she'll get a quarter of whatever you sell it for, which probably won't be much. I doubt that he's maintained it properly for all these years, and it was never Versailles." It had been a pretty country château, in good order when she owned it. It had been impeccably maintained until she turned it over to him, and neglected ever since. He hadn't mentioned or thought of it in years, and had lost interest in it very quickly once it was his to maintain and run. Taking care of it properly would have required too much work, and money he didn't have or didn't wish to spend on a property in France he never used. It was typically Paul. Out of sight, out of mind. And out of pocket, even more so.

"Well, I can tell you right now, I want to sell it," Timmie said without hesitation after they ordered dinner. "The last thing I need is part ownership in a château in France, and all the headaches that go with it. It sounds like a money pit to me."

"It always was," Véronique confirmed, and she knew it made no sense for her daughters to keep it. The only time they went to France now was for a week in the summer to visit her, and they weren't even coming this year. Their days of vacationing together seemed to be over. Their lives were too separate now, with different schedules, obligations, and needs. And keeping a château, with all its upkeep, for a few days a year was absurd.

"I don't want a château in France either," Joy said, with a look of panic. "I need to work in L.A. and go to auditions. I don't even live on the East Coast, and it's too hard to get to from L.A. Besides, I can't afford it." More important, she didn't want to.

"Don't you think we should at least see it before we decide?" Juliette said cautiously. None of them had been there in twenty years and had only vague memories of it from their childhood. "Maybe it's worth hanging on to. We could rent it out, which would give us income to maintain it, and maybe even make a profit, which we could all use."

"After we pour a fortune into it," Timmie said, sounding definite about it. "I'm not going to spend what Dad left me to start a safe house or homeless shelter on a château in France I'll never use." And Joy felt the same way.

"I want to take a look at it before we sell it," Juliette persisted. "I could go over in August, since the shop will be closed." She had decided to stay closed for the rest of July and all of August, because of her father's death, so she had time on her hands. She looked pointedly at her younger sister then. "Will you come with me?" It was obvious that Timmie wasn't going to leave her clients to look at a château in the South of France. And her mind was made up about selling it, sight unseen, whatever condition it was in.

"I don't know. Maybe. If I'm not working," Joy said vaguely. All she could think about now were the auditions she would go to, and the parts she might get, especially with a new agent and manager, thanks to her father.

"What about you, Mom?" Juliette wanted to organize a reconnaissance trip. She had been thinking about it all afternoon.

"I could meet you there," Véronique said thoughtfully. She had never expected to see the place again, and had memories there. It would be bittersweet for her.

"What about Sophie?" Juliette inquired. "I think we should meet her, too." Both her sisters and her mother looked shocked at what she said. "We should find out who we're dealing with, and she's our sister after all."

"Half-sister," Timmie corrected her with a stern look, in deference to their mother. She had felt sorry for her that morning when the truth came out about their father's love child and affair. It was so typical of him to just drop it on them after he had checked out, instead of having the guts to tell them when he was alive. And such a rotten thing to do to their mother, particularly after his death. He had managed to shatter even her last shred of faith in their marriage. Timmie viewed it as a huge slap in Véronique's face. With one hand he had given each of them their dream, and with the other hand he had taken away all hope of respecting him as a husband and father.

And Timmie especially hated the pain she saw in her mother's eyes now. It wasn't just loss, it was betrayal, which was worse. She wasn't close to her mother, and Timmie wasn't a warm person. But she respected her and was loyal and hated this final blow to her. The painting he had left her out of sentiment was no compensation for what he'd done.

"I don't want to meet her," Timmie said bluntly about Sophie, and Joy looked pensive as she thought about it. She loved her mother, but a newly discovered sister could not be ignored.

"I don't know if I do or not. What if she's awful, or tries to get more money from the estate?" Joy said, looking worried.

"That would be Bertie," Timmie said drily. "I don't think he's going to take what Dad did lying down. We haven't heard the last of him yet. All we need now are two of them on our necks. One here and one in France."

"Can you have her checked out, Mom?" Joy said sensibly.

"I suppose I could call a detective service. It shouldn't be too hard to find something out." She was worried that Sophie and her mother might expect more from them, although they had never contacted her or the girls or gone after Paul legally. If they had, she would have known about it. And he had admitted in his will that he had never done anything for her until now. But it still wouldn't hurt to discover more about them, and Véronique was curious, too—how long the affair had gone on, and how they'd met. It still shocked her that she'd never learned about it or even suspected it. She hadn't heard a word about Elisabeth Marnier and their child. And it was hard to accept even now. "I'll make some calls when I go back."

Once that was settled, they continued talking about their father's will, and the unusual gifts he had left them. They were grateful for the opportunities he was giving them, but with the discovery of their unknown half-sister, they had mixed feelings, and it was all very bittersweet.

"It's kind of a crazy will," Joy commented, but he had tailored what he left each of them to their specific needs, which showed a rare insight for him.

"Bertie certainly thought so," Timmie said with a grin, and they all laughed, even their mother, as they discussed what an ugly scene it had been in Arnold's office, only moments after they had been told about Sophie.

"I think I went into shock," Juliette admitted, more relaxed after the wine and a good dinner.

"Yeah, me, too," Joy seconded.

Véronique sighed. She had certainly been shocked, and deeply hurt when she heard how old his hidden daughter was, and when she'd been born. "Maybe she's a nice girl," she said, trying to be generous, but unconvinced.

"Not likely, knowing the kind of women he went out with," Timmie said, which they all knew was true. He hadn't had a serious or worthwhile relationship with a decent woman since Véronique. It was all about his ego and their looks. He had been sixty when they divorced, and Timmie said he would have married again if he had found a woman with enough money, but his reputation preceded him by then. No one had wanted to marry him after Véronique, which she knew was true. And he was having too much fun, and living too well on her settlement to care.

They ended the meal with vague plans to meet in France in August, depending on what their mother was able to find out about the Marniers. But they agreed that they needed to see the château, to make a good decision about it, except for Timmie, who staunchly said she wanted out no matter what, even if it turned out to look like Versailles.

Juliette still wanted to see it, and Joy said she'd come along for the ride, if she wasn't working, but agreed with Timmie. She didn't want the responsibility or expense of a château in France. It sounded like a nightmare to her.

"When are you going back, Mom?" Timmie asked her as they left the restaurant.

"I don't know yet. In a few days, I guess." She had taken all her things from the house in St. Tropez when she left, so she didn't need to go back for the rest of the rental, but she had nothing to do in New York, and she realized that she wanted to go back to Europe for the rest of the summer. She had no firm plans, but maybe Paris in July and August wouldn't be so bad, even if it was quiet. She wasn't in a festive mood now anyway. And Paris seemed better than New York, which was stifling.

"What about the painting Dad left you?" Juliette asked her. They had spent the entire dinner talking about Bertie, Sophie, and the château. "Is it real?"

"I never thought so," Véronique said quietly. "Sometimes it's hard to tell with Renaissance paintings like that. It could have been painted by one of his students, several of them in the school, the master himself, or a clever forger. I always meant to research it, but I never did. And your father took it when he left. It's a very handsome painting even if it's a fake." Véronique looked wistful as she said it. After the reading of the will, the memories it evoked were too poignant now.

"You should check it out," Joy said gently, feeling more tender toward her mother after that morning. Her mother hadn't made a single unpleasant comment about her father helping her with her career. She respected his decisions and was too shaken by the discovery of Sophie. It had had the effect of uniting her and the three girls. Whatever their differences, they were forgotten now, faced with something far more serious, and a common enemy they were all prepared to despise. Not to mention Bertie, who had declared war on all four of them. They had enemies on all sides.

"Maybe I will research the painting," Véronique said, looking tired. "I could go to Italy for a while instead of France." She always loved spending time in Rome, Florence, and Venice, visiting museums and churches. She thought about it again when she went home that night, but she also wanted to hire a detective in Paris to investigate the Marnier women. That was a priority to her now, for herself and the girls. She had much to think about.

She decided what she wanted to do the next morning. Arnold called her to see how she was, and apologized for what a shock she must have had at the reading of the will the day before.

"I begged him to tell you himself," Arnold said gently, "but he wouldn't. He wanted me to handle it for him. He wasn't good about things like that." Arnold sighed. They both knew it was true. Paul only did what was easy, never what was hard.

"It doesn't matter now," Véronique said graciously, wishing it were true. But it did matter to her, and had left a bad taste in her mouth about who he was. He had disappointed her once too often, and hurt his children this time, too, in spite of the thoughtful way he had disposed of his estate. And then she remembered something she wanted to ask Arnold after her conversation with the girls the night before. "Can you get me a photograph of the painting he left me? I'm sure he has one in a file somewhere."

"I can have the painting delivered to you fairly soon," he said helpfully, but she wasn't ready for that. It was a very large painting, and she had no space for it on her walls. She would have to move some other things to make room, and she didn't know if she wanted to do that, particularly for a fake, if it was. And it evoked conflicting emotions now of hurt and tender memories that were long past.

"I'd rather just have a photograph for now. I'll have to put it in storage anyway."

"I'll take a look," he promised. "Would you like me to give you the photograph over dinner?" he asked hopefully. He never gave up.

"To be honest, I'm still too upset. You gave us a lot to digest yesterday. And I'm going to leave for France in a few days. I need to get organized and pack." She wasn't in the mood to fend off Arnold's gentle, persistent advances. "I'm going to hire a detective in Paris to investigate the two Marnier women for the girls," she told him, to change the subject, and he said he thought it was a good idea, and promised to get her the photograph of the alleged Bellini before she left.

"Are you going to check that out, too?" he asked her.

"Maybe. Eventually. I don't know if I'll have time now. There's a monastery in Venice, with incredible archives, that pursues the veracity of paintings, particularly those in dispute as to their authenticity. It would be interesting to visit them anyway. I went there once with my mother, after my grandfather wrote about the monastery in a book. She was always fascinated by forgeries. I caught the bug from her. If I go to Italy, I might visit them again."

"When will you be back?"

"I don't know. Late August. Maybe September. I'm going to visit the château with the girls."

"Are they planning to keep it?" he asked with interest.

"I doubt it. They don't want the burden of a château in France. They're much too busy with their lives here." They both knew that she could take on the responsibility of the château for them, but she didn't want to. She had given it to Paul, and it was a relic of ancient history for her.

"I'll get you the photograph before you leave," he promised again. "It sounds fascinating. Let me know what you find out. And about Sophie and her mother, too." Paul had certainly left a trail of mysteries and problems in his wake, which was so like him, an odd mixture of joy and pain, while he thought only of himself.

Véronique was packing and getting organized two days later, when she heard from Arnold again. He had received a letter from an attorney representing Bertie, who was registering strong displeasure over the disposition of his father's estate. He was offering his sisters an opportunity to settle it with him and include him in their share of the château, and a monetary amount "to true things up," particularly from Timmie, who had gotten the largest share. And if they failed to do so, he was giving them fair warning that he would attack them individually, and the estate, and file a lawsuit to overturn the will.

Véronique sighed as she listened, when Arnold read it to her, but she wasn't surprised.

"I thought he might do something like that. It's his only hope of getting something out of Paul now, and the girls." She sounded unhappy about it.

"He'd have gone after you if he could, but you neither have ownership in the château, nor got a monetary bequest. And he's obviously not interested in the painting you think is a fraud anyway."

"It's foolish of him," she said to Arnold. "If it's real, it's worth a fortune."

"He wants a safer bet, and faster money. What he really wants is a settlement, not a lawsuit. He's trying to scare the girls." It was obvious to Arnold, and Véronique had figured that out, too. "Do you think they'll give him something to get rid of him?" Arnold asked her.

"Not a chance," Véronique said with certainty. They had hated their half-brother for years and knew him for what he was. And they were far less charitable than Véronique. "And they're right. He doesn't deserve a penny now. Paul and I gave him more than enough, and he wasted it all. He'd do it again." Arnold agreed with her. "What do we do now?"

"Wait to see if he sues, and deal with it then. He won't get far with a suit, given the history, and Paul had the right to do what he wanted with what he had. The most Bertie can do is harass the girls for a settlement. I think a lawsuit would be unsuccessful, but he can try." Véronique still thought he might.

All three of the girls called her later that day, when Arnold faxed Bertie's letter to them. All of them were outraged but not surprised.

"We'll nail him to the wall if he tries to sue us," Timmie said succinctly, and Véronique was sure they would. The girls had no sentiment about him, and Timmie least of all, who always said he was a worm and had hated him even as a child and seen right through him, with his lying and wheedling ways. Arnold had said Bertie might even try to go after Sophie's share, since she had never been recognized by their father during his lifetime, but he doubted Bertie would succeed with that tack, unless he terrorized Sophie and she caved. Bertie didn't have a leg to stand on. All he had on his side were jealousy, venom, and greed, which wouldn't get him anything in court.

Juliette was more anxious about it when she called her mother, she didn't want the stress of getting sued. Véronique tried to reassure her and went out to Brooklyn to see her the next day, to give her a hug before she left for France. They had a nice visit in Juliette's tiny apartment, and Véronique promised to let her know what the detective said about Sophie Marnier.

That night Véronique dropped by Timmie's apartment for a few minutes to say goodbye to her as well. She usually said goodbye to them over the phone, but this time, since they had just lost their father, she wanted to see them in person before she left. She was flying to Paris the next day, nine days after she'd arrived from Nice. And she felt as though she'd been back for ten years. It had been a painful visit, full of hard emotions, good and bad surprises, and all the turmoil Paul had left in his wake. She couldn't wait to leave and get back to her peaceful apartment in Paris on the Île St. Louis.

Arnold found a photograph of the Bellini for her. If she went to Italy, she would try to track it down. The photograph was in her hand luggage, with a copy of Bertie's recent letter and another of the will.

Then Véronique called Joy in L.A. to say goodbye to her as well. She was busy and in good spirits. She had quit her waitressing job when she got back, and was thrilled, and she was meeting with drama coaches and agents to select the right ones. Her mother sounded pleased for her. They had turned a corner, and Véronique was trying to be more supportive about Joy's acting, following the example Paul had set. Joy was impressed by how much nicer her mother was being about it.

Véronique had decided to make her peace with it. Joy was twenty-six years old, after all, and had worked hard at acting for five years, which showed dedication. She had genuine talent and was serious about doing everything she could to get ahead. Véronique felt that she no longer had a right to stand in her way. It was Joy's life, and her dream.

When Véronique got on the plane the following afternoon, she left with a heavy heart. So much had happened, the last of her illusions about Paul and their marriage had been shattered. And the only good that had come of it was that she felt closer to her daughters than she had before. But she felt strangely alone as the plane took off. Paul was gone now, there was nothing left of him to hang on to, either as a husband or even a friend. And as much as she loved her daughters, they were grown women with their own lives. And she'd realized that she had relied on them emotionally for too long. She had never really built a life for herself after Paul. The children had been very little, and she had clung to them, and to him in a different way. Now, with his death, the umbilical cord had been severed. And as New York shrank beneath her, she had never felt so lonely in her life.

Chapter 5

The plane landed at Charles de Gaulle airport at six o'clock the next morning, and Véronique took a cab into the city just as dawn was breaking in the sky over Paris with brilliant pinks and oranges. It looked like one of her Impressionist paintings, and she nearly cried it was so beautiful and she was so happy to be back. There was something about Paris that always soothed her and consoled her. Even though she had lived in other cities, and in New York for many years, Paris always felt like coming home.

She had left her housekeeper a message that she was arriving, and when she got into her apartment with the slightly sloping floors and breathtaking view of the Seine, she found everything in good order, a fresh baguette in the kitchen, a basket of fruit that looked like a still life on the table, and her favorite foods in the fridge. And her bed with the perfectly pressed sheets had been left open in case she wanted to go to sleep. She loved Carmina in New York, but there was nothing in the world like her apartment in Paris and the impeccable way her housekeeper in Paris kept it ready and waiting for her.

She ate an apple, made herself a cup of coffee, and sat looking out the window from the kitchen table with a feeling of peace. She already felt better than she had the night before. After she took a shower, she went to bed for a while. She had a list of things she wanted to do that day, but she wanted to relax first and settle in. And she could tell it was going to be a hot day. She didn't have air conditioning in her apartment, and didn't care. She liked the heat, and the already half-deserted city in July felt peaceful to her, and the pace slower than usual. Half the country took vacation in July now, and the other half in August, when it was even quieter in Paris, and many businesses and restaurants were closed.

She slept for two hours after slipping between the cool Porthault sheets, and it was nearly noon when she woke up, and called a lawyer she knew to recommend a detective. When she called the detective he suggested, she was relieved to find that he wasn't on vacation. She explained the situation to him and gave him the names of the two Marnier women and said that they lived in or around St. Paul de Vence. He promised to get in touch with her by e-mail as soon as he had some information for her, about where they were living, what their jobs were, their marital status, and any other details about their life. He didn't seem to think it would be a difficult task, as long as they were still in the area and hadn't disappeared, which Véronique already knew from Arnold they hadn't.

She felt relieved after that, as though she had completed her mission, and she sent an e-mail to all three girls to tell them that the investigation had been started about Sophie Agnès Marnier and her mother. And then she put it out of her mind and went for a walk.

She wandered past the bookstalls along the Seine, the little displays of art for tourists, and some photographs of Paris, and eventually stopped at a café and had a cup of coffee and something to eat, watching the passersby and the tourists, and then she walked to Notre Dame and back to her apartment on the Quai de Béthune.

Her grandfather's and later her parents' home was nearby, but she didn't go there. She had no reason to, and did only when she had to make a decision about something that needed to be replaced or repaired. She kept it like a shrine to her past, but she much preferred her cheerful apartment overlooking the Seine. And she went back to it trying to decide what to do for the next few weeks. She had nothing but time on her hands. And as she thought about it, she took out the photograph of the supposed Bellini painting and looked at it long and hard. She liked the idea of going to Venice to try to track down its history and veracity at the monastery she knew there. Venice was crowded and hot in the summer, but it would give her a project that appealed to her. And if it was part of her estate now, she wanted to know if it was genuine, so she could tell the girls.

She put the photograph back in the folder she'd brought with her and then, on the spur of the moment, decided to go to Rome. She loved the city and always had fun there, even if she went alone, and from there she could go to Venice, to research the painting. Italy always buoyed her spirits, and she needed some of that now. The weeks since Paul's death had been very hard. Her girls had gone back to their lives, and she knew she had to find her own. Her world felt different now without Paul. In a strange way, his dying and their discovery of his final betrayal had freed her from her ties to him, and she felt liberated in a way that she never had since the divorce. But she missed him, too. There had always remained an unseen bond between them, which had been severed now at last. Suddenly she wanted to do something for herself. And Rome seemed like a good place to start. She only wanted to spend a day there before moving on to Venice.

She made a reservation at the Hotel Cipriani in Venice, and at the Hassler in Rome, and made a plane reservation to Rome for the next day. She felt free traveling alone, not having to adjust to anyone else's plans or worry about what they wanted to do. She packed a small bag, and the next morning she was ready. She had the photograph of the painting with her, and she was excited about going to the monastery. But just being in Italy would be fun. It was going to be an adventure.

The plane landed at Fiumicino Airport in Rome, and she took a cab into the city. The Hassler was in the center of town, near all the best shops, above the Fontana di Trevi, at the top of the Spanish Steps. The rooms were old fashioned and elegant, and she loved the hotel, even though she had always stayed there with Paul. She pushed the thought out of her mind as she checked in and was shown to her room, with a pretty view. Everything in the room was yellow satin, and there was a canopy over the bed.

She didn't linger in the room long, and went out for a walk half an hour after she'd arrived. The streets were crowded, and it was hot. She wore a white cotton dress and sandals. She had stopped wearing black for Paul after the reading of the will. She wanted to close the door on the past now, but she had no idea what lay ahead.

She walked for hours, in and out of small churches, and went to her favorite shops. She bought some pretty shoes and had them sent to the hotel. And everywhere she went, she noticed couples embracing or walking arm in arm, and families with young children, and by the time she got back to the Fontana di Trevi, she felt lonely again. It would have been nice to share the city with someone, but those days were in the past for her. She stood thinking about it as she watched people making wishes in the fountain.

A little beggar boy ran up to her and offered to exchange her euros for coins. She smiled and made the trade for him and gave him a coin for himself, and then she stood for a long moment with the coins in her hand. She had no idea what to wish for, and the little boy told her in Italian that one wish was for luck, another for true love, and the third was to return to Rome. She understood enough Italian to know what he had said.

She stood looking at the fountain for a long time, and then noticed a man in jeans and a blue shirt watching her. He had a serious expression and a heavy camera in his hand, poised to shoot, pointed at her, but he stopped when he saw her watching him. Their eyes met for a moment, and then she looked away. He had a young face and salt-and-pepper hair, and he looked European to her. There was something very distinctive about him. A moment later he disappeared, and she concentrated on her wishes again.

She finally tossed the three coins in, wishing, as the little boy had told her to, for luck, love, and a return to Rome, feeling melancholy for a moment as she did so. Then she walked away. She decided to wander the streets some more before she went back to the hotel. The traffic was heavy and chaotic, pedestrians were everywhere, she could hear half a dozen languages around her, and everything was so lively that she didn't want to go back to her room and be alone. Rome was a city to share, and it saddened her not to be able to, there was so much beauty around her.

She strolled for another hour, found two more exquisite small churches, and was walking back toward the fountain and the Spanish Steps on the way to the hotel, when a snarl of traffic exploded around her. She found herself in the middle of the street with cars rushing past her on either side, and scooters darting between the cars. She felt paralyzed and didn't know which way to turn. She saw a red Ferrari coming toward her, head on, at full speed. She looked at it as if it were a raging bull, and for an instant she was frozen in time, knowing it was going to hit her and she might be killed. The moment was mesmerizing, and she couldn't move, as she saw the driver and the speeding car, and suddenly she no longer cared what happened. Paul had betrayed her, her children no longer needed her, there was nothing she still wanted to do, she could feel her life racing past her, and suddenly it no longer mattered if she lived or died. It seemed totally unimportant. What did it matter if she was killed on the streets of Rome?

She heard someone scream as they watched her, and just at the moment when she decided not to move, for reasons she could no longer fathom later, she felt a force stronger than any she had ever felt push her, and she flew through the air, and landed on her hands and knees on the pavement as the Ferrari whizzed past her and screeched to a stop a few feet away. Horns were blaring, people were shouting in Italian, and suddenly a tall, heavyset man with dark hair was bending over her with a look of terror and trying to help her up.

She was shaky on her legs when he did so, and she had scraped her knees and hands badly and was bleeding all over her white dress. It was a frightening scene, but no more so than the fact that she had almost been killed by the Ferrari and had very nearly let it happen. Something had pushed her out of the way. She had no idea who or what it was, and there was no one standing near her. The driver helped her to her feet, and he looked as shaken as she did, and his face was as ashen as hers. He guided her to the sidewalk, where she sat down on the curb, and he handed her a handkerchief to clean the blood flowing from her hands and knees. She was too stunned by what had happened to even feel any pain, as the man leaned over her and spoke in heavily accented English.

"I almost killed you," he said, and she saw that his hand was trembling as he held out his handkerchief. He was well dressed in a linen jacket and gray trousers and was wearing a heavy gold watch. She was almost sure his accent was Russian. "I will take you to a hospital," he offered, as people swirled around them, and cars honked at his stopped car.

"No, no, I'm fine," Véronique insisted in a barely audible voice as she looked up at him, mortally embarrassed by the condition she was in, but even more so that she had almost let him hit her, and she didn't know why. She had never had an impulse like that before. Paul's death, and everything she had discovered since, had taken a toll. "I'm sorry. I think I got scared and froze on the spot." She wanted to believe that her momentary paralysis had been that and nothing worse.

"You need a doctor," he insisted, pointing at the blood-soaked handkerchief she had used to wipe her legs. He had strong features, piercing blue eyes, and a deep voice. He looked like a man who was used to command. He exuded power and was about her age.

"Really, it's just scrapes, it's fine," she said weakly, shaking from head to foot as she tried to regain her composure.

"I will take you to my hotel, and we'll call a doctor." He pointed at the Hassler as he said it, and she smiled wanly, as someone handed her the handbag that had flown off her arm. It was a shocking pink canvas bag that she had worn to go shopping, and the woman who handed it to her smiled sympathetically. Véronique's dress was torn and covered with blood, and she knew she must look a mess. She felt pathetic sitting there, but she was sick and slightly dizzy and was beginning to think a doctor wasn't such a bad idea.

"I'm staying there, too," she said, as he helped her up off the curb, and led her to the Ferrari, as she dabbed at her knees again with his handkerchief. She didn't want to bleed all over his car, but he didn't seem concerned. He was just grateful she wasn't dead.

"Rome is a very dangerous place," he said as he started the car, and drove up the hill to the hotel. "Too much traffic, too much cars and motorcycles. Crazy drivers." They were at the hotel a moment later, and he took her arm as they walked into the lobby and he propelled her toward the desk, where he requested a doctor for her. She was still feeling weak and slightly faint as the assistant manager looked at him with respect and addressed him as Mr. Petrovich. The manager could see that her hands were bleeding and looked concerned. "We had an accident in the street," Petrovich explained, as Véronique gave the man at the desk her room number and asked for her key. They promised to send a doctor immediately.

The Russian escorted her to her room, apologized profusely again, and asked if she felt well enough to be alone. She assured him she did, as he looked at her with relief. "I really thought I killed you," he said miserably. "I've never had an accident before."

"It was my fault," she said again, as much to reassure him as herself. "I'm fine." She felt considerably less than fine, and was still trembling, but she had caused him enough trouble for one afternoon.

"I will have the doctor come to my room," he told her. "I will call you when he comes." She didn't like the idea but didn't have the strength to argue with him as she unlocked her door. All she wanted now was to get out of her blood-soaked dress, put some cold water on her face, and lie down. And she would have much preferred to see the doctor in her own room. But a moment later he was gone. There was something familiar about his face, but she couldn't place it, and she was too distracted to think straight after what had happened.

She was horrified when she saw herself in the mirror in her bathroom. She looked a mess. She took off the dress, and tossed it onto the floor. She wanted to take a shower but was still too dizzy and afraid she might faint, so she washed her legs and hands with water from the sink, and went to lie down on the bed. She had a pounding headache, and five minutes later the phone rang. It was Mr. Petrovich to tell her the doctor was waiting for her in his suite. He must have flown. But it had been easy to see that the hotel management was vastly impressed by whoever the Russian was.

He gave her his suite number, which was on the sixth floor, two floors above hers, and she put on another cotton dress and went upstairs. Petrovich was waiting for her when she got off the elevator, and he led her into a spectacular suite, with an enormous wrap-around terrace with a view of all of Rome. It was the presidential suite. A doctor was waiting for her in the living room, and there was a beautiful woman lying on the couch. Petrovich spoke to her in Russian, and with a glance at Véronique and the doctor, the girl disappeared into the bedroom without a word. She looked very young, and had been wearing shorts and a halter top and had the body of a goddess.

Véronique felt slightly overwhelmed, as Petrovich told her to sit down, and the doctor examined her hands and knees. She had noticed that there was dirt from the road in both. And her host was obviously someone who was used to telling people what to do. He treated her like a child as she sat there, just as he had the girl he sent to the next room. And the doctor looked in awe of him, too, while Petrovich explained what had happened. The doctor asked her then if she had hit her head, or been unconscious, and she said she hadn't. She had fallen on her hands and knees when she was thrown, or pushed, or whatever had occurred, which she still didn't understand. Something or someone behind her had pushed her out of the way with superhuman force. Either a person or her destiny.

The doctor cleaned her wounds with disinfectant and confirmed that she didn't need stitches. The cuts were superficial and not deep, and most of the bleeding was from scrapes. He said there were no broken bones.

The tall Russian looked relieved. "I almost killed her," he confessed unhappily to the doctor, who smiled at them both. He could see that they were both badly shaken by the experience, but he assured them she'd recover quickly and no serious damage had been done.

"Fortunately, you didn't," he said cheerfully. "She will be fine." And by then Véronique was feeling better and smiled at them both. She was mortified by all the fuss that had been made. The doctor asked for her name then, so he could write it down for his report. She told him, and the Russian looked at her and said his name was Nikolai Petrovich, and she realized instantly who he was. He was one of the most powerful men in Russia, a multibillionaire who kept yachts all over the world, had homes in Paris and London, and was known for his vast collection of fast cars and beautiful girls. She had inadvertently picked a very important man to run her down. And the doctor left discreetly as Nikolai opened a bottle of champagne, poured a glass, and handed it to her.

"Drink, you will feel better. I am very sorry I hurt you," he said, as he poured a glass for himself.

"I'm very sorry I didn't move," she said again, as he indicated the terrace and opened the door, and she followed him out, still holding the glass of champagne. And as soon as she was outside, she was in awe of the breathtaking view. It had to be the best view in the city. You could see everything. They walked around, then sat down on two deck chairs, and she finally started to relax after a sip of champagne.

"I always stay here, for the view," he said, looking out at the city again, and then he turned to gaze at her. "You have beautiful eyes," he commented, "like sapphires." He was clearly a man of expensive tastes, but there was something rough about him. He was simple and direct to the point of being blunt. "Where do you live?"

"Most of the time in New York, and sometimes in Paris."

"You're here alone?" She nodded, and he seemed surprised. "You're not married?" He had looked for a ring, and her hands were bare.

"Neither am I," he said matter-of-factly. She had assumed he wasn't, judging by the girl she'd seen on the couch when she walked into the suite. She hadn't reappeared. "I'm divorced," he said almost proudly, as though it were a status symbol of some kind. "My ex-wife hates me," he announced out of the blue, and the way he said it made her laugh. "I was a very bad husband." He smiled at her then. Paul had been, too, but she didn't say it.

"My ex-husband just died. I've been upset about it, which is why I was probably distracted when I was crossing the street. We were good friends."

"You must be a good woman to be friends with your ex-husband," Petrovich said, looking at her intently.

"We'd been divorced for a long time." She didn't know why, but they were exchanging all the details of their lives, as though they mattered, but maybe nearly dying under the wheels of his car had created an instant bond between them. He seemed to want to know everything about her.

"Do you have children?" She looked young to him, and he guessed her for younger than she was.

"I have three daughters. Two are in New York, one is in L.A."

"You shouldn't travel alone," he scolded her. "It's too dangerous for a beautiful woman."

"Thank you," she said with a smile. She didn't say that she had no choice. And she didn't feel beautiful, she felt disheveled, her hands and knees were hurting more than they had at first, and the disinfectant had burned. She could still feel it, although the champagne had calmed her nerves.

"I have four daughters," he volunteered. "I always wanted to have a son." She nodded and thought wistfully about Bertie, who had been such a disappointment, despite the love she'd lavished on him.

"Girls always love their fathers," she said gently, as he smiled and admitted that that was true.

"Do you like boats?" he asked her, and she nodded. "You must come to dinner on one of my boats. Do you go to the South of France?"

"I'll be there in a few weeks with my daughters. Sometime in August."

"You must all come to dinner." He laughed then and looked more relaxed. The incident had frightened him, too. "We will celebrate that I didn't kill you."

"I think someone pushed me out of the way," Véronique said pensively, thinking about it again.

"It wasn't your destiny to die," he said solemnly. "Now you must enjoy your life more than before, because you are alive." He struggled with the words. His English was fluent but far from perfect, but she understood what he was saying. "Every day is a gift." She hadn't thought of it that way, but he was right. She felt as though she'd just been given a second chance at life. If something hadn't moved her out of the way, her children could have been burying her, too. It was a sobering thought. They both sat for a long moment, admiring the view. It was peaceful under the Roman sky at dusk. He walked to the railing then, and she joined him as they looked down at the spot where he had almost run her over. The traffic looked insane from there, and the fountain more beautiful than ever.

"I made three wishes today," she said wistfully, thinking of the three coins she had thrown in.

"Then they will come true," he said, smiling at her. "Wishes are magic. You're a good person—that's why you were saved today."

"I'm not so sure of that," she said with a cautious

smile, beginning to feel the effect of the champagne. He had filled her glass again. "I think I was just lucky."

"We get the luck we deserve," he said, sounding profound, as he set down his glass and looked at her. "Will you have dinner with me?" She was startled by the invitation and wondered what had happened to the girl in the bedroom. He didn't seem concerned.

"I'm not in any state to go out," she said, indicating the wrinkled dress she had pulled out of her suitcase in haste to see the doctor, and her battered knees and hands.

"We can have dinner here. The food is very good," he said simply. In spite of the fancy car and obviously expensive trappings of his life, he was without artifice, and he liked talking to her. He never met women like her, and spent all his time with young girls who were there for the money. Véronique was from a different world. He handed her the room service menu then and ordered for her.

They sat chatting on the roof, about Rome, and art. They talked about Venice, and the painting Paul had left her. Their dinner arrived half an hour later with three waiters to serve it. She had ordered truffle pasta and lobster salad at his insistence, and he had ordered caviar as their first course. It was a sumptuous meal, and the sommelier had chosen an excellent wine to go with it, a Chassagne-Montrachet.

By the end of dinner, Véronique was relaxed, had

had a wonderful time talking to him, and felt a little tipsy. Not drunk, but pleasantly relaxed and giddy. It had turned into a most unusual day, she had almost been killed on the streets of Rome, and now she was having dinner on the most extraordinary terrace in the world, with one of the most powerful men on the planet. She couldn't even imagine explaining it to her daughters. And she knew that what he had said was true. She had to seize life with both hands and enjoy every moment. He looked as though he did, with his yachts and planes and houses, exotic cars, and racy women. And he was clearly having a good time with her.

After the waiters left and took the tray away, Véronique thanked him for dinner and said she thought she should go to bed. It had been an exciting day, and he had told her he was leaving early in the morning on his plane to go to London—he had business there.

He walked her back to her suite and handed her his business card. All his numbers were on it, and he had asked for hers before they left his suite. He promised to call her, and reminded her of his dinner invitation in the South of France.

"And be careful crossing the street!" he admonished her, looking fatherly for an instant, and she smiled.

"I had a lovely time tonight, Nikolai. Thank you, and I'm sorry I was so much trouble." She still felt guilty for her part in their near disaster. He had more than made it up to her for what had happened. He had been kind and attentive and generous with his time, and the meal. It had been entirely unexpected, and she appreciated it.

"You're a very troublesome woman"—he wagged a finger at her—"and a dangerous one with those big blue eyes." No one had ever called her dangerous before, and it startled her. Their lives had almost been changed irreparably that day, and they were both grateful that nothing terrible had happened. In fact, it had turned into a perfect evening, and she knew she had made a new friend. "We will see each other again, in the South of France, or before. You'll hear from me," he promised, and then gave her a warm hug after she opened her door. He was a big bear of a man. "Take care of yourself, Véronique," he said, and then strode back to the elevator with a smile as she waved and closed the door. She felt as though she had been living someone else's life for the past several hours. She didn't know whose, but definitely not hers. She got a text message from him, telling her to sleep well and have sweet dreams. She was already half asleep when she read it and followed his advice. And by then, he was in the arms of the girl who had been waiting in his bedroom for hours, and she knew better than to complain. And he had had a delightful evening with Véronique.

Chapter 6

Nikolai had already checked out of the hotel when Véronique woke up the next day. And she groaned when she saw herself in the mirror. Her knees looked like hamburger, and there were bruises up and down her legs. Her hands still hurt, and she had a hangover from the champagne.

"You are a mess," she said to her reflection, and then got into the bathtub, to soak her bruises and relax. She felt better by the time she dressed and smiled when she thought of the remarkable evening she'd had on the terrace of the presidential suite. Nikolai was an extraordinary man, and she wondered if she'd ever hear from him again. It seemed unlikely, but it would be fun to introduce him to her daughters if he actually did show up in the South of France. They would be astounded that she'd met him, and she was still surprised herself. He wasn't the sort of person she normally ran into in her quiet life, and on the surface they had nothing in common, but he had been interesting to talk to, and he was wise about life. He was a person who obviously lived each day to the fullest, and had advised her to do the same. It had amounted to nothing more than a mild flirtation, but there was no denying he was a very intriguing and attractive man. She couldn't imagine becoming romantically involved with him, they were too different, and given his reputation, she was much too old, but he would be fun to know, and she hoped she'd hear from him again.

She was in good spirits when she checked out of the hotel. The concierge had rented a car for her, and she drove to Venice on her own. She could have flown, but she preferred to drive and enjoy the Tuscan scenery along the way. She left at noon and arrived in Venice in the late afternoon. The trip had been easy, mostly on highways, as she circled Florence and Bologna on the way. The Hotel Cipriani, where she had a reservation, had a boat waiting for her at the parking stand where she returned her rental car, and they took her to the hotel, where she was given a suite with a view of the lagoon. It was a beautiful warm night, and after she unpacked, she had one of the hotel's boats take her to the Piazza San Marco so she could walk around. She couldn't wait to explore Venice again. It had been years since she'd been there.

The city was even more beautiful than she remembered, with the enormous church, the Doge's

Palace, and outdoor cafés where people were eating and drinking wine. There were tourists everywhere, but she didn't mind. She felt safe and at ease as she walked around for two hours, bought a gelato from a street vendor, looked at the cathedral all lit up at night, and watched people getting into gondolas to glide under the Bridge of Sighs. She thought it was the most romantic city in the world. It brought back memories of her honeymoon with Paul, and she tried not to think about it. As Nikolai had said the night before, the past was gone, and it was time to look ahead to the future and enjoy today. It was good advice. And she was pleasantly tired when she got into the boat to return to her hotel. She looked at the lights of Venice as she crossed the lagoon to the Cipriani.

She stood on her small balcony when she got back to her room, remembering the incredible view of Rome she'd seen the night before. She thought of Nikolai, her dinner with him, and their near disaster, and then she went to bed. She got a text from him just before she fell asleep, and she smiled when she saw it. He said he hoped she was feeling better and was no longer suffering the ill effects of the day before. She responded immediately, thanked him again for dinner, and assured him that she was fine and was thoroughly enjoying Venice, and hoped to see him again.

She woke up early the next morning, had breakfast on her balcony, and got dropped off at Piazza

San Marco again, and this time she intended to explore the town in depth. There were narrow serpentine alleyways, and every time she thought she was lost, she would find herself in a familiar place again. Streets seemed to double back and intersect, and little by little she began to find her way. She walked into small beautiful churches, and admired the intricate marble designs and the exquisite frescoes in every church and made new discoveries everywhere she went. The art was so breathtaking that it was exciting just being there. After several hours of walking, she sat down on a bench in a small square and looked around. She had no idea where she was, but it didn't matter, because she knew she'd find her way back to Piazza San Marco, and every inch of Venice was beautiful to look at.

She had been sitting there for a few minutes, when a man sat down next to her. She didn't know why, but he seemed vaguely familiar, and he had a camera hanging from a strap on his shoulder. She had the feeling that she'd seen him somewhere, but she couldn't place his face. She saw that he glanced at her, too, and he winced when he saw her battered knees in her short pink dress. Her knees were much better than they'd been the day before and didn't hurt as much, and they hadn't slowed her down. She knew they still appeared terrible, but they were healing. She looked as though she'd been dragged behind a horse on her knees, and he winced again when he saw her hands.

"That must have been a nasty fall," he said sympathetically with a noticeably British accent. He knew she spoke English from the guidebook she had next to her on the bench. She had been trying to figure out where she was, and couldn't. She smiled at him. He had a young face, salt-and-pepper gray hair, and serious dark brown eyes.

"I had a close encounter with a car in Rome," she explained easily. "It's not as bad as it looks." He didn't seem convinced. The bruises on her legs had turned purple by then. She'd clearly been in the wars, but she didn't seem upset about it. She was too fascinated by her surroundings to think about her scrapes and bruises.

"At least you won't get run over by a car here," he said, amused. And then he mentioned a church that he'd just seen and thought was worth a visit. She thanked him and picked up her guidebook to find a description of it, and a few minutes later he walked away. She still had the feeling that she'd seen him somewhere, but decided it was her imagination and forgot about it. She thought about backtracking to the church he had suggested, but was afraid she'd get lost again when she saw it on the map. It was down several alleys and was complicated to reach. So she kept moving forward, and as she thought she would, she eventually wound up back at Piazza San Marco. Her morning of exploring had been successful, and she'd seen wonderful things, and many tiny churches and chapels filled with the Renaissance art so typical of Venice. Once in the square again, she stopped at a sidewalk café, sat down at a table, ordered coffee and gelato, took a notebook out of her bag, and began to sketch. She was hungering to draw, after all the art she'd seen there and in Rome the day before. She sketched the faces of some of the people sitting in the café, and was engrossed in what she was doing. She sipped her coffee, ate some of the gelato, and didn't look up until she finished a small drawing of a woman a few tables away. And as she glanced around when she set her notebook down on the table, she noticed the man with the camera again. He was sitting two tables away, smiled when she noticed him, and pointed at her with a quizzical expression.

"Are you following me?" he asked, and she laughed at the question, and shook her head. It was the second time their paths had crossed that day, but Venice was a tiny city, and all paths led back to Piazza San Marco.

"I think you're following me," she accused him jokingly, and he denied it. Without asking, when the table between them became free, he sat down next to her, and observed admiringly what she'd drawn.

"You're very good," he complimented her, and she was embarrassed and put the notebook away. She never liked showing off her work and was shy about it. And she rarely even sketched anymore. But she'd been inspired since that morning. And being in Italy made her want to paint again. "So explain something to me," the man with the intense brown eyes and gray hair said casually, "why are you following me all over Venice? Are you CIA or KGB?" He pretended to be serious but had a mischievous glint in his eyes. There was something vaguely sarcastic about him, and it made Véronique laugh the way he said it. But they were visiting all the same places, and it was easy to run into the same people. He was just more distinctive-looking than the other tourists she'd seen on her walk around the city, so she recognized him each time. "Have you been to the Doge's Palace yet?" he asked with interest.

"I was there this morning—it's spectacular. I tried to get into the cathedral, but the line was endless." She didn't usually talk to strangers, but there was something very easy and open about him, and the conversation was harmless, so she didn't mind talking to him as they sat at their tables at the café.

"I'll tell you a trick to get into the cathedral," he said, lowering his voice conspiratorially. "If you tell one of the guards you're going to mass, they let you in immediately. A friend told me about it, and it works. I tried it today."

"Seriously?" She glanced at him in surprise, grateful for the tip. She didn't want to wait in line for hours in the heat.

"Seriously. Try it," he advised her, as his eyes seemed to search hers.

"I will, thank you." She smiled at him, and had

that same haunting feeling that she'd seen him somewhere other than on the bench that morning. It was a powerful sense of déjà vu. She glanced at his camera then, and suddenly she remembered. She had seen him at the Fontana di Trevi in Rome, when she was about to make her three wishes. She had seen him watching her as he held his camera, and then he'd disappeared, and she'd forgotten all about him until then. "I saw you two days ago in Rome," she said pensively. "I think you were about to take a picture of me, when I was going to throw coins into the fountain." He nodded. He had recognized her earlier. He had been struck by how beautiful she was and the unusual color of her eyes, somewhere between lavender and blue.

"I saw you again after that," he said, with a guilty expression, and pointed at her knees. "I'm afraid I'm responsible for those."

She shook her head. "No, I almost got hit by a car," she said and then she remembered the force of the push that had saved her from the Ferrari, and wondered what he meant.

"I'm afraid I got a little carried away. I thought you were going to be killed." He watched her eyes as he said it.

"**You** pushed me?" She was stunned as he nodded with a sheepish look. "I thought somebody had pushed me, but I couldn't tell. I thought it was the hand of destiny," she said, smiling at him gratefully.

"No, it was just me. You didn't seem like you

were going to move. You were too frightened to react." She didn't want to admit to him that she still didn't know why she had stayed rooted to the spot, watching Nikolai's car barrel toward her. "You were lighter and flew farther than I thought. I hit you damn hard," he said apologetically. "I felt terrible when I saw your knees this morning."

"You saved my life," she said with amazement. "Why didn't you stick around? I looked around afterward and I didn't see anyone, and after that I was sitting on the curb, and I was pretty shocked."

"I saw the driver get out of the car to help you, and there were people all over you after you fell. I didn't think you needed me around, too. I knew you'd be all right then," he said quietly. She was still amazed that it had been him and that they'd met again in Venice.

"Do you do that a lot? Go around saving people's lives when they're about to be run over?" She was seriously impressed to be meeting her benefactor and to be able to thank him in person. He had pushed her so hard that she had literally flown to safety, despite the awkward landing.

"Never. I'm a terrible person. Normally I push old ladies down the stairs." But he was far less believable as a villain than a hero. "Besides, you were standing right in front of me, and I thought if he hit you, he might hit me, too. So it was a totally selfish act." He was mischievous again. He had a dry sense of humor.

"I don't believe you," she said, and he laughed.

"Anyway, you owe those lovely knees to me, and your hands. I apologize for the brutality."

"They don't even hurt. Getting hit by the car would have been a lot worse," she said gently.

"Yes, it would. Messy, too," he said, sounding very British.

"I actually flew through the air," she informed him. "The poor driver was scared to death."

"He should have been. He was driving too fast, and he damn near hit you." Her benefactor seemed upset. "Everyone drives too fast in Rome." They both knew it was true, but the man with the camera thought the driver of the Ferrari was entirely to blame, and she'd been very lucky.

"It was really my fault. I didn't get out of the way. I don't know why, but I just froze," she confessed.

"Which is why I pushed you as hard as I did. I didn't realize the landing would be so rough. I'm glad you didn't break anything," he said, sounding relieved. He had thought of her the night it happened. The experience had been powerful for him, as he saw her about to die. "I'm Aidan Smith, by the way." He held out a hand, and they shook hands properly.

"Véronique Parker," she said politely.

"It's nice to meet you," he said pleasantly, mock serious again. "Now stop following me, Véronique

Parker." He stood up then, paid for his coffee, and was preparing to leave as she stood up, too.

"I'll try to," she promised. "I'm going back to my hotel now, so you don't need to worry." She was laughing as she said it, and so was he.

"Where are you staying?"

"The Cipriani." It didn't surprise him. It was one of the best hotels in Venice, and she was right for the part.

"How elegant. I'm staying at a little inn on the Calle Priuli dei Cavalletti. It's one step above a youth hostel, but it's cheap." Which the Cipriani emphatically was not.

"Are you a photographer?" she asked as they strolled across the square together. The camera he carried looked very professional.

"Yes, I am, a chronicler of the evils of the world, of which there are many," he said with an ironic tone.

"Then why were you photographing me at the fountain? There's nothing evil about that."

"You were so beautiful," he said kindly, as his face softened. "I wanted to capture it forever. The sun was picking up the color of your eyes, and there was something very poignant about your expression. Part hope and part sadness as you thought about your wishes. I hope they come true." He smiled down at her, and there was something very gentle in his face. And at other times, she had noticed, he was very intense and serious. She suspected that he was a man of many facets and moods. "Well, don't get run over by a gondola," he said as he walked her to the Cipriani shuttle.

"I won't. Thank you for saving me in Rome," she said sincerely, deeply grateful. In fact, he had saved her from herself, in that fraction of a second when recent events had overwhelmed her and she had abandoned herself to the fates, and then he intervened.

"Anytime. It was a pleasure. And I'm sorry about the hands and knees. I'll be gentler next time, if it happens again."

"I hope it won't," she said fervently, remembering Nikolai's Ferrari heading straight toward her, until Aidan's superhuman push.

"I hope so, too. See you around somewhere tomorrow," he said casually.

"I won't follow you, I promise," Véronique said, smiling.

"You don't have to. I kept seeing the same people again and again all day. That's because I was lost most of the afternoon," he confessed, and they both laughed as she got into the boat.

She waved at him as the boat pulled away, and he waved back, watching her go and wondering if he'd ever see her again. Fate had intervened three times so far. At the Fontana di Trevi, when he pushed her out of the way of the Ferrari, and now twice in Venice. It seemed too much to hope for destiny a fourth time, and he doubted that it would. No one could be that lucky, he told himself, as he walked away, thinking about the color of her eyes. She was even more beautiful than he'd remembered when he saw her at the fountain in Rome. She looked like a raven-haired angel to him. And it was odd the way fate and coincidence kept putting her on his path. He knew where she was staying now, but he didn't want to intrude on her. They were strangers, and all he could hope was that somewhere on the streets of Venice, he would run into her again.

Chapter 7

Véronique got into the Basilica San Marco early the next morning, using the ruse that Aidan had suggested. When she told one of the guards that she was there to attend mass, he immediately lifted the rope and let her in. And in the end she stayed for the service anyway. It was a simple, beautiful mass in the extraordinarily exquisite church. She couldn't stop gazing up at the ceiling and the art all around her. She lit candles for Paul and her daughters before she left the church. And she realized that indirectly, she had come back to Venice because of him, to try to authenticate the Bellini they had wondered about for thirty years.

She visited countless small churches once again, also Santa Maria della Salute, which was one of the city's landmarks, and the Cloister of San Gregorio nearby, and Santa Maria dei Miracoli, which she remembered visiting with Paul. By lunchtime, she was all churched out and stopped at a trattoria for a slice of pizza, and then she went back to meandering through the narrow streets, glancing into shop windows, and she peeked into several jewelers on the Rialto Bridge and stopped to watch the gondolas sliding beneath it.

She wanted to take a gondola ride but hadn't had time yet, she was too busy visiting churches and admiring the art, and she was just emerging from another tiny chapel she'd discovered when she ran into Aidan again. He was eating a chocolate gelato, and it was dribbling down his chin as he saw her and grinned. He had been hoping he would see her again, but was determined to let fate make the decision for him. She was friendly and polite, but he could easily see that their worlds were far apart. He was staying at one of the cheapest hotels in Venice and content to do so, and she was at the most elegant hotel at the Lido, which to her was commonplace. And in Aidan's opinion, the two worlds didn't mix, but he was happy to see her by chance.

"I got into San Marco this morning, thanks to you." She smiled broadly when she saw him, as he wiped the gelato off his chin and popped the rest of the cone in his mouth. It was another minute before he could speak, and he was silently observing her eyes again. Their lush violet color was mesmerizing. "But then I decided to be honest about it," she admitted, "and I went to mass, too. The church is incredibly beautiful. What did you do today?" They acted like old friends, and he had finished the cone by then and could talk.

"I've been photographing frescoes and people in the streets. The faces are so good here, almost as good as the art." As always, he had his camera in his hand.

"Do you sell the photographs to magazines and newspapers afterward?" She was curious about him, and he was obviously a pro.

"I'm not that kind of photographer." He smiled as they walked side by side. "I do gallery shows of my work, and I hope to be in museums one day. I'm fascinated by the offbeat, the mysterious, and the grim. I'm having a show in Berlin soon. I have a very good rep, and he gets me into some interesting shows." Véronique knew that the art scene in Berlin was very advanced, and many American artists showed their work there, but she had never been to Berlin. "I had a show in London last year. I got some fairly decent reviews, if that means anything, which of course it doesn't. Reviewers can be jealous little people with no talent and small minds." He dismissed them summarily with an irritated look. "Have you ever had a show of your artwork?" he asked, equally curious about her. He had seen how skilled she was from her sketch at the café the day before. They were both chroniclers of life and the human condition, which fascinated him.

"Only once when I was very young, but it wasn't

a real show. My father organized it for his friends. I was still a student then, at the Beaux-Arts. It was very embarrassing, and I got some commissions out of it. I really haven't painted in a long time," she said, always modest and dismissive about her talent.

"Why not?" Aidan pressed her, sounding as though he disapproved. He hadn't had a camera out of his hands since he was in his teens. He always said the camera was his eyes and he couldn't see without it. And thought she would be the same about her art. He was very militant about using the talents one had been given, and not wasting them. He pushed himself hard and expected a lot of those around him.

"I was busy," she said, to explain not painting for many years, as they wandered down the street, "married, raising children, and too lazy now." She dismissed the question easily, but Aidan was never satisfied with superficial answers, though she didn't know that about him. He went straight to the core of every issue, which showed in his photography, too. Even simple honesty was never enough for him—he always wanted more.

"Those are poor excuses for not using your talent," he said critically. "Maybe you're not lazy, you're scared." She was startled by what he said and was silent as they walked along, as she thought about it, and then she looked at him.

"You're probably right," she said thoughtfully.

She was an honest woman, particularly about herself, and never put on airs. "I've been afraid to paint for a long time, particularly since my kids grew up, and I can no longer blame not painting on them."

"Afraid of what?" He delved deeper, always wanting the real answers and not the easy ones.

"Maybe afraid that I have no talent, that I'm an artistic fraud. It's easy to paint a portrait that makes people happy. You correct the obvious flaws, do something gentle that idealizes them. If you painted the truth, and what's in their soul, it would scare the hell out of them, and they'd never buy it. I was always kind in my work, and painted the ideal more than the real. I don't want to do that anymore. I never really did. And I didn't want to be a commercially pleasing artist, which you really have to be, so I stopped."

"Then paint what you really see and how you feel," he said simply. It seemed obvious to him, but his subjects were criminals and convicts, prostitutes and derelicts, drug addicts and people in the streets. He didn't have to please anyone but himself.

"And who would I paint for, Aidan?" she said, looking him in the eye with her violet laser glance. Her gaze was as intense as his, and he liked that about her.

"You paint it for yourself, not for them," he insisted.

"Not with portraits, or no one would let you paint them. It would terrify them."

"Can't you do both? Be honest and be real, and still true to yourself?"

"Maybe. I never worked that out. I was very young when I stopped painting."

"You try to make it sound like you're old," he said with an air of disapproval. "You're not."

"I'm old enough," she said honestly, and she had more experience about life than he did. Despite the gray in his dark hair, he looked young. "Older than you are," she said with a cautious smile. She felt as though they were becoming friends. It was a serious conversation for two strangers to be having on a Venetian street, only days after they'd seen each other for the first time. But Aidan wasn't a trivial person—he was intense.

"I'm forty-one," he challenged her, convinced that she was younger than he, though not by much.

"I'm eleven years older than you are, I'm fifty-two." He was stunned and hadn't expected that at all.

"I thought you were thirty-five, or late thirties tops." She had a youthful way about her and a gentle style that made her seem younger than she was. And there was no age to the way she dressed. Her face had been very little touched by the passing years. "I'm impressed."

"Thank you," she said with a broad smile.

"I think age is irrelevant. It's about what you're doing and thinking, how alive your spirit is, not what your passport says. I've known people half my age who were dead. I photographed a hundred-year-old man last year, and his spirit was younger than mine."

"Unfortunately, I don't see my spirit when I look in the mirror," she said, laughing, "I see my face. That's a little scary at times."

"You look like a kid," he said, glancing at her. "How many children do you have?" There was something fascinating about her, in every way, physically, philosophically, and he wanted to know more about her life. She was equally intrigued about him. He had a dark mysterious quality to him, and then the sunshine would burst through the clouds when he smiled or said something kind.

"I have three daughters. They're in their twenties, work hard, and have busy lives." Busier than hers, which was a problem for her now, trying to figure out what to do with herself. All signs recently seemed to be pointing to her going back to painting. Paul had suggested it in his will, and now Aidan, who barely knew her, was pushing her in that direction, too.

"What do they do?"

"A social worker, a baker, and an actress." She had to admit, it was an odd mix when she said it like that, but it was true.

"Interesting. You must have given them a lot of leeway to be themselves."

"No." She laughed at his comment. "They're all

very headstrong young women and do what they want." She sounded as though she admired them for it when she said it, and he heard that, too.

"And are you headstrong, too?" he asked her, searching her eyes, wanting to discover who she was.

"No"—she shook her head—"not as much as they are. That's the privilege of youth, not having responsibilities and answering only to yourself. What about you?"

"I'm hell on wheels," he said proudly and she laughed, not sure if it was the truth, although she could imagine him being difficult. He had his own ideas and wasn't afraid to voice them, even with someone he didn't know well. "I've never been married, have no kids, and never wanted any. I think I'd be a lousy parent. I'm too independent to be a good influence on a child, and maybe I'm too selfish by now. I've lived with two women. One hates my guts for not marrying her after five years. The other woman and I have ended up good friends. We lived together for eight years. I ended it because I was bored—we both were. We stopped growing together, and I wanted out before we hated each other. It's not easy to make relationships work, and we were very different. She was a barrister from a wealthy aristocratic family, and I was too bohemian for her, or at least her family thought so. She married a member of the House of Lords, and they were thrilled. I was her little detour before she settled down." He sounded slightly bitter as he said it, and Véronique could hear it in his voice.

"You don't like aristocrats?" she asked him boldly, which was unlike her, but he'd been candid with her.

"I'm allergic to them," he said with fervor, "particularly if they have money. I grew up dirt poor, and I believe in the honesty of the masses. When I was a kid, I always envied the rich. I always thought they were happier than we were, and then I discovered they're just as miserable—they're just politer and use bigger words." She laughed at what he said as they continued walking.

"Not all rich people are bad, although some certainly are," she admitted, thinking of how corrupted Bertie had become by his pursuit of money, greed, and envy of everyone.

"And not all poor people are good," he conceded. "They tend to be more honest, though. If they hate you, you usually know it when they tell you to sod off. I can't stand pretense and hypocrisy. Arabella's family drove me mad—they were never honest about anything, just incredibly well bred and polite. I'd rather have a poor man spit in my eye than a rich one shake my hand. My father's family were coal miners from the North, and my mother's family was slightly more genteel. Their families hated each other, and they were miserable with each other for most of their marriage. Chalk and cheese, as we British say. Those matches don't work. Like marrying fish to birds." He had very definite ideas. She wondered what he'd think of her family, and Paul, who had married her for her money and lived off her shamelessly for thirty years. It wasn't admirable, but they had had ten good years together, and she got three nice children out of it, which made her feel it had been worth whatever it cost her. "You're divorced?" Aidan asked her then, and she nodded.

"We stayed close. My ex-husband died two weeks ago, and we were all very sad about it. It's a bit complicated. He wasn't a great husband or father, but he wasn't a bad man," although he had cheated on her, lied, and spent as much of her money as he could. She was having mixed feelings about him ever since he died, after the revelation of the daughter he had fathered during her marriage. It was one transgression too many. But she didn't say any of that to Aidan.

"He must have been young to die," Aidan commented. "Accident or heart attack?"

"He had a stroke a year ago. He was a lot older than I am. He was eighty when he died. My kids are still very upset. It will take time to settle down." That and the shock of Sophie. She wondered if they'd ever get over that. She didn't think she would, given the circumstances. In the last two weeks, it had tainted everything she'd felt about him. And she felt oddly adrift as she talked to this stranger about people he didn't know.

"I must sound like a Communist to you," Aidan said, smiling, as they sat down on a bench facing some trees and a small park where children were playing and their mothers were watching them.

"No, just very clear about what you think. And not very fond of rich people," she said, smiling back at him. "Sometimes I'm not either. And I don't like hypocrisy and lies. But I don't think that's particular to the rich. I'm sure people without money lie, too."

"Constantly," Aidan said with a grin. "It's the nature of man, and some women." But he seemed unusually honest, even about himself, and cut to the heart of things, seeking the truth.

They sat on the bench in silence for a while, observing the children. Scenes like it always reminded her of the happy days when her own children were small. It was hard not to miss that now.

"You're thinking about your children?" he asked her, as though he could read her mind. She nodded and turned to him, and he could read volumes in her eyes. He had a sense that she was very much alone in life, and not entirely happy. "What made you come here?" he asked, wishing he could take a photograph of her, but he didn't want to bother her or make her feel scrutinized. He could tell she didn't like too much attention focused on her. And as a photographer, neither did he.

"I had some time on my hands, and I actually came to research a painting my ex-husband left me. We bought it here on our honeymoon. I always thought it was a fake, and he thought it was real. A Bellini. It's hard to tell if it was painted by a student, the master himself, or a brilliant forger. There's a monastery here known for researching works like that, and pursuing provenances. I always meant to come here about it and never did. So now here I am." She smiled, and he looked intrigued.

"Could I go with you? It must be fascinating."

"They have one of the most extensive art libraries in the world, mostly from the Renaissance, illuminated manuscripts and more recent books to research provenance. They've found many stolen works, authenticated some real mysteries, and debunked some paintings that private collectors and museums paid a fortune for. I've brought a photograph to see if they can trace this one. I feel like I owe it to my children to check it out."

"Will you love it even if they say it's a fake?"

"It has sentimental value to me. That's different," she said, thinking of Paul. It was a relic of a better time than their later years or his shocking revelation at the end.

Aidan was impressed by how much she knew about art and obviously loved it, and asked her about how she came to be so knowledgeable, as they chatted and watched passersby from where they sat.

"My grandfather was a famous art dealer in Paris,

and my mother taught me a lot about art. She passed her love for it on to me before she died. It always fascinated me, and still does." He could tell it was her passion, the way photography had always been his.

"Are you hungry?" he asked her after a while, and she nodded. "I found a funny little trattoria yesterday by accident. Want to give it a try?"

"Sure." She smiled at him, amused by the friendship they had struck up—fellow travelers in Venice, who kept bumping into each other, after he'd saved her life in Rome. It was very picturesque and would make a good story when she went home, if she bothered to tell the girls. It was the kind of anecdote that wouldn't interest them much. They were too busy to wonder how she spent her time, and had their own lives to think about, not hers. They paid attention when they needed her help or serious advice, but not the rest of the time, for her daily pursuits. She was on her own now, and even more so without Paul to check in from time to time. And she had grown more solitary than she intended over the years. It made a chance encounter like the one with Aidan all the more entertaining, and she had time to enjoy it now.

The trattoria he took her to was lively and fun and noisy. There were mostly locals and a few tourists, the food was delicious, and they both had pesto pasta, mozzarella, and a big green salad, and **granite di limone** for dessert. It was the perfect meal for a hot day, and she would have gone back to her hotel to lie by the pool, but there was so much left they wanted to see. They walked the streets together all day, stopped in Piazza San Marco at the end of it, and both admitted they were exhausted and couldn't wait to get back to their respective hotels, but they'd had fun together. Véronique invited him to come to the monastery with her the next day, and he was delighted to accept.

"I was planning to go to Siena and Florence after Venice," Aidan said, looking relaxed as they drank lemonade at a sidewalk café, while she waited for the boat from the Cipriani to pick her up. "Can I interest you in joining me?" She had the time, but didn't know him, yet they had enjoyed each other's company. She was sure her children would be horrified to hear about her traveling with a stranger, but she had looked him up on the Internet the night before at the hotel, and he appeared to be a real photographer, with a long list of gallery shows to his credit. He was what he said, if nothing else. "I have some time to kill before my show in Berlin. I have to go to prepare it in the next month, but until then I decided to take a break and wander around Italy. I wanted to come back to Venice, and a few of my favorite cities. Siena is wonderful. If you've never been there, you'd love it. And Florence is my favorite city for art." She had been there many times and loved it, too.

She was thinking about his offer to travel with

him. "I'd like that," Véronique said cautiously, deciding to trust him, and not sure why she did. She could always leave at any point, if he made her uncomfortable or acted crazy. But he hadn't so far, and despite some of his radical ideas, he was pleasant, interesting, polite, and respectful, as well as outspoken and intelligent.

"Italy is so perfect this time of year." She couldn't disagree with him, and there was nowhere she had to be until St. Paul de Vence in another month to see the château. She had the time, too.

They agreed to meet in Piazza San Marco the next day at eleven o'clock to go to the monastery about the painting, and continue their sightseeing. He suggested Harry's Bar for dinner the following night. It was an institution in Venice, and she liked the idea of going there, too. And the following day they would leave for Siena. He said he had a car in the parking lot, an old Austin-Healey he had been nursing for years. Although it wasn't as impressive as Nikolai's Ferrari, it sounded like fun to her. It was an adventure, which fit in with her current philosophy since Paul's death, that life was short and you had to seize it with both hands while you could. Aidan seemed to live that way, too.

He walked her to the boat dock, and she went back to the Cipriani, had a quick swim and dinner in her room. It had been a thoroughly enjoyable day, and Aidan had been good company.

She took out the photograph of the Bellini, and laid it on the desk for the next day. She could hardly wait to hear what the monks would say about it. And although she considered it unlikely, it would be amazing if it was real!

Chapter 8

The next morning Véronique met Aidan at the Piazza San Marco, where he was enjoying an espresso at his favorite café. He saw her coming toward him and waved, and she sat down next to him, and he ordered an espresso for her, too. They chatted peacefully in the sunshine for a few minutes, and he asked to see the photograph of the Bellini. She took it out and showed him, and he studied it for a moment in silence, concentrating on the details.

"Beautiful painting," he said admiringly. "It looks real to me." It did to her, too, a little too much so, which was why she'd been suspicious of it since the beginning. She explained that to him as they drank their coffee.

"When it's too perfect, there's usually something wrong with it. Very few paintings have this kind of flawless precision, and if they do, they've been in museums for the last two hundred years. It may be by the school of Bellini, possibly even worked on by several of his students, but I just don't think it's by the master himself. I'm sure the monks will want to see the original, but at least they can start tracing the provenance, and where it's been for the last six hundred years." The painting had certainly been painted in the fifteenth century—the question was by whom, an unknown or a master.

"This should be very exciting," he said, fascinated by the story. He was catching the bug from her.

They finished their coffee, and Véronique had the address of the monastery, which was farther afield than they had ventured so far around Venice. It was the monastery of San Gregorio de la Luce, and they guessed that it would take them twenty minutes to walk there if they didn't lose their way. It was a Gregorian monastery that dated back to the fifteenth century, like so much of Venice. They had no appointment and were planning to drop in, and she hoped that at least one of the monks would speak French or English. She could manage in Italian, but not well enough to give them all the pertinent details of the painting.

Aidan gave her back the photograph, and she felt as if she were carrying the Holy Grail. Part of her wished that the painting would turn out to be genuine, it would be an incredible legacy to leave her children. But for the most part, she was prepared to hear ultimately that it was a fraud. They had bought it from an antique shop that didn't even exist anymore. The owner had brought it out of the back room, and had sold it to them for very little. She had gone back to look for the shop on her first day in Venice, and it was no longer there.

And as they walked in the direction of the monastery, it was hard not to stop at some of the beautiful small churches they saw. They promised each other to do so on their way back to the square. And they chatted easily as they walked along. Aidan said he had gone for a long stroll the night before, and had made new discoveries around his hotel, including a small restaurant where he'd had dinner. He said the food was fabulous, but they had already agreed to go to Harry's Bar that night, which was Véronique's favorite, and she was dreaming of their risotto Milanese, which she said was the best in the world. Aidan said he'd never been there but was excited to try it with her. It was one of the most famous restaurants in Venice, and known around the world. It had spawned many namesakes but none as good as the original, and she promised him a delicious meal.

It took them slightly longer than expected to reach the monastery, and when they got there, they found heavy bronze doors open to reveal a large courtyard where several monks were standing and talking. Véronique approached them, and asked if there was an office or library where she could consult someone about the provenance of a painting. Its veracity was a whole other issue and too complicated to explain. One of the brothers understood her mission immediately, and directed them to a small door, which was locked, and they rang a bell. It took a few minutes, but a monk in a brown habit came to the door and looked at them both. Véronique explained again. The monk told them to follow him, as they heard the church bells ring in the chapel and they saw all the monks in the courtyard go inside.

They were led into a small waiting room that looked almost like a cell, and a few minutes later a young brother in the habit and sandals of the order came to greet them and escort them deeper into the monastery. Véronique already had the photograph in her hand.

They were led down a long, narrow stone hallway and from there into a large room. It was a library, with stone floors, wood paneling, and shelves lined with enormous ancient books. There were two tall ladders and several monks carefully dusting and cleaning the books, and a very old monk at a desk. He glanced up when they entered and smiled at them, as Véronique and Aidan approached. There was something very holy about the atmosphere, and a wonderful smell of old parchment and leather from the books.

The older monk stood up when they reached his desk. He was small and round, his head was shaved as required by the order, and he had a snow-white beard. He would have looked like Santa Claus if it weren't for the monastic robe. He invited them to sit down on two straight-backed chairs, and smiled at them from across the desk.

"What brings you here?" he asked them in English, after hearing them talking to each other. He had an accent but spoke it well. He gazed from one to the other, and Véronique answered him in a hushed tone. She explained the history of the painting to him, in her life, and was candid about her doubts about it, but she said she had always wanted to know more, and had finally come to Venice to find out. She handed him the photograph.

He put on rimless spectacles, held the photograph close to his face, and frowned. Then he turned the photograph slowly around, holding it upside down for a long time. Véronique described the quality of the paint surface to him, and the few flaws it had, which were mostly due to time, since she genuinely believed it was of the era they said it was. The artist was in question, not the fact that it had been painted during the Renaissance. And it was obvious that she was knowledgeable about fifteenth-century art, and painting in general. She gave him a very good description of the technical aspects of the painting. Once again, as he had been when they talked about it, Aidan was impressed. She was a very learned woman about art, and the monk, who had said he was Brother Tommaso, seemed to think so, too. He studied the photograph for a long time, and then set it down on his desk and turned to Véronique.

"I can see why you're intrigued by it. It's a very interesting piece. It's a subject he painted several times, though never in quite this way." It was a painting of the Virgin Mary, holding her infant son, surrounded by angels that seemed to fill the heavens. And although it was a religious painting, the detail was exquisite, the face of the Virgin was astoundingly beautiful, and the angels floated in a sky at dawn over Venice. "**If** this is real," Brother Tommaso said carefully, "it was painted by Jacopo Bellini, the father, who was a student of Gentile da Fabriano. I don't think that this was painted by either of Jacopo's sons, Gentile or Giovanni, who weren't as fond of angels as their father, and didn't have the same ethereal quality to their themes." Véronique listened with fascination. She had researched Bellini, so the names were familiar to her, and she also knew about Bellini's son-in-law Andrea Mantegna, who painted with them as part of their community of artists.

Paul had always loved the painting because he said the Virgin looked like Véronique, and Brother Tommaso noticed it, too, and commented on it, much to Véronique's surprise, since she didn't think she did. And then Brother Tommaso surprised her further, and told her there was a similar painting that he wanted to show her.

He led them into another enormous library room, and from that one into several others, with bookshelves going up to the high ceilings, with ladders to reach them. In the fifth room of its kind, he asked a young monk to reach a high bookshelf that he pointed to, and told him which book he wanted. He knew exactly where it was located, and the young monk put it in his hand a moment later. Brother Tommaso opened it and found a reproduction of a painting similar to Véronique's, with an almost identical theme.

"Either your artist was inspired by this painting, or it's one of a series Bellini did himself, and we have simply lost track of this one over the years. You have given us a very interesting project, my dear. Let me do some work on the provenance, and then you can ship me the original for further study." He took them into another room then, filled with paintings that had been sent by museums and collectors to be verified. The monastery was extraordinary in the meticulous research the monks did.

And then he led them into a smaller room that was incongruous, compared to all the ancient books they'd seen in the monastery's libraries. This was the computer room they used to do modern research, and to contact museums and art resources around the world. They even had a direct connection with Interpol, to research stolen paintings. Several of the younger monks were working at the computers when they walked in. Véronique's project was in good hands. Brother Tommaso told her that he couldn't say when, but they would be in touch with her when they were ready for the next step, to examine the painting itself.

They spent two hours there, and when they left, Aidan was in awe of what they'd seen. They both agreed that they could have spent hours in the library rooms, examining the old books.

"Thank you for taking me with you. It was fascinating," he said, still amazed. They went to their favorite little trattoria then, on their way back to Piazza San Marco.

"How long do you think it will take to hear from them?" he asked her over a delicious bowl of pasta, curious about the process he was learning about from her.

"Probably several months," she said thoughtfully. "Maybe longer. Nothing moves quickly in the art world. And they have six centuries of history to dig through on this painting, before they even look at it to see if it's a forgery. And if there's no trace of it before this, that's a whole other story, and could mean it's a fraud, too, or even rarer than we hope. I just don't know."

"It's like a mystery, waiting to unravel," Aidan said. He had loved sharing the morning with her and meeting Brother Tommaso. "How do you know about this place?"

"My grandfather mentioned it in a book he wrote nearly seventy years ago. They've always been one of the definitive verification sources. Every museum knows about them and uses them as a resource, and I heard great things about them when I was at the Beaux-Arts as a student."

"Amazing stuff," he said, smiling at her. He loved learning new things, and what she was sharing with him. He knew a great deal about photography, but her expertise in art was a whole other world.

They looked at a few more churches that afternoon that they had missed earlier, but they had each seen enough by then. Véronique left him to do a little shopping in the shops that bordered the square, and Aidan wanted to go off and take some photographs of skulls and relics in one of the churches. And he was planning to pick up some maps for their trip to Siena the next day, and they agreed to meet at the boat dock to go to dinner.

She left him and was very happy with her purchases, including a handbag at Prada, and a small, pretty, typically Venetian blackamoor brooch at Nardi. She knew it wasn't politically correct, but the brooch was part of the history of Venice, and it had tiny diamond earrings. She thought it might look nice on a black suit in Paris, and she was sure her girls wouldn't approve of it. To Véronique it was simply Venetian, a brooch of a Moor, and not offensive. Fashionable women had been wearing Nardi's blackamoors for years.

When she went back to the Cipriani, she had just

enough time to dress for dinner and meet Aidan at the boat dock. He was wearing a well-cut beige linen suit, a shirt and tie, and proper shoes. And she was wearing high heels and a short red dress, and her knees and legs were looking a lot better and not so battered. They made a handsome couple as they took a water taxi to dinner.

The food at Harry's Bar was as excellent as she had promised. She had the risotto Milanese she'd been longing for, with zucchini blossoms to start with, and Aidan had linguine vongole, followed by a steak he said was delicious. And their conversation was lively.

As she had, he had spent time in Hong Kong when he was younger, and they talked about their experiences there. After that, he had lived in Shanghai and Singapore before moving back to London, and he'd also spent time in New York and Paris, so they shared common geography, even if not similar backgrounds. He was still startled that she had married so young, and had a much older husband.

"I was lost when my father died," she explained over the Chianti he had ordered. It had been a delicious meal and a very pleasant evening so far. "I had no parents. I didn't know how to manage what my father had left me. I was alone in an enormous house, with no one to guide me. Paul took over the role of father and mentor, and it was easy for me when we got married. I had no one to take care of me, without him."

"You probably could have taken care of yourself," Aidan said quietly.

"I became prey for a lot of very unnerving people. Paul shielded me from all that, and protected me, and then we married and started having babies and I was very much in love with him. I felt safe in my life with him. The good times lasted for eleven years. It doesn't seem like long now, but we were very happy." She looked peaceful as she said it. "They were the best years of my life."

"And after?"

"It was pretty rocky in the beginning, alone with three children. And I was used to being married. But I had the children to keep me busy and distract me. And the next thing I knew, they were teenagers, and then off to college. The time flew by, and then one day I woke up and they were gone, and it was over. My youngest daughter left for college eight years ago, and it's been very quiet since then."

"No men in your life during all that time?" He was surprised at that, given what she looked like.

"A few, but not serious ones. My girls wouldn't have liked that. They were very outspoken about the men I went out with. No one was ever good enough, in their opinion, or measured up to their father. And I never met anyone I was seriously in love with. Maybe one I could have made a life with, but he had difficult children, too, and a troublesome ex-wife I didn't want to deal with. It's not so easy meeting someone new when you have children," she told him, smiling. She had made her peace with it, which Aidan could see and thought was unfortunate. "And Paul was always on the fringes of my life, to offer advice and companionship when I needed it. Between his romances, we went to things together. And he always spent the holidays with us. I think it kind of diminished my motivation to get seriously involved again. And then I felt that I was too old to meet somebody. Men want to go out with women my daughters' ages, not mine."

"That's crap, and you know it," Aidan objected as they ordered coffee. "You weren't even trying. And what right did your girls have to tell you who you should be dating?" She laughed at the question.

"Children don't hesitate to tell you what you should be doing. And they were very loyal to their father, even if he didn't deserve it. As they got older, they saw where he fell short as a father, except for my middle daughter, who always thought he was perfect. But they never saw where he failed as a husband, and I didn't discuss it with them, out of fairness to him. So they compared everyone to him unfavorably. Until a few weeks ago," she said quietly.

"What happened a few weeks ago?" He looked puzzled. She had made some vague reference to it before, without going into detail.

"Some things came up at the reading of the will that shocked everyone. It spelled it out very clearly even to them that he hadn't been much of a husband. He even admitted it himself in the will. I had always tried to protect him in their eyes, but I discovered after we separated that he was very badly behaved when we were married, even worse than I knew. He had an unfailing eye for pretty young women. We divorced over an affair he was having, but there were others I didn't know about."

"Did you stay with him because he had money?" Aidan asked her bluntly. He wanted to know what she was about, and she almost laughed at the question.

"No, not because he had money. I loved him, and we had ten very happy married years, until he fell madly in love with a famous model. He was so blatant about it that the damage became irreparable. I forgave him eventually, but our marriage was dead by then. And there were other things I was unaware of, so it was just as well we parted." She didn't sound bitter as she said it, just sad and matter-of-fact about what had happened, which touched him. And she didn't want to tell a man she barely knew that Paul hadn't had a penny and had married her for her money, and was happily blazing his way through it at the time, in answer to Aidan's question. She wanted to give Paul's memory more respect than to tell Aidan that, and she didn't want to make a point of her having a great deal of money. She was discreet about it, and Aidan hadn't guessed.

"That's why I never married," Aidan said as they

finished their coffee. "People do such rotten things to each other. It seems easier to get out of it if you're not married. At least you got three nice kids." She nodded, and agreed. She was having trouble defending the institution of marriage these days, too. It had made sense at the time, but now that she knew just how dishonest he'd been with her, her whole marriage felt like a sham. He'd been in love with someone else and having a baby when she still thought they were happily married. It made her feel like a fool.

She offered to pay for dinner, or at least split it with him, but he wouldn't hear of it, and picked up the check, and left a handsome tip. In spite of what he called his "dirt poor" background, he acted like a gentleman with her, had very nice manners, and was perfectly polite, in a normal, relaxed way.

As they left the restaurant, Aidan suggested they go to the casino and gamble. It was located at Ca' Vendramin Calergi, right in Venice, so they would have to take a water taxi, a five-minute trip to reach the casino. It sounded fun and different to her, and she agreed.

When they got there, it was a classic Venetian building, and the casino had been in existence since the seventeenth century. The entrance to the building was elegant, and the gaming rooms surprisingly simple. They were crowded with well-dressed women in cocktail dresses and men in suits, so they blended easily into the crowd. Véronique stood behind him while he played blackjack, and he won a thousand euros. He looked as though he was practiced at it, and then they played a few hands of poker, and left before it got too late. He said he had one last stop to make in Venice before taking her back to the hotel.

Aidan wouldn't say what the last stop was, when they got into the water taxi, and he directed the driver to Piazza San Marco. And as soon as they got out, he hired a gondola. She hadn't been in one yet, although she had promised herself to every day. She'd been too busy walking, visiting churches, and exploring the city with Aidan. She had wanted to visit the glass factory in Murano, and hadn't gotten to that either. But Aidan insisted that a ride in a gondola was a must, and she couldn't leave Venice without being in a gondola at least once.

The gondolier Aidan hired was wearing the traditional striped sweater, and the gondola was a particularly pretty one. They settled into their seat, and Aidan had already told him where they wanted to go. It was a perfect last night in Venice, with the moon shining overhead and the gondolier singing softly. It was a very romantic scene as Véronique looked at Aidan with a smile and thanked him. He had thought of everything, and it had been a fun evening, from Harry's Bar to the casino and now a gondola ride. She didn't have the feeling that he was trying to woo her—he just wanted her to have a good time. And then when they reached the

Bridge of Sighs, the gondolier explained that they had to kiss while they went under it if they wanted to be together forever. Véronique laughed when he said it since they had only just met.

"What's so funny about that?" Aidan teased her.

"The last thing you need is to be stuck with me 'forever,'" Véronique said to him. "You don't know any of my bad habits or what a rotten cook I am." He didn't, but he had already figured out what a good person she was. He just smiled as she said it, didn't comment, and a moment later they were under the bridge, as the gondolier crooned an Italian love song to them. The beauty around them was awesome, it had been a lovely evening, and she'd had a great time. Every moment with him was an adventure. And as she closed her eyes, enjoying the moment and listening to the gondolier singing, suddenly she felt gentle lips on hers. She opened her eyes, and looked into Aidan's eyes with amazement, and then closed her eyes again. It was a serious kiss, her first in a long time. And he kissed her until they were clear of the bridge and the moonlight was shining brightly all around them when she opened her eyes and gazed at him.

"I saved your life," he said calmly. "I figure I might as well keep you around forever," he added lightly, "otherwise, what's the point?" He put his hands out in a very Italian gesture, and she laughed at his words. But she was very startled by the kiss. She had no idea if there were romantic overtones to it. He acted perfectly normal for the rest of the ride. She felt slightly confused by the kiss and the Chianti they had drunk. He helped her out of the gondola when the ride was over, and gave the driver an extra tip. He was pleased with his blackjack winnings at the casino. The entire evening had gone extremely well, for both of them.

And he took her all the way back to the Cipriani, and told her he would meet her there the next morning. She invited him to a last drink at the bar, and this time it was her treat. He had paid for everything until then. She told him what a wonderful time she'd had, and neither of them mentioned the kiss in the gondola. She was sure he had kissed her to be nice, or out of local tradition, but it had swept her away for a minute. And she suddenly realized that there was a very sensual side to him, although he kissed her chastely on the cheek when he said goodnight. He didn't want her worrying about the trip to Siena, or thinking he was doing it to seduce her. He just enjoyed being with her, more than he had any woman in a long time.

"Goodnight, Aidan. I had a fantastic evening," she said, and meant it. He had made her trip to Venice infinitely better for her in every way.

"So did I. See you in the morning." And then he looked worried. Seeing the hotel she was staying in, it suddenly occurred to him that she might be traveling with a mountain of bags. He hadn't thought of it before. "How many bags do you have with you, by the way?" His Austin-Healey had a tiny trunk and a tiny makeshift backseat, barely big enough for a small dog, where he could put his backpack but not much else.

"Just four big suitcases and two trunks," she said innocently with her huge blue eyes. "Is that okay?" He looked panicked and wondered how they'd get to Siena and Florence, and realized he might have to rent a car for the trip. And then he saw that she was laughing and making fun of him. "I have one small bag, the size of a carry-on, and a tote," she reassured him, and he laughed.

"You had me worried for a minute. That'll work." He said goodnight to her again, and saw her into the elevator, and then he left, took the boat to San Marco, and walked to his hotel with a broad grin. She was the kind of woman he'd always dreamed of, just in a different package than he'd ever expected. She obviously came from money or a fancy family of some kind, and had probably been married to a rich man, and she was eleven years older than he. But he didn't care what she came from, who she'd been married to, or how many years older she was, he had never met anyone as wonderful in his life, as smart, as beautiful, or as sexy. And he could hardly wait to go to Siena the next day. And in the meantime, their time together in Venice had been perfect, and he liked her better every day. She had a graceful, gracious way about her, an innate elegance, and a gentleness he had never found in any other woman. Véronique Parker, whoever she was, and whatever she came from, was the woman of his dreams. And as he walked into his tiny little hotel on a back street of Venice, he was smiling from ear to ear. He had thoroughly loved their first kiss. And he had managed it under the Bridge of Sighs. He felt like a kid as he thought to himself, it didn't get better than that. He was whistling and wanted to do a little jig as he walked up to his room, excited about their trip the next day.

Chapter 9

Aidan met her at the Cipriani in the morning, with his backpack and small suitcase, and they took the hotel boat to the huge parking lot that served all residents and visitors to Venice. It took him a few minutes to locate his Austin-Healey. And she loved his car when she saw it. It was a dark, very British-looking racing green, and suited him perfectly. They filled the trunk and the miniature backseat with their things. She had thought to bring along a box of sandwiches from the hotel in case they didn't want to stop and eat. She was wearing pink jeans and a white T-shirt, and a pair of sandals she had bought in Venice. She looked fresh and pretty on the hot July day. Aidan wore a shirt with the sleeves rolled up and jeans. He put the top down, and they both put on dark glasses and got in the car. They looked perfectly matched and totally at ease with each other, and no one would have guessed a difference in their age, or that they had been strangers until very recently. Her children would have been astounded to see them together. And Véronique was surprised at herself.

"All set?" He turned to smile at her, and she nodded, and they took off for the three-hour drive to Siena. They admired the scenery and chatted occasionally. She offered him a sandwich after an hour, and he ate half of it, while she ate an apple, and she thought of their kiss the night before but didn't say anything. He was so relaxed and casual with her that she wondered if it was simply a one-time event. He acted as if they were old friends. She was comfortable with that, but the night before when he kissed her, she'd been suddenly aware of wanting more with him. She was conflicted about it, and not sure what she wanted or which way she wanted their friendship to go, and it was all so new.

They reached Siena shortly after lunchtime, and decided to look around the city, before they checked into a hotel. He had already made vague reference to getting two rooms, to put her mind at ease. So she wasn't worried about it and concentrated on what they were going to see.

They walked around the Piazza del Campo, and visited the enormous Palazzo Pubblico and the cathedral with a remarkable striped facade. The entire town had been built in the Middle Ages in the thirteenth century, and seemed even older than Venice. They had just missed the festivities of the Palio, which happened every year in July, and again in August, with thousands of spectators, trumpets, costumes, and horse races. Aidan had been in Siena for it once and described it to her, and told her it was really worth seeing one day. It took over the entire town, and people came from all over Italy and Europe to be part of it, and he said the horse races were incredible. They readily agreed that there was nothing to beat the charm of Italy. Even France, which they both loved, never seemed as warm and enticing as this. And every step of the way, Aidan took photographs, including many of Véronique.

In the late afternoon, they made their way to a small hotel that Aidan remembered, and took two rooms. The rooms were next to each other, and the hotel was very sweet. The innkeeper couldn't do enough for them, and recommended a small restaurant for dinner, which they both enjoyed. It was entirely different from Venice, but it was lovely to see. Véronique admitted to him as they walked back to the hotel after dinner that for her Venice had been the highlight of the trip.

"Should I give up now trying to charm you with the rest of Italy?" he asked, looking crestfallen, and she laughed at him. They both agreed that based on past visits, they liked Florence, too, and were looking forward to it.

They drove on to Florence the next day, after coffee and pastry at their hotel, and they each paid for their own rooms. Aidan offered to pay for both, but Véronique wouldn't let him do it. They were traveling as friends. And in spite of that, he seemed to be paying for every meal, which didn't happen often to her. She didn't know his circumstances, and was touched by how generous he was, and how well he was treating her.

Aidan was amused to see that Véronique could hardly contain herself as they approached Florence. She acted as though they were going to Mecca, and she talked about the Uffizi Gallery and how much she loved it, the Duomo, the cathedral, the Palazzo Vecchio. She kept telling him about all the art treasures she had seen there. She had gone there many times with her parents, and later alone with her father, and she could hardly wait to show her favorite places to Aidan. They checked into the Excelsior Hotel in Piazza Ognissanti as soon as they got there, parked the car, and started out on foot.

They went to the Cathedral of Santa Maria del Fiore first, and then the museum behind the cathedral. She knew all about the works of Donatello, Della Robbia, and other artists, and shared her extensive knowledge with him, which he found fascinating. And from there they went to the Uffizi Gallery, which was heaven for her. Aidan loved visiting it with her. She knew stories about almost every artist, details about their work, and compared one work of art to another in ways he would never have thought of. And her eyes were ablaze with light and excitement when she talked about it. She brought the Renaissance alive for him. And she was equally excited when, at other times, they talked about the Impressionists. It was a thrill for Aidan to be there with her.

And on their way back to the hotel, they stopped at the Piazza della Signoria, and bought gelato again. She seemed to live on a steady diet of it, despite how thin she was. They agreed to come back to the piazza that night, to have dinner there after resting at the hotel for a while. It was nice being outdoors in the warm nights.

And that night at dinner, they almost got into an argument, when he said that the only reason she hadn't continued painting was that she could afford not to, and she said she was busy bringing up her children.

"That's no excuse. If you have a God-given talent, you have to use it. You can't just ignore it for twenty years. That's criminal. If you were poor, you'd have worked at it."

"If I were poor, I'd have been a waitress somewhere, to support my kids, and I wouldn't have been sitting around doing portraits either." She looked faintly miffed and was defensive on the subject.

"Maybe you'd have done artwork commercially. But you wouldn't have just ignored it." It was hard to know what she'd have done. And never having had any, he had no idea how time-consuming children were. And she had always thought her kids more important than her art and said so to him.

"It would have been better for them to know that

they had a talented mother who was serious about it and respected her gift. That would have been a great example for them."

"They're all following their passions. Just as I did mine for all these years," she said quietly. She was touched that he admired her drawing and love of art, but her children had always been more important to her, and spending time with them, and with Paul when they were married. But that whole value system was foreign to Aidan. His whole life was about using his own talent, and developing it, which she respected. But he had no children or partner to take care of or focus on, so it was all about him. Her life had been very different, dedicated to her family. They were her priority.

They were still discussing it at the end of dinner, when she got a text message. She glanced at it to make sure it wasn't from her children, and saw that it was from Nikolai. He was just checking to see that she was well and had recovered from their encounter in Rome. And he said he hoped to see her soon. She smiled as she read it, and then mentioned it to Aidan.

"The text was from Nikolai Petrovich. He was checking to make sure I'm okay." She didn't answer it and thought she would later. She didn't want to be rude and respond to his text in front of Aidan. And she was surprised to see him look annoyed when she told him.

"What's that about? Why is he writing to you?

You said you told him you were fine when you left Rome. What's he after?"

"Nothing," she said, startled by his reaction. "He's just being friendly, and responsible, after the accident."

"Just tell him you're fine and to leave you alone," Aidan growled at her. "He's probably part of the Russian Mafia anyway. Nobody makes that kind of money honestly." He was said to be worth eighty billion dollars, according to the press.

"That's certainly possible," she admitted. She didn't know Nikolai well enough to defend him, nor how he made his fortune. "But he was very nice to me," she said fairly.

"After he tried to kill you. He's probably afraid you'll sue him."

"Of course not," she said, trying to calm him, and then realized that he was jealous. It made her wonder if the kiss in Venice had meant more than just a touristic gesture, although they hadn't kissed since, and he had been very circumspect and respectful with her, but he looked genuinely upset over Nikolai texting her. "You were the hero of the piece, Aidan," she said gently, trying to reassure him. "You were the one who saved me." She patted his hand then, and saw his ruffled feathers start to smooth into place. She had to force herself not to smile then. She thought his mild fit over the Russian was very sweet.

"Be careful about guys like that," Aidan warned

her, trying to put her off him. "You don't know him. He's a rough guy. There's no telling what someone like that would do. Men with that much power and money think they own the world and everyone in it. You don't want him to think he could own you." The way he said it touched her. He treated her as though she were young and naïve.

"I don't think I'll hear from him again. I think he was just being polite. I was pretty banged up after I hit the pavement." She tried to mollify him, but Aidan looked chagrined.

"That was my fault, not his."

"No, you saved me," she insisted. "If you hadn't pushed me that hard, I'd have been worse than banged up. I would have been dead." He smiled at her then.

"I'm sorry you got hurt," he said, and meant it.

"I'm not," she said easily. "Maybe I'd never have met you then." He nodded, and the evening went smoothly after that, although it reminded her that he had a chip on his shoulder about anyone he considered "rich," and Nikolai certainly fit that bill, far more than she did. The money she had inherited was paltry compared to his. But people with money made Aidan uneasy, no matter how it had come to them.

The subject came up again after they visited the Palazzo Vecchio and the Palazzo Pitti and saw the signs of the great wealth in Florence at the time. It launched him into one of his philosophical diatribes about rich people and how they never understand anything about real life, and she politely disagreed with him.

"Money doesn't keep you from having real problems, Aidan," she tried to explain to him. "My mother died when I was fifteen, and my father when I was twenty-one. Money didn't change that, although I wish it could have. Rich people die, get sick, and get their hearts broken like everyone else. Money just keeps you more comfortable while bad things are happening to you." But he still bristled whenever the subject came up, although it was only when she admitted to him in a quiet moment over dinner one night that for a split second in Rome, she hadn't wanted to avoid the Ferrari, and had stood there tempting the fates, that she truly upset him. She confessed that Paul's death had saddened her profoundly, and the ugly revelations at the reading of the will, and with her kids grown and gone, there was much less meaning to her life. He looked horrified by what she said.

"Let me tell you something about me," he said in a pained voice, his eyes locking into hers. "My mother committed suicide when I was twelve, because she had a miserable life. She was tired of being dirt poor and barely having enough to put food on the table, no matter how hard she worked. My father drank every penny she made, cheated on her with the neighbors, and beat her up whenever he got too drunk. So she killed herself, which must have seemed like the only way out to her." Véronique was stunned into silence by what he told her, and not knowing what else to do, she reached across the table and took his hand. The look in his eyes nearly broke her heart. She could suddenly imagine the little boy he had been when his mother died. And he went on, "My father drank himself to death when I was seventeen. I left after the funeral and never looked back. I guess it's why I never wanted to get married or have kids. I didn't want them to have a childhood like mine."

"You wouldn't be a father like that," she said gently. "You're a very different man." He nodded at what she said, and she could see that there were tears in his eyes, and he had trusted her with the dark secrets of his youth.

"My father was a son of a bitch, to everyone. My mother was a sweet woman, and didn't deserve someone like him." Véronique nodded sympathetically and continued to hold his hand. It explained a lot about him—how angry he was at times, how frightened of the responsibility of marriage and children, his hatred of poverty and what it did to people—and he chose to blame the rich for all the world's ills. Someone had to be responsible for the miseries of the world, and as far as Aidan was concerned, they were it. He demonized anyone with wealth, which worried Véronique, but she sympathized with the agonies of his childhood.

He insisted that poor people and rich people

were different. He couldn't imagine that people with money would ever suffer heartbreak the way he had. But Véronique knew that heartbreak came in all shapes and colors, and wasn't reserved only for poor people. Rich people lived tragedies, too.

"Some people are just bad people, Aidan. It doesn't matter if they're rich or poor."

"I guess not," he said with a sigh, as he squeezed her hand. She was a compassionate person, and he could see her caring in her eyes. "I hated every minute of my childhood, especially my father." They went for a walk after dinner, and Aidan put an arm around her shoulders. They were both thinking about what he'd said. It gave her greater insight into him, as they got comfortable with each other. There was an abrasive quality to him at times, but she could tell that inside he was all heart, and a good person, and more sensitive and vulnerable then he wanted to admit. But he seemed closer to her after he had told her about his parents' deaths.

They went back to their separate rooms at the hotel and the next day continued their pilgrimage to admire art. They did all the important galleries and went back to the Uffizi, and after five days steeped in art in Florence, they agreed that they had done it, and there was nothing left that they wanted to see again. Aidan looked at her over lunch.

"What do we do now?" he asked her. He still had several weeks before he had to go to Berlin. And he had no desire to leave her. In spite of their occasional philosophical disagreements, they were having a wonderful time together. And from strangers initially, they had become friends.

"I don't know. I suppose I could check in with my children. Two of them are coming over here, and I ought to find out when."

"Why are they coming to meet you? Just for a vacation?"

"No, I rented a house in St. Tropez earlier this summer, and none of them showed up. They have busy lives. They're coming over on family business, just for a few days." He could see the loneliness in her eyes as she said it. She had been alone now for a long time, with no one to spend time with, and no one to love her, even if she did have three daughters. They were no longer part of her daily life. It brought the point home to him of just how solitary she was. And he suspected it was harder for her than she let on.

She called Timmie that night—it was afternoon for her, and she was busy in her office. Timmie didn't ask where she was or how she'd been—she assumed she was in Paris. Véronique tried to reach Juliette, and she never answered. And the message on Joy's voice mail said she would be busy shooting a commercial all week and didn't have time to return calls.

"When do you think the girls are coming to look at the château?" She thought Timmie might know, even if she wasn't planning to come herself.

"I don't know. You have to ask them, Mom. I talked to Juliette two days ago, and she said in a few weeks. I think she went away to stay with friends in Vermont. She's still very upset about Dad."

"If you talk to them, tell them I need a little warning before they just show up," Véronique said reasonably, and Timmie sounded surprised.

"Why? Are you doing something special?"

"I might want to make some plans myself. I don't want to just sit here waiting for them to arrive. Joy's not returning calls, and Juliette is impossible to reach now that the sandwich shop is closed for the summer." Until then, she'd been at her shop day and night, and easy to reach. Now she was MIA.

"Send them both a text," Timmie said practically, and Véronique refrained from saying that it was a difficult way to have a relationship with one's children. They assumed that she had nothing to do, and just sat around waiting for them, and would drop everything for them when they wanted to come. And that had certainly been true for many years. But suddenly she wanted more of a life than that. She had felt that way since Paul died, and now Aidan was a part of it. She was having fun with him. And he was becoming more important to her day by day, although he had a life of his own, too, and had a gallery show to organize in Berlin. But for now they were both free, she even more so than he, with no professional obligations of her own.

"I'll do that," she said in answer to Timmie's suggestion to send both girls text messages. "And how are you?"

"Busy, crazy. Nothing ever changes here." It could now, with her father's bequest, but she hadn't come to any decisions about it yet. She wanted to look for a building, but hadn't had time.

"Well, try not to work too hard. Are you getting away at all?"

"I'm going to stay with friends in the Hamptons this weekend. It's the first break I've had."

"Good. Well, have fun," Véronique said, told her she loved her, and realized when she hung up that Timmie hadn't asked her a thing about her, or how she was. It never even occurred to any of them.

She reported to Aidan the next morning that she didn't know when her daughters were coming, maybe not for a few weeks, although she hadn't been able to reach the two who were coming, so she had no news from them.

"That doesn't sound considerate," he said practically, as they ate breakfast at the hotel. "Are you just supposed to drop everything when they show up?" He looked somewhat shocked. He thought it an odd way for adults to behave even if she was their mother.

"They're not considerate anymore," she said honestly. "I can't expect them to organize their lives around me, but they expect me to be free when they want to come. They think I have nothing else to do. It's a little trying at times."

"Maybe you should tell them you're busy, and retrain them a little. It sounds like they need a wake-up call that you're not their slave." She smiled at what he said. "It sounds like you've been too available to them for a long time." It was true, and had happened because there was no man in her life, she wasn't working, and she was alone, and missed them so much. So they always assumed that she'd be free for them, and so far she always had been, even if it meant canceling her own plans to be with them, which she often did. The plans were never as important to her as her kids.

"You're right," she conceded to Aidan. "I've given them bad habits. But this time they're not coming over to have fun. They're coming to look at a château their father left them near St. Paul de Vence. I think they'll probably sell it. It hasn't been used in years. But they should look at it first."

"See what I mean about rich people?" Aidan said. "Their father had a château he didn't even use. How spoiled is that?" She smiled at him, wondering what he would say if she told him that she had given Paul the château. She could tell that he thought Paul had the money, and she was doing nothing to dispel the illusion. Given Aidan's very harsh opinions about wealthy people, she was afraid now to admit to him that the fortune was hers and not Paul's, that he hadn't had a penny until they married. It seemed more information than Aidan needed for now. She didn't like giving him the impression that she was one of those women who had been living off alimony and a settlement for the past twenty years, but for now it seemed better than the alternative, and telling him the truth.

"Where are you meeting your daughters?" Aidan asked her.

"Cap d'Antibes. I have nothing to do till then," she admitted. "I'd love you to meet my girls one day." She smiled at him, but he shook his head.

"I don't know if we'd get along. I don't like the way they treat you. They don't seem very attentive. Your relationship with them sounds like a one-way street, with all the love and attention coming from you." He wasn't wrong, yet it sounded harsh when he said it. But she couldn't deny that she often felt that way, too, and he had picked it up from what she'd said.

"That's not always the case," she said, trying to be fair about them. "We had some good talks for a couple of days when their father died. The rest of the time, they're just busy." And after Paul died, they had needed her help, so they had made time. But at other times, Aidan was right. And a text message was not the same as a call, when they could talk, or laugh, or catch up. They rarely filled her in on their lives, and didn't ask about hers.

"They sound a little too self-involved to me, not unlike the way you describe their father. Maybe he set the tone for them, about how to treat you." He was critical, but not entirely wrong in his assessment.

"He was actually nicer to me than they are," Véronique said, looking pensive. Or was he? She was no longer sure. "I guess in your twenties, you don't have time for your parents. At their ages, I had three kids and a husband, which teaches you to think about people other than yourself. All they have to focus on is themselves and what works for them."

"Fine. Then to hell with them," Aidan said bluntly. "What are **we** going to do now? I think we've exhausted Florence. Do you want to do some more traveling together? I have the time." He didn't want to leave her unless she told him to, and he was hoping she wouldn't. Their days together had been magical, since Venice and in Siena and Florence. Aidan wanted more.

She was looking at him shyly across the table. "I'd love it," she said to him. She had no idea what this was, friendship or something else, despite the difference in their ages. It seemed unlikely, but at times it felt like being part of a couple, particularly when they argued about their views of life, but the discussions were respectful and the arguments resolved quickly. This seemed like a strange parenthesis in their lives, but it was working for both of them, and she was loving every minute of it. She didn't want it to stop, and neither did he. He looked pleased with her answer.

"Why don't we drive toward France?" he said. "We can hang around in the South of France for a while, and take our time. And we'll wind up where you need to be. How does that sound?"

"Wonderful," she said, smiling broadly. They agreed to leave Florence the next day, after one more trip to the Uffizi, and they would head toward France in a leisurely way, stopping wherever they wanted.

After breakfast, they walked back toward their rooms, pleased with the plan, and when they reached Véronique's door, Aidan reached an arm toward her and pulled her to him as though he had something to tell her. She looked up at him, and saw the warm chocolate brown of his eyes as he came closer, and he pulled her into his arms and kissed her, more profoundly than he had in the gondola, and with deeper meaning now that he had gotten to know her. They kissed for a long time, and were breathless when they stopped. She leaned against the door of her room, and he kissed her again, and there was no question now about what this was. They were falling in love. They had no idea if it would last, or if it could ever work, but for right now, in the moment, it was all they both wanted, and it was perfect.

Chapter 10

Aidan and Véronique left Florence the next day and drove to Lucca, where they stayed at a small inn, and went for long walks in the countryside for two days. It was relaxing and peaceful. They talked and laughed, and he took photographs of her constantly. He always got her in her unguarded, pensive moments, which was how he liked her best. On the second night, the detective she had hired in Paris called her on her cell phone. He had completed his report on the Marniers and wanted to know where to send it. He said the information had been easy to obtain. They had lived in the same place all their lives. She had him fax it to the hotel, and she read it carefully, with a serious expression. Aidan watched her, and was concerned. He waited until she was finished reading to ask her about it. The report was only five pages long, so he didn't have long to wait, and she seemed sobered by it when she was through.

"Bad news?" he asked her, looking worried, and she shook her head, but she didn't seem happy either.

"Old news," she said with a sigh. She hated to burden him with the ugly details of her life, and her late ex-husband's transgressions. "At the reading of Paul's will, we all discovered that he had an illegitimate daughter, by a woman he had had an affair with when we were married. I found out after we were separated that he'd had a lot of affairs." She had told Aidan about that earlier. "But this is the only one that bore children. It was a shock for all of us. And he gave his daughter a quarter of his estate with my girls. She owns a quarter of the château with them. So I've been trying to find out something about her and her mother. That's what I was just reading. I hired a detective in Paris before I left for Rome." Aidan suddenly looked as serious as she did.

"That must have been a hell of a shock for you, as well as your children. You never suspected?"

"No, never. Not about this one. When I heard about the others, this woman's name was never mentioned. He hid her well, and he never told me, right till the end."

"Cowardly of him," Aidan said sternly, and Véronique didn't deny it, "to leave it till after he was gone."

"That was Paul. He never did anything difficult or unpleasant. He left it all to me. And I'm sure he figured I'd pick up the pieces now, and I suppose I will, as much as anyone can. They're going to have to deal with her. She's their sister, or half-sister."

"I'm surprised you stayed such good friends with him," Aidan said quietly. It was hard for him to understand. He sounded like a bastard to him, and in some ways he had been. But a charming one at all times.

"At first I did it for the children. And probably because I still loved him when I divorced him. And then it just became habit that we were friends. I wasn't in love with him in the end, so the bad behavior didn't matter to me anymore. I have no family except my children, so he was part of my history. Like a badly behaved older brother. But this last escapade of his, or the discovery of it, changed everything for me. I'm not feeling too kindly toward him at the moment." Aidan nodded and said nothing as it all sank in.

"What did the detective say about them?"

"Apparently the girl is a medical student, and her mother is the local doctor. She's very well thought of in the community, and respected. She must have been a medical student herself when Paul met her and they had the affair. He never supported his daughter, but sent them occasional 'gifts of money,' rarely, which doesn't surprise me. He was never responsible about money, and he probably forgot about her when it suited him. He only saw the child a few times, and not recently. The child's mother never married, but lived with another local doctor for many years, until he died two years ago. He was the only father this girl ever knew. Apparently, her mother never told her Paul was her father. Until recently, she thought he was an old friend of the family who visited once in a while. And I'm sure Paul was perfectly happy to play that charade." Hearing about him, there was absolutely nothing Aidan liked or respected about Paul Parker. And the pain in Véronique's eyes, as she talked about it, made him furious at Paul and ache for her. He could see just how betrayed she felt.

"According to the report," Véronique went on, "people in the area say she's a very nice young girl, very responsible and serious and a good student. And her mother is supposedly a lovely woman. They both sound better than Paul deserved. He could have wound up with a real disaster on his hands, especially at the time, if the girl's mother had been after money or wanted to cause a scandal, blackmail him, or create an explosion with me. She never did. And now the mess is ours. I'm sure Paul leaving the girl in his will came as a surprise to them, too, but in their case a good one. According to the report, they have very little money, just what the mother makes in her medical practice, which can't be much. So this will be a windfall to them. And a headache for my girls, to own a piece of property with a half-sister they never knew they had."

It didn't sound like a good situation to him, but at least they appeared to be decent people. He had no tolerance whatsoever for men like Paul. Aidan took Véronique in his arms then and kissed her, sorry for what she'd had to go through with a man she had obviously been kind and loyal to. And she was grateful for Aidan's kindness and support. They spent a quiet evening talking about it, and she faxed the report to all three girls, although she had no idea when Juliette would get it since she was in Vermont, but she knew the other two would tell her about it when she called. And Juliette always stayed in close touch with Timmie. In some ways the report was good news because the Marniers sounded like respectable people, but the whole situation was unpleasant for them all.

They drove on the next day, and Véronique didn't mention the report again, so Aidan didn't bring it up. She didn't want to think about it, but the day after, all three girls called her on her cell to talk about it. They had the same reaction she had, that at least they sounded like reasonable people. But they were all dreading meeting their half-sister and her mother, and after talking to them, Véronique admitted to Aidan that she didn't want to meet them either.

"Then don't," Aidan said simply. "You didn't inherit the property, your kids did. If you don't want to meet these women, why should you have to deal with something painful? To hell with them. Let your kids deal with them. They're grown women."

It had never occurred to Véronique to think that way, but what he said made sense to her and gave her a feeling of freedom.

"You're under no obligation to put yourself through pain, in honor of a man who sounds like he hurt you most of the time, as long as he was having fun. If you want to meet them, do it. But if not, just let the girls see them, and you stay away." She smiled at him after he said it, and leaned over to kiss him.

"You're a wonderful man," she said to him. "Thank you. I'm glad you saved my life."

"So am I," he said, and kissed her again. They were kissing a lot, but had managed to stay out of bed so far. Neither of them wanted to do something hasty, or in the heat of passion, that they'd regret. They hadn't figured out what they were doing yet, and their leisurely flirtation worked for both of them. They didn't want to hurt each other, or get hurt.

"I've never had a relationship like this," he confessed to her one afternoon as they drove to Portofino. "Usually, I sleep with women and don't love them. Now I'm in love with you, and not sleeping with you. One of these days I'll get it right." He laughed, and she smiled at him. She had never had a relationship like this either, with a man who treated her as well, and actually cared how she felt, even though he barely knew her. Paul had never thought of anyone but himself, as witnessed by the situation her daughters had to deal with now in France.

They spent three days in Portofino at a charming small hotel in the little port town, and then a day in Cinque Terre. Their days were spent exploring, while he took photographs, or being on local beaches, and at night they went to restaurants in the romantic setting.

They crossed the border into France after four days, and headed on a meandering course toward the South of France. They wanted to see Èze in the Maritime Alps, and had decided to settle in Antibes after that. He knew a small hotel in the Old Town, and it was close to the hotel where she planned to stay with the girls.

The drive to Èze was as beautiful as they hoped it would be. The town had cobblestoned streets, and old men were playing boules when they walked around. The views were spectacular, looking down at the coast. They had an excellent lunch, and then drove down the mountain to Antibes, and found Aidan's tiny hotel, where they were given two small bedrooms side by side. They walked around the old part of the town, and had an elegant dinner in a restaurant on the ramparts that night, where they could see big yachts and sailboats of all sizes drift by. There was a handsome yacht harbor in Antibes, and the town was a nice place to relax, with several beaches to choose from.

They walked back slowly to the hotel after dinner. Aidan had his arm around her waist, and they stopped and watched the boats for a while. Their time together was a peaceful respite from real life, and he finally voiced the concern she'd had for days.

"What are we going to do after this? Will you visit me in London, Véronique?" He was afraid he'd never see her again after their trip. Their worlds seemed light-years apart. More so than their ages, which didn't seem to bother either of them. They felt the same age most of the time, except when she talked about her kids, since it was hard for him to relate, as he had none of his own.

"I could come to London. And you could come to visit me in Paris or New York," she suggested to him.

"Will you come see my show in Berlin?" he asked. He wanted to make her part of his life, to show her where he lived and how he worked. And they both knew that it would be harder for him to enter her world than for her to visit his. At some point, if they continued seeing each other, he would have to meet her daughters, and Véronique didn't know how they'd react to anyone in her life, let alone Aidan, who was younger. They'd probably be shocked at how young he was. The age difference between them wasn't ridiculous, but it was there.

She suspected that they'd be most upset that she was involved with a man at all. They were used to her being alone and never thought of her as a woman, just as their mother, who existed only in relation to them, and for whatever they needed from her, in terms of attention or emotional support.

"I could come after the girls leave," she said thoughtfully. "I doubt they'll stay long."

"I'd really like that," he said, smiling at her. He loved the idea of her coming to his show.

"So would I." She was happy he'd invited her, and with that settled, they walked back to the hotel arm in arm.

Juliette called her that night and told her she and Joy were coming in a week. They were thinking of staying for five or six days, maybe a week, which was what Véronique had guessed. And as she hung up afterward, she realized that their visit felt like an intrusion. She wanted to be with Aidan and, for once, not with them. She felt guilty as she thought it, and told Aidan about Juliette's call the next day, as they drove to Cap Ferrat for the day. And they were going to have dinner at the Voile d'Or, overlooking the port in St. Jean Cap Ferrat that night, and this time, as the restaurant was expensive, she had insisted it was her treat.

Knowing they had a week left together made every moment even more precious to Aidan and Véronique. They drove to different towns along the coast, tried out new beaches, swam together, and went to fun restaurants at night. They talked for hours, shared their dreams and secrets, argued occasionally, delighted and annoyed each other, kissed frequently, and had fun together. She had never felt as comfortable with anyone, nor had he. And spending every waking hour together every day taught them much about their characters. And they liked everything they'd seen so far. Aidan said he'd never been as happy with any woman as he was with her, and even though they hadn't slept with each other, they shared a rare intimacy, and anyone who saw them together would have assumed they were married, or at least lovers. They were totally at ease.

The days sped by, and on the last day, they talked again about her coming to Berlin to see his show. She promised to be at the opening in a couple of weeks, or she might even come before and help him set it up. He was hoping she would, and told her it would mean a lot to him. She was going back to Paris after the girls left, and flying to Berlin from there. On the last night, they had dinner at a pizzeria in the old part of town, and walked through the crowds of people roaming the streets on their way back. They had their arms around each other, and he kissed her just before they got to the hotel.

"I'm going to miss you so much," he said softly to her. It was hard to imagine a day without her now, and she felt exactly the same way. It was going to be strange to see her children, and not have them know how important Aidan was to her, or even that they'd met. But she didn't feel ready to tell them, and she wanted to protect what she and Aidan had. It seemed precious, fragile, and rare.

He kissed her again before they went to their rooms that night. She lay in bed thinking about him, and wondering if he was sleeping yet. She had booked a reservation for herself and the girls at the Eden Roc, where they always stayed. He was going to take her there the next morning, and have lunch with her, and then drive to Berlin. Juliette and Joy were coming in that night. She and Aidan had spent every moment together that they could, and as she thought of leaving him the next day, her eyes filled with tears. She was in bed unable to sleep for the next hour, and then got up to stare at the sea in the moonlight, and heard a soft knock at her door. She went to answer it, and Aidan was standing there in his underwear and bare feet, with a sheepish expression.

"Are you awake?" he whispered, and she smiled, happy to see him. He looked like a kid in the dark hall.

"Yes, I can't sleep," she whispered back, and held open the door. Without another word, he took her in his arms. He couldn't leave her without making love to her finally. It felt as though they had waited an eternity, and it felt right to both of them. They both wanted the reassurance of this final bond before they left each other the next day. Without saying anything, they climbed into her bed, took off their clothes, and lay in each other's arms, and slowly their bodies joined. The moonlight washed over them as they made love and lay together afterward, peaceful and united at last. And when morning came, they were sound asleep side by side. When they woke up, Aidan looked at Véronique, and they both knew they'd done the right thing the night before. He kissed her before they got up.

"Are you sorry?" he asked her, looking worried, after they kissed.

"No." She smiled at him. "Are you?"

"I don't know how we're going to make this work," he said to her, "but I know we'll find a way." It was all she needed to hear.

She wanted him to be right, and for it not to be a summer romance, or a fling. It didn't feel like either one to her. He ran his hands over her breasts and belly again, still hungry for her. This was only the beginning for them.

"I wish you could come to Berlin with me today," he said sadly.

"I'll be there soon," she promised, and then kissed him. He had a startlingly beautiful body. They made love one last time, before they had to face the world.

He went to shower and dress in his own room, and was back a short while later. He looked at her differently when he came back to her room. She was his now, and whatever happened, they would deal with it together. Their lovemaking had been an end to their old lives, and the beginning of their new one. And neither of them was alone anymore. A bond between them had been sealed in the tiny room the night before.

He took her bags down to his car, and she followed him a few minutes later. She felt as though they'd just been on their honeymoon. He put the car in gear as soon as she got in, and they took off for Cap d'Antibes, taking with them everything they had shared and built and done and given for the past few weeks. They were both smiling, and he leaned over and kissed her as the elegant old hotel where she'd be staying came into view.

She didn't want to leave him, but she knew she had to, to see her girls. There was more to her life now than just traveling with Aidan, going to long dinners together, and waking up in his arms. She had responsibilities, and he had work to do in Berlin. And somewhere in the midst of all of it, they would find time to be together. All they had to do now was figure out how to make this work. And as she got out at the familiar hotel where she had stayed with her family for years, she vowed to herself, she would. Aidan already meant too much to her to lose him now. He was the best thing that had ever happened to her, and when their eyes met as they got out of the sports car, she could see that he felt exactly the same way.

Chapter 11

The Eden Roc was part of the distinguished Hôtel du Cap in Cap d'Antibes, only a few miles from the friendly little town of Antibes, where they'd been staying, and the tiny hotel where their relationship had finally been consummated. The Hôtel du Cap was one of the most beautiful, exclusive, and illustrious hotels in Europe, with prices to match. The main building had marble halls, high ceilings, and magnificent rooms and suites, most of them looking out at the sea shimmering like glass. There was an impressive outdoor staircase leading down to the even more exclusive Eden Roc, with gardens on either side of the wide path and closer to the water. It was the vacation spot for aristocrats, royalty, the immensely rich, and in recent years jetsetters, Russian tycoons, and movie stars, many of whom preferred to stay at the less formal lower building, with smaller but still elegantly appointed suites, and even better views of the sea from their balconies.

There was a very elegant restaurant that serviced both hotels and, below it on what looked like the deck of a ship, a less formal one where hotel guests gathered for lunch, at astronomical prices. There was an infinity pool, and a host of private cabanas, where you could eat, relax, and lie around naked, unseen by other guests. The cabanas were more expensive than rooms at other fine hotels. The Hôtel du Cap and the Eden Roc were a world unto themselves, with guests who came back faithfully year after year, alone or with their families or their mistresses. It was a magical kingdom secluded from the real world, full of elegant, famous people who wanted to be waited on hand and foot and pampered while they were there. Even the staff remained the same from year to year. And they knew Véronique and her children well. She had even gone there as a child herself, with her parents, and had taken Paul there as soon as they were married. They had spent part of their honeymoon there. It was like a second home to her. And as soon as she arrived, the concierge and both his assistants came out into the driveway to greet her, along with the doormen and two porters who were waiting to carry her bags. Aidan looked instantly uncomfortable the moment they approached, as though he thought they might attack him. He stopped them as they started to take his bags out of the Austin's tiny trunk. He handed them Véronique's bags, and one of the porters disappeared into the hotel.

They were standing under the portico covered with vines and flowers, and Véronique walked slowly inside, surrounded by the uniformed employees greeting her, while Aidan followed, feeling like an intruder who had wandered into the wrong hotel and would be thrown out as soon as they realized he was an imposter and didn't belong there. Véronique was chatting easily with all of them, as they led her to her familiar suite. She had had the same rooms for thirty years, and the children and their nanny at the time had had a suite of rooms on the floor just above her. The concierge opened the door to her suite with a flourish and stepped back, as Aidan hesitated behind the crowd.

Véronique turned to find him, and beckoned him in with her, and after she introduced Aidan to the concierge, he followed her into the room, which took his breath away when he saw the elegant rooms and the view. She had a bedroom, living room, with balconies on both, and two bathrooms. It reeked of luxury and comfort, with beautifully upholstered furniture in blue and white, and what looked like antiques to him, although they weren't. The porter set down her bag on a luggage stand, the concierge bowed and wished her a good stay with them, and the entire group disappeared, accompanied by two maids who had offered to unpack her pathetically small suitcase, and Véronique smilingly declined. And she and Aidan were finally alone.

"I wish you were staying here with me," she said, as she walked to him and put her arms around his neck, just as he noticed a huge box of chocolates on the desk. They thought of everything. The hotel was dedicated to serving every whim of their guests.

"I'd be afraid to leave the room," Aidan said, looking anxious.

"Why?" She was surprised, and pulled him into a comfortable chair with her, big enough for them both. Everything in the room was elegant, luxurious, and inviting, but Aidan seemed frightened to sit down, and sat stiffly next to her.

"I don't belong here," he said nervously. He hadn't realized that her life was quite as luxurious as this, although the Cipriani in Venice had been pretty grand, and he knew she had money. But this was about more than money. It was about opulence in a discreet way to a degree he had never seen. Most of the guests who stayed here came from Old Money, and a few were billionaires like Nikolai who were enjoying it thoroughly. The place shrieked of money. "If I hadn't been with you when we got here, they'd have thrown me out," he said nervously, jutting out his chin, which she knew he did when he felt extremely uncomfortable, as he was now. And she wanted him to like the hotel as much as she did, and come here with her one day. It was the most romantic place in the world, both the geographic setting at the water's edge, and the hotel itself. There was even a boat dock for people coming off their yachts, and there were always half a dozen of them anchored in front of the hotel.

"Don't be silly," Véronique tried to reassure him. "Some of the people who stay here look like bums when they relax. You look perfectly civilized, and as appropriate as any of the other guests." He didn't look any more at ease about it than when they'd arrived.

"I can't breathe here. I told you, I'm allergic to rich people, and it doesn't get richer than this," he said, looking panicked.

"What's bothering you?" she asked gently, disappointed by his reaction. "Do you think you don't deserve it?"

"Maybe," he said pensively. "I just don't approve of people who live like this, when there are millions of starving people in the world. I don't even want to know what staying in a place like this would cost." He shuddered at the thought.

"A lot," Véronique confirmed. "No one has to live like this every day. But it's a nice treat for a holiday. I love it here." She was honest with him. "Do you think you could ever get used to coming here? Just as a treat, once in a while?" As she said it, she handed him the box of chocolates, and he put two in his mouth at once, and she laughed. Sometimes he was like a child. And at other times, he was more adult and more caring and protective of her than any man she had ever known. And one thing was for sure, he certainly wasn't spoiled, or looking to be, or he wouldn't have been so uncomfortable there. He looked as if he were crawling out of his skin.

"I just can't see myself staying in a place like this," he said, looking around the room again, "although the chocolates are damn good," he added with a sudden grin and helped himself to another one as she laughed.

"What difference does it make, if I can afford it?" she asked him honestly.

"That's nice for you. But the problem is I can't. And I'm not looking to become a gigolo when I grow up. I don't want to take advantage of you, Véronique. I've never done that in my life, and I don't intend to start now." This was the flip side of the coin of being with a decent person who didn't want her for what she had. A less honorable man would have leaped into it with both feet.

"Why can't we have both? Some simple times, like the hotel we just stayed at, and some of this? What you're telling me is that I'm too 'rich' for you. That's not fair. I would never tell you that you're too poor for me. That's discrimination. Can't you be a little more relaxed about the rich?"

"Maybe," he said thoughtfully. "You're the first one I've ever liked." And as he said it, he reached over and kissed her, pulled her into his arms, and slipped a hand under her blouse. And their conversations about rich and poor were forgotten for a minute. They continued kissing and found their way to the luxurious bed. She pulled back the covers, and they climbed into it, and a moment later their clothes were in a heap on the floor and they were making love, even more passionately than the night before. And when they stopped, he leaned back breathlessly among the pillows and smiled at her as the Mediterranean glistened in the sunlight outside. “Maybe this place isn’t so bad,” he said, still out of breath. She wished she could ask him to stay for a few days, but there was no hope of that with her girls about to arrive. He rolled over in the bed with her then, visibly more at ease than he had been when he arrived. Their lovemaking had relaxed him. She suggested they take a bath, in her marble bathroom, and he followed her in, as she ran a tub for them.

They sat in the bathtub, talking for a while, about her visit to the château the next day, and whether she would meet the Marniers. She still didn’t want to, and he encouraged her to do whatever suited her. He fully supported her in that, and a little while later, they got out of the bath, and toweled each other off. He put on a terrycloth robe, and went back to eat another chocolate.

“Now I can see how prostitutes do it,” he said with a sigh. “You’ve corrupted me in an hour. I’ve eaten half your box of chocolates, the robe is very nice, the bed was fabulous, almost as good as what happened in it, and I love the tub. Give me a week here, and I'll do whatever you want." He laughed, but she knew him better than that now. He was still Aidan, and always true to himself, but he seemed like he was having fun, and she was glad.

They walked to the building next door where the fancy restaurant was, with a huge buffet spread out, and opted for the more casual restaurant downstairs, near the pool. They had lunch on the terrace, and sat enjoying the view after a delicious meal. There were half a dozen spectacular yachts at anchor.

"I'm going to miss you," Aidan said seriously. "Call me whenever you want. I won't get to Berlin till tomorrow, but you can reach me on my cell phone anytime. At least now I can visualize where you are." Véronique didn't know if that was a good thing or a bad thing, but he looked happier than he had at first. Aidan had strong opinions and social ideals, and prejudices about the rich, how they lived and what they stood for, but he had relaxed about it long enough to make love to her and have lunch. It made for a nicer farewell before they parted for the next couple of weeks. She was going to try and join him in Berlin after the girls left. She had some things to do in Paris, but after that, she wanted to see him again as soon as she could, and it was all he wanted, too. He was going to be lonely without her now.

He walked her back to her room for a moment alone, kissed her longingly again, and then she walked him to his car. The valet brought it to him, and the battered little Austin-Healey sat among two Rollses, a Bentley, and a Ferrari. They exchanged a smile when he saw it, but he didn't look upset. And however much he had disapproved of lives like hers until then, he was shoulder to shoulder with the rich and super rich, whether he liked it or not. She just hoped he could adjust to it enough to stick around. And other than occasional indulgences like her stays at the Eden Roc, Véronique didn't live a showy life. Her life in Paris was quiet, her apartment manageable and human scale, and even the apartment in New York was luxurious but not overwhelming, although she wondered if it would be to him. She wasn't quite sure yet where his limits were. Clearly the Hôtel du Cap was well above them, but that was an extreme case. Even she could concede that, and in the end, he was fine with it.

He kissed her again as he stood by the car. "Take care of yourself. Don't let the girls upset you or beat you up, or anyone else!" he whispered, and she nodded. "Remember that I love you. I'll call you tonight." They kissed one last time, he got in the Austin-Healey, and with a roar of the engine, and a blast of the exhaust, he waved and drove off, as the valet watched with a straight face, and bowed when she went back inside.

She sat on the balcony of her room, thinking about him. The bed had been made while they were at lunch, so there was no sign of their lovemaking. It was hard to believe all that had happened, and how much he already meant to her. It was as though they had been together forever, not just a few weeks since they'd first glimpsed each other in Rome and met in Venice. So much had happened since then. She felt like a different woman, and as though she had Aidan's name stamped all over her. She wondered if her girls would see it, or sense a change. She had no intention of saying anything to them about him yet. It was much too early, and she wanted to give their relationship time to settle in and take hold, before she introduced him to them. She didn't know when that would be, but definitely not now.

She walked around the grounds after that, listening to the crickets, which were very loud, and sat in the cabana she'd rented, waiting for the girls. They were landing at four o'clock in Nice, and it was almost six as she walked back to her room at the Eden Roc building. She saw a chauffeur-driven Mercedes pull up, and Joy and Juliette got out. They both looked very pretty. Juliette had traveled in jeans with a T-shirt and sweater, while Joy was wearing shorts and a T-shirt and, as always, was spectacular. And both girls turned when she called their names, and were happy to see her. She walked them to the room they were sharing next to hers.

"Are you tired?" she asked them, and both of them shook their heads.

"We slept on the flight," Juliette volunteered. "I had lunch, and as usual Miss Beautiful ate two lettuce leaves and an olive. I had foie gras." Juliette looked pleased and didn't feel guilty. She didn't mind being a few pounds heavier than the others. They all agreed that both Joy and Timmie had a tendency to be too thin—Timmie due to anxiety and stress, and Joy by design for her work.

"What do you want to do?" their mother asked them, and they both answered at once that they wanted to go for a swim. They loved the pool here. And she followed them down to it when they were ready, and sat at the edge, dangling her feet in the pool, but she didn't want to go swimming. She was pleasantly relaxed and enjoyed watching them. And afterward they all went back to the room to dress for dinner. It was always a relatively formal affair, with elegantly dressed women, wearing jewels, and men wearing jackets, although in recent years they were no longer required to wear ties. When Véronique and Paul came here, the men had worn suits. It was more casual now, but the women still looked well put together in cocktail dresses, and a few of the younger ones were wearing diaphanous chiffon dresses to the floor. They looked ethereal and sexy. Juliette and Joy opted for short black dresses, while Véronique was wearing white satin palazzo pants and a shocking pink silk blouse and diamond earrings. They were the only dressy things she'd taken to Rome, and now she was glad she had. She would have to figure out something else for the next day.

The subject of Sophie Marnier and her mother didn't come up until halfway through dinner, when Joy asked Véronique if she was going to meet her. Juliette had made an appointment with them at ten o'clock the next morning, before they went to the château.

"You can meet us after that, Mom," Juliette said gently, "and go straight to the château. You don't have to meet them." The girls felt they had no other choice. They owned a piece of property with Sophie now, and she was their half-sister, they wanted to lay eyes on her. And they had promised to relate everything to Timmie, who was dying to know how it went.

"I don't know. I don't think I want to meet the mother, and then when I think that, I realize it was such a long time ago, maybe I should. To satisfy my curiosity if nothing else. And I should be there for you two girls." She still felt torn.

"You can decide in the morning," Joy said easily, and then she told her about the new manager she'd hired. She had liked what he'd said, and he had a great reputation as an up-and-coming talent manager, even though he was only thirty-two years old. His name was Ron Maguire. And he had recommended her new agent. The agent was already turning up better acting parts for her, and Ron, the manager, had great contacts for national ad campaigns, through ad agencies he worked with. She was excited about what she was doing, and about the fact that her father had opened new doors for her so she could pursue her dream. It was something that Véronique had never done, given how she felt about Joy's acting career. She felt a little guilty about it now, listening to Joy, but at least Paul had finally done something for her. She could see how much it meant to Joy, so maybe he was right. It started her thinking that she needed to be more accepting and supportive of all of their careers. They were old enough to make good decisions even if different from her own.

They stayed at the table for a long time, talking. Juliette hadn't opened the sandwich shop again since her father's death, and didn't intend to until after Labor Day, but she had decided to hire the people she needed so that she could travel a little more, and she wanted to make some improvements to the bakery, as her father had suggested. And although she was still angry at him herself, Véronique was touched by what he'd done for the girls, helping to fulfill their dreams. It had mellowed her a little about Joy's acting career, and maybe being a baker really did suit Juliette, even if that was hard for Véronique to understand. And Joy looked happier and more relaxed than she had in years. She was auditioning for better parts, and was excited about it. Timmie hadn't even thought about opening her own shelter yet, but both girls said they thought she would in time, and would be happier when she did than she was in her current job.

And as they walked back to their rooms in the adjacent building, Véronique thought about the Marniers again. She didn't want to meet Elisabeth, Sophie's mother, but she was curious about the girl. She would sleep on it, as Joy had suggested, and decide in the morning. And when she got back to her room after saying goodnight to the girls, Aidan called her. He had just stopped for the night in Stuttgart, on the way to Berlin. He had been driving for many hours and hadn't even stopped for dinner. And every step of the way, he said he had thought about her.

"I've been thinking about you, too," Véronique said softly. "I miss you." She was sitting on the balcony in the moonlight as they talked. And it was nice knowing they had made love in her bed before he left. It made him part of all this now, despite his hesitations. And she would remember him too in the bathtub whenever she bathed.

"How are the girls?" He sounded as though he knew them.

"They're fine. Everyone is nervous about tomorrow. It's a big deal meeting a half-sister you never knew you had."

"I'll say it is. What did you decide to do? Are you going, or just meeting them at the château?"

"I'll figure it out in the morning, depending on

how I feel." She still had mixed emotions about all of it, even seeing the château again that she had once loved.

"I'll be sending you good thoughts," he said warmly, and sounded tired. She knew he was anxious to get to Berlin the next day, and start setting up his show.

They chatted for a few more minutes and hung up. She sat there thinking about him afterward, looking at the view, and then slowly lowered the electric shutters over the windows that made the room completely dark so you could sleep late in the morning.

She lay in bed, remembering their lovemaking the night before and that day at the hotel. Their relationship had a surrealistic quality to it, from the way they had met, their meeting again in Venice, their travels afterward, and his bringing her to the Eden Roc that day. It had all happened so suddenly that sometimes it was hard to believe he was real. And yet he was, he had just called her, he had said he loved her, and she believed him, and he was waiting for her to meet him in Berlin. She loved his dignity and integrity, his pride, his intelligence, his tenderness and kindness. She remembered special moments with him in the last weeks, and whatever happened in the future, she knew with her entire being that for now, however remarkable and amazing it seemed, in all the ways that mattered, this was real.

Chapter 12

Right up until the moment Joy and Juliette left for St. Paul de Vence for their meeting with Sophie Marnier and her mother, Véronique was still of two minds about going with them. The three of them had breakfast on her terrace, with birds fluttering in and out, and the delicious breakfast the hotel served. She decided not to join them, and then when she saw them leaving, she changed her mind at the last minute.

"I'll come!" Véronique said hastily, grabbed her handbag, and ran out the door with them. She was wearing white jeans, a white blouse, and flat pink shoes for their exploration of the château after the meeting. And she jumped into the car with the two girls. They had a driver and they knew that St. Paul de Vence was half an hour away, and the little town where the château was was just a few minutes farther.

Véronique sat in the back of the car next to Juliette, looked out the window, and said not a word. Joy was in the front seat, chatting with the driver. And Véronique was thinking back to the day she'd bought the château at Paul's insistence. He had even talked about their moving there at first. He had been in love with the beautiful old eighteenth-century château. Véronique had loved it, too, but restoring it and then maintaining it was a lot of work. The project had been expensive, but Paul had been crazy about the place, so Véronique thought it was worth it. She and the girls stopped going there when she gave it to him in the divorce, and Paul never took the children there again. He spent time there in the summer with friends, and eventually stopped going entirely, particularly once the house needed to be maintained. He just boarded it up, and hired local caretakers to keep an eye on it for him and do minor repairs. The house had been the victim of deferred maintenance for twenty years, and now it had become the responsibility of the girls, or whoever bought it from them. For their sake, Véronique hoped they would put it on the market soon, to avoid it becoming a burden on them. It made no sense in any of their lives. It hadn't made much sense in her and Paul's life, even as a family, but even less now in theirs. And Véronique didn't want to invest in maintaining or repairing it for them. The Château de Brize was a money pit and always had been.

They drove slowly through St. Paul de Vence and

saw the main square. Old people were sitting under the trees and talking, in front of the local restaurant. And Véronique could see the familiar stone path that wended its way up a steep hill to the church. It was a few feet wide and only open to foot traffic in the medieval town. And then they drove through it to Biot, a few kilometers away. It still had old fortifications, and was a pretty little town. They had the Marniers' address and were meeting them at Elisabeth's medical office, which she said was a few feet from their home. Sophie lived with her. And a few minutes later the Mercedes stopped in front of a small picturesque stone cottage. It looked like a mouse house in a fairy tale. There was a shingle outside with Elisabeth Marnier's name on it, with the words "Médecine Générale" underneath it. She was the local GP.

All three women got out of the car. There was no one around. Juliette and Véronique followed Joy to the front door, where she rang a bell they could hear, and no one came to the door for a minute. And then a thin, spare blond woman opened the door, wearing a wrinkled gray linen dress, with her blond hair pulled back. She was wearing flat shoes and a man's watch on her wrist, and her eyes were serious as she looked from one of the women to the other. She had intense blue eyes, and a lined face, as though she had taken too much sun in her youth, and she wore no makeup. She had glasses pushed up on her head. She looked like a country doctor, there were no frills about her, and she smiled cautiously, as Véronique and Juliette walked up the few steps to the porch.

"I'm Elisabeth Marnier," she said simply, and they could smell the disinfectant from her small, spare medical office. She looked straight at Véronique as she introduced herself and held out her hand. "I owe you an apology," Elisabeth said quietly in reasonable English. "I never wanted to trouble you, or for you to know. It was a terrible mistake." Véronique hadn't expected the directness of her words, and they took her by surprise. Tears filled her eyes as she nodded and shook Elisabeth's hand. There was a faded quality to her, as though she must have been pretty once but no longer was. And although she was five years younger than Véronique, she looked a decade older or more. Véronique still had something youthful in her face, and perfect skin. Elisabeth was a different kind of woman, hadn't had an easy life, worked hard, kept long hours tending to her patients, and it showed. There was nothing frivolous about her, and it was difficult to imagine Paul in love with her, even if she had been pretty as a young girl. Their affair must have been born of boredom, one summer at the château. And Sophie's date of birth nine months after the summer, in May, suggested that was the case. He had never denied himself anything he wanted, particularly if there were women involved. She suddenly felt sorry for this woman, if she had found herself pregnant as a young girl, by a man who didn't care. Or not for long. Véronique wondered if having another child had fed his ego, or if he had simply been careless, while dallying with a country girl. If so, Elisabeth had paid a high price for his self-indulgence by bearing a child he almost never saw.

"Won't you come in?" she said politely after shaking hands with Joy and Juliette, and led them into her office, where everything looked old and threadbare but was immaculately clean. A nurse was sterilizing instruments when they walked in, and disappeared the moment they sat down in the chairs across from Elisabeth's desk. She put her glasses on then, and addressed the two girls, while Véronique tried to compose herself after their emotional greeting.

"I know this must have been very hard for all of you. And I'm so sorry about that. Sophie and I never expected anything from your father. He hadn't seen her since she was a little girl, and I hadn't heard from him in ten years. This whole business about the château came as a shock to us as well. Sophie is pursuing her studies in Grenoble. She hopes to do her training in Paris one day and work there, or come back here to join me in my practice. She has no desire to keep the château." As her mother spoke for her, they wondered where Sophie was, and if she had decided not to meet them after all. "I think she would be more than happy to concede her share of it to you, for a small price, whatever is fair. It would help her with living expenses during her studies, but she has no intention of taking advantage of you in any way. The faster she can get out of this, the better for us all."

Elisabeth didn't mention the rest of the bequest, but after what Paul had left his legitimate daughters, Arnold had said it would be very small. Particularly after the share he had left Timmie to establish her homeless facility, there was going to be barely enough for the others, and just a pittance for his child in France.

"Are you planning to sell the château?" Elisabeth asked the two young women, who nodded. They were impressed by her. She seemed like a nice woman and everything she said was fair. They had been prepared to hate her and their newly discovered half-sister, but there was nothing to hate about her yet.

"We don't want to undertake the work repairing it," Joy explained to her. "None of us live here. We don't come to France in the summer anymore, except for a week with our mother. My sisters live in New York, and I live in L.A. It just doesn't make sense." Véronique said not a word, and just listened to the exchange.

"Have you seen it yet?" Elisabeth asked sympathetically, and both girls shook their heads. "I hear it's in very poor condition. I believe your father stopped maintaining it a long time ago. I don't think he'd even seen it in about thirteen years, since the last time he saw Sophie when she was ten. He never came back again." She said it without reproach or accusation. She seemed to have nothing good or bad to say about him. And they all remembered the detective's report that said that she had lived with another man for twenty years, who had died two years before, her partner in her medical office. And he had acted as Sophie's father, far more than Paul, whom she had only seen a few times.

"We're going there today," Juliette chimed in, as Elisabeth nodded. And as she said it, a young girl appeared in the doorway. She looked like she was in her teens. She was very slight and had a child-like, innocent face, and huge green eyes. The girls thought she might be Sophie's younger sister, but the moment Véronique saw her, she knew exactly who she was. She was a tiny, delicate miniature of Paul. She looked just like him, and could have been Timmie's child, too, since she looked so much like her father. And she had a strong resemblance to Juliette as well, in a diminutive version. She looked nothing like Véronique or Joy. She was totally Paul. She had similar coloring to her mother, who was blond, too, but there was no denying who her father was. It took Véronique's breath away to see her. The girl smiled shyly at them all, as she walked into the room and stood near her mother. She was graceful and light on her feet, with blond hair that hung down her back. She looked like Alice in Wonderland, with a sweet face.

"This is Sophie," her mother introduced her. "She's very nervous about meeting you." Elisabeth smiled at them. "So was I. We had no idea how you felt about us. I appreciate how kind you've been." And then she smiled at her daughter and spoke to her in French, which only Véronique understood fully. She was reassuring her that they were not angry and they were very nice. And then Elisabeth turned to them again. "Her English is not so good." Sophie nodded when she said it, with a shy smile, and it was hard to imagine her as a medical student—she looked about fifteen. "She's studying to be a pediatrician." Sophie nodded then, she understood what her mother was saying, but was too shy to speak to them, as Joy held out a hand to her with a warm smile. There was nothing threatening about this girl. She looked young and shy and scared, and both of her half-sisters felt sorry for her.

"Hi, Sophie, I'm Joy. I'm the youngest, I'm three years older than you are. I live in L.A." Sophie smiled at her and nodded.

"I go to medical school," she said in careful English. "I want to be a doctor, and be like my mother."

"And I'm a cook," Juliette said with a smile. "I live in New York and make sandwiches and cookies—**gateaux,**" she added, patting her hips, and they all laughed. "I have a sandwich shop and patisserie. I'm twenty-eight. And our older sister Timmie works with homeless people." She wasn't sure if

Sophie would understand the term, and Elisabeth added, "SDF," the French term for homeless. "She's twenty-nine and lives in New York, too. And none of us are married." It seemed like all the pertinent initial information, and then Juliette added, "You look just like our father, and like Timmie . . . and I guess like me." She sounded sad as she said it. "Except Timmie is very tall."

They chatted for a few more minutes and Elisabeth offered them all tea, but no one wanted any, and finally Véronique spoke up and asked Elisabeth if she and Sophie would like to come to the château to see it with them.

"Sophie should see it," she said quietly, and Elisabeth agreed. Sophie addressed her sisters then, vehemently shaking her head.

"I do not want the Château de Brize," she said clearly. "Too much expensive for me."

"It's too much expensive for us, too," Joy said to her, smiling. "We want to sell it, but we want to see it first, to see how bad it looks." Sophie nodded, she understood and agreed, and a few minutes later, they all went outside. Elisabeth agreed to come with them, and the girls invited Sophie to ride between them in the backseat. Elisabeth followed in her car, and as they drove the few miles down a familiar back road, Véronique felt as if she were in some kind of dream. She had just met one of her ex-husband's mistresses, and they were riding to their old château, with his illegitimate child between two of her daughters. It was surreal. But they seemed to be nice women, and Sophie was very sweet. She was young in her demeanor, but she seemed bright. And her mother was dignified and respectful of the awkward situation they were all in. She had been no older than Sophie when she got involved with Paul Parker, and maybe just as naïve. And it had been so wrong of him to pursue her and start an affair with her. They were all in agreement on that.

They rounded the last bend, and the château came into sight. For a moment, it took Véronique's breath away. It looked no different than it had thirty years before, when she'd bought it for him. It stood elegant and noble against the summer sky, surrounded by beautiful old trees. It was made of stone, and there were a number of outbuildings, which they could already see were in bad shape. The hedges around the property had been recently trimmed, and there were rosebushes outside the guardian's cottage that looked like something in a fairy tale. As they got out of the car, a big friendly dog bounded up to them, wagging his tail. And the ancient guardian and his wife came out of the cottage shortly after to greet them. They were so old that it was hard to believe they could take care of anything, but the husband still seemed pretty spry.

Véronique explained to them in French who they were and why they had come. She said that these were the children of Monsieur Parker, and they had come to tour the house. The guardian said he had expected them, and that Monsieur Parker's lawyer had sent them a letter advising them that the family would come soon. He didn't recognize Véronique, and had been hired after she left.

He went to get the keys, which were the original keys on a huge ring. And then he went to open the enormous doors and let them in. Véronique could see the stables in the distance, where she had kept horses for the children. She and Paul had been good horsemen and had gone riding across the fields and in the woods.

The door creaked like something in a horror movie as he opened it and pushed it wide. He told Elisabeth and Véronique that his wife cleaned the house once a week, which seemed unlikely, and Véronique noticed cobwebs almost the moment they walked in, but she didn't disagree with him. There was a long Aubusson runner in the front hall. At a noise, Juliette ducked with a scream.

"Oh shit! Do you think there are bats in here?" she asked her mother, as the others laughed.

"Probably," Véronique said, "but they sleep in the daytime." Juliette made a terrible face, and they followed the guardian into the enormous living room. The furniture was still there, covered with sheets, and the curtains were the same, faded almost beyond recognition. There were two beautiful Aubusson rugs that had been rolled up, and an enormous fireplace. The house was still fully furnished. And the guardian opened the shutters and let the sun in. Véronique could see that it was still a magnificent room. She could instantly envision the children playing there when they were little.

There was an enormous dining room with a table that seated thirty people, several smaller reception rooms, and a library full of old books. And the kitchen was a relic from another century, with big iron kettles and a round table where she used to feed the kids.

There was a long elegant staircase, and all five women walked upstairs silently to discover a multitude of lovely bedrooms, all with views of the grounds, and the master suite, which brought back painful memories for Véronique now. She had thought they were happy there, for most of the time anyway, and now knew it wasn't true. Elisabeth and Sophie were living proof of that.

And the bathrooms were antiquated and wonderful. There were six or eight bedrooms on that floor. And above it, under the mansard roof, with oeil-de-boeuf windows, were at least a dozen smaller servants' rooms. The caretaker said there was a huge wine cellar in the basement, storage space, the furnace, and a place to hang meat.

The place looked less damaged than Véronique had expected it to, but in almost every room, she could see the evidence of leaks. The plumbing had been problematic years before, the electricity looked dubious now, the kitchen would be a nightmare to use and had to be gutted and renovated. The guardian readily admitted that the roof leaked throughout the house. And Véronique could see that the windows had almost rotted through. There was a huge amount of work to do, and no point doing it. The girls would never use it. However beautiful it still was—and in many ways, it was even lovelier than Véronique remembered—it made absolutely no sense to have a home like this for three young women pursuing lives and careers on their own. Even for her, as a single woman living in Paris part time, it made just as little sense as it did for them. Elisabeth was shaking her head as she looked around, impressed by the size and splendor of it, but it was like visiting an ancient museum, and Sophie looked on the verge of panic. She addressed both of her half-sisters as they came back downstairs to the main floor.

"For me, no no no no," she said, wagging a finger and pointing at herself, and then spreading her arms wide, referring to its size. "Too big for me and my **maman.**" She then pantomimed vacuuming and sweeping and rolled her eyes, and the two girls laughed.

"Yeah, me, too, **moi aussi,**" Joy said immediately. "Too big, too much, too old, too expensive." She pretended to pull at her hair, and Sophie laughed and nodded agreement.

"Trop cher à réparer," too expensive to repair, and her mother was nodding, too, and then turned to Véronique in admiration.

"What a beautiful château," Elisabeth said to Véronique. "It's wonderful, but Sophie could never use it. We live in a tiny house near my office, and I'm alone there now most of the time."

"My girls will never use it either," Véronique said sadly, thinking that it was a shame that the house had gone unloved for so long. She couldn't imagine herself there now either. It would probably sell to a Russian, who would turn it into a palace worthy of Louis XIV. No one else would want to do the work it would take to restore it, nor could afford it. The only one who could was Véronique, and she didn't want the headache. Joy and Sophie were pantomiming a lengthy conversation about it, and seemed in full agreement, as Juliette wandered around on her own. And when they were ready to leave, to visit the stables, they couldn't find her. She had gone back upstairs. And she finally came downstairs with a dreamy look in her eyes.

"Please don't tell me you're falling in love with it," Joy said with visible irritation. "Did you see the leaks in every room and the windows? They're about to fall in. And Mom says the guardian said the roof leaks like a sieve. We need to sell it," Joy said with determination, and she knew that Timmie, even without seeing it, would agree with her. "I can't take this on," Joy said with a look of panic.

"I live in L.A., and I can't afford it, and neither can you."

"It would make a fabulous hotel," Juliette said as they walked to the stables through tall overgrown grass.

"Not unless you put millions of dollars into it," Joy said practically. Juliette was always the dreamer, but this was one dream Joy wanted no part of, and neither would Timmie. "Stop looking like that. We have to sell it," she said sternly.

"Dad loved this place," Juliette said sadly.

"The hell he did. He hadn't been here in thirteen years. He didn't want the headache either. Even Sophie agrees with me." She pointed at her new half-sister, who understood what they were saying and nodded vehemently. She had been terrified they would expect money from her to do repairs, and Elisabeth had been worried about that, too. They couldn't afford it. They could barely afford the tiny house they lived in.

They visited the stables, and all the cottages and buildings, including the guardian's cottage, which was a mess and smelled of some kind of stew. And three hours after they'd gotten there, they had seen everything, including some old chandeliers that had been stored in the stables, which Véronique remembered buying and never using, and was surprised to see again. Paul had done nothing since she left.

They headed back to Elisabeth's office, where she

said she had patients to see that afternoon, and Joy confirmed to Sophie and her mother that there was no question, they would be selling the Château de Brize, and hoped Sophie agreed, which she did. Joy promised to stay in touch with them, and Sophie kissed both her sisters on both cheeks and Véronique with an awed, respectful expression. They were even more beautiful than she expected and had been far nicer to her than she'd hoped. The meeting had gone very well, given the possibilities. All five women were civilized and nice people, and Elisabeth and Véronique shook hands. Véronique liked her much better than she wanted to, and felt sorry for her again as they left. Paul had given Elisabeth an even worse deal than he had given her. He had done nothing for her at all. And Sophie was obviously a lovely girl. Paul had lucked out again, surrounding himself with people who were nicer than he deserved.

Véronique and the two girls headed back to the Hôtel du Cap, as Joy commented on the condition of the house, and Juliette was suspiciously quiet, as she gazed at the countryside with a faraway gaze. Véronique was feeling nostalgic after seeing the house, but was totally in agreement that they should sell. Everyone agreed. It required way too much work, and there was no rational reason to keep it.

"I still think it would make such a beautiful hotel," Juliette said wistfully, staring out the window, and looking at neither of them, as though talking to herself. "It's close to St. Paul de Vence, and half an hour from the coast. The location is perfect, and it can't be **that** much work," she said, turning back to Joy.

"Are you insane? Did you see the condition it was in? I thought the roof was going to fall on our heads. The kitchen is out of the dark ages, and looks like witches should be cooking there, like in **Macbeth.** And the windows are ready to fall out. Don't give me that look, Juliette. This is not a sandwich shop in Brooklyn. This is a château we can't afford to own, and Dad couldn't either. Let's get rid of it as fast as we can. I'd rather have the money, and so would you. Timmie wants it to help start her shelter, and it sounds like Sophie needs it, too. I don't want to hear some crazy plan about turning it into a hotel. If you want a hotel, buy one. But count me out on this."

Juliette had tears in her eyes as she listened to her sister, and she was silent when they walked back into the hotel. Joy called Timmie immediately and told her all about the meeting with Sophie and Elisabeth and how nice they were. Timmie sounded relieved and asked about the château.

"It's a mess," Joy confirmed to her. "I hope we can get rid of it. Someone will have to want to sink a fortune into it."

"Can you list it with a realtor before you leave?" It sounded like a good idea to Joy, too. She was still talking to Timmie, when Juliette walked into her mother's room. Véronique was sitting on the terrace, thinking about the château. It had been a sad déjà vu for her, and an emotional meeting with Elisabeth and Sophie, more than her daughters seemed to realize.

"Can I talk to you for a minute, Mom?" Juliette asked as she sat down on the terrace. "Are you okay?"

"I'm fine. It was just kind of an emotional overload going there today."

"I'm sorry." Juliette paused for a long minute, wondering if it was the wrong time. "I know this sounds crazy, but how much do you think it would cost to buy the others out of the château?"

"I don't know," Véronique said seriously. "We'd have to have it appraised. It's probably not worth much in the condition it's in. There's a lot of work to do."

"I know," Juliette said seriously. She had fallen in love with it, and her mother could see it in her eyes. "Would you lend me the money to buy it, against my inheritance? I could use the money Dad left me to fix it up, and maybe sell the sandwich shop, and do some of the work myself, if I could find someone locally to help me do it. What do you think? Is that something you would ever do? Help me buy it, I mean? I just felt like it was calling to me to love it." They were almost the identical words Paul had used with her when he wanted her to buy it.

It was yet another déjà vu. "Could I afford it from my inheritance?" Juliette asked her, and Véronique nodded. Easily, but she didn't say it to Juliette.

"If that's what you really want to do. I think you should think about it, and be sure. You don't live here. You'd have to consider how much you'd use it."

"I'd probably have to move here," Juliette said, as though that made sense. "I couldn't do the work from far away."

"Would you really want to live here?" Véronique was startled. None of them had ever wanted to live in France. It was a battle getting them to come over for a week a year.

"Maybe I do. I think I've finally found the place I want to be."

"Give it some thought before you make any serious decisions," Véronique advised her, and then smiled at her. Juliette looked happier than her mother had ever seen her. "What did you think of Sophie?" she couldn't resist asking.

"She's really sweet," Juliette commented. "She's like a little kid. And she looks just like Dad, doesn't she?"

"And like Timmie and you," Véronique said with a sigh.

Juliette went back to her own room a few minutes later. Joy was off the phone by then and glanced at Juliette suspiciously. "What are you up to?" She didn't trust her not to go off on one of her tangents, just like when she had given up her career plans in art history and bought a bakery in Brooklyn. In Joy's opinion, she was always doing crazy things, like taking in lame guys.

"I think I might want to buy it," Juliette said seriously, and Joy could see she meant it. "It would make a beautiful hotel."

"You don't know anything about running a hotel," Joy reminded her, irritated by how unrealistic her sister always was.

"I didn't know anything about running a bakery either, and it's worked out pretty well."

"What about the money Dad gave you for the sandwich shop?" Joy asked her pointedly.

"Dad gave us each the money to fulfill our dreams. Timmie so she could start her own homeless shelter. You for your acting career, so you could hire the right manager, get a better agent, and take acting lessons so you can get better parts and stop waiting on tables. And if my dream turns out to be turning the château into a hotel, I don't think it's so terrible, it's still my dream. What's so wrong with that?" Joy fell silent as she listened to her, and could see that she meant it, and then she shook her head.

"I love you, but I think you're now officially crazy. It'll cost a fortune to fix that place up. How the hell are you going to do that?"

"I could do a lot of the work myself, and Mom could lend me the money, if you all agree to let me buy you out."

"You're serious about this, aren't you?" Joy looked at her with amazement. Juliette nodded. She had never been as serious about anything in her entire life. She felt as if it were meant to be, a final gift from their father who wanted her to do more with her life than make sandwiches in Brooklyn, and now she would. She could turn the Château de Brize into a beautiful small hotel, and run it herself. Maybe she'd even run the kitchen and do the baking. Her mind was going in a million different directions, as they changed and went out to the pool. Véronique joined them a little while later, and they sat in the cabana for a while, relaxing and lying in the sun, while a waiter brought them cold drinks. It was a totally luxurious life and good to be together. And Aidan called Véronique that afternoon when she got back to her room.

"How did it go? Did you meet them?" He sounded worried about her.

"Sophie looks like an angel, and just like her father," Véronique said wistfully. "And her mother seems like a very decent woman. She's a sensible, no-nonsense, serious, respectable person, and she must have been as crazy about him as I was when she was a young girl. She's a nice, wholesome country doctor, and she apologized to me when we got there. All things considered, it went fine. It was just emotionally draining. And the five of us went to the château."

"How was that?" he asked with interest. She

sounded tired, but he could tell that she was at peace about the meeting, and he was relieved.

"The house is even prettier than I remembered, and in just the kind of shape I thought it would be in. It's like Rip Van Winkle's castle, and looks like it hasn't been touched in a hundred years. It will cost a fortune to fix it up. Timmie, Joy, and now Sophie want to sell it. And her mother is very anxious for her to do that. They can't afford to keep it and maintain it, and they need the money. But Juliette fell in love with it, and wants to turn it into a hotel. She's the family dreamer, but I think she's serious about it. She wants to buy out her sisters, and do the work herself if she can find someone to help her."

"Can she afford to do that?" He sounded surprised.

"She wants me to lend her the money. I could, but I want permission from her sisters. I don't want them to think I'm favoring her." She was always very careful about that and fair to all.

"Just do it," Aidan said, sounding tense. "Don't hold out on her. If you can afford it, help her. Maybe this is her destiny, not just her dream."

"If it is, we'll find a way," Véronique said calmly, touched by what he'd said, for a girl he didn't even know.

"She'll never forget it, if you do it, or forgive you, if you don't." She had pretty much decided to lend Juliette the money after she left her room, but she wanted to talk to the others, too. For a man who had no children, he had a lot of very definite ideas about what she should do. But she agreed with him, too—he wasn't wrong.

"We have a lot to talk about when we get home. She wants to sell her bakery and move here."

"She must **really** be serious about it then." Aidan sounded impressed and Véronique was, too.

"I think she is."

"Well, it sounds like everything went better than expected," Aidan said. She was happy to talk to him. It was nice to know that someone cared what was happening in her life. That was new for her.

"It did. How's your show coming?"

"I haven't been to the gallery since I arrived. My rep is here—he came to check it out. I haven't seen him yet. I wanted to call you first." She also loved being a priority to him. "How much longer are the girls staying?" He was eager for her to meet him in Berlin.

"I don't know yet. Another couple of days. They won't stay more than that."

"Well, tell them to hurry up and go home. I'm waiting for you in Berlin," he said impatiently. "I miss you, Véronique."

"I miss you, too," she said, smiling broadly. It was so good talking to him. It was just what she needed after the sadness of seeing the château again. It had been like visiting all her shattered dreams. And with Aidan, everything was new. It made her feel young and full of hope just talking to him.

Chapter 13

Joy and Juliette had dinner with their mother at the Eden Roc in the hotel's formal dining room that night. They had a lot to talk about after seeing the château and meeting the Marniers. All of them had been pleasantly surprised by Elisabeth and Sophie, and Juliette couldn't stop talking about the château. Joy thought she was crazy to want to buy it. She was very clear that she wanted to unload it as soon as possible, and repeated it to her sister when they went back to their room.

"I think I could do something terrific with it," Juliette said with a determination Véronique had never seen in her before. And she spoke to her mother again the next day about borrowing the money. Véronique wasn't opposed to it, if Joy and Timmie were amenable, and she wanted to get an appraisal of what the property was worth, so they could assess the value of each girl's share. Juliette said she would stay in the South of France long enough to get a proper appraisal, and talk to an architect about the cost of the work. She was serious about it, called a realtor in St. Paul de Vence that morning, and made an appointment with him for the following afternoon.

Joy had already said that she was leaving the next day. Her new agent had e-mailed her about an audition for a better part on a soap than she had had so far, which could mean her being on the show for as long as a month, and her manager wanted to talk to her about a possible national ad campaign for a cosmetics line. Both were great opportunities she didn't want to miss. She was anxious to get back and had heard from her manager several times. He texted her constantly, and she said he was nice and a really smart young guy. Juliette had asked her jokingly if she was going out with him, and Joy said it was strictly business, although he was handsome, too. Véronique had wondered as well. He seemed unusually attentive, but Joy insisted they were only working on her career, and nothing else, and said he had a great reputation in Hollywood for making stars.

The three of them enjoyed a leisurely afternoon in the cabana and at the pool, and Joy and Juliette swam out to the raft, just as they had as kids. Véronique was alone in the cabana when she got a text from Nikolai Petrovich, asking where she was in the world at the moment, and she texted back that she was at the Hôtel du Cap with two of her daughters. He responded immediately, said he was on his boat in St. Jean Cap Ferrat, and was heading in her direction that afternoon. Would she and her daughters like to have dinner on his yacht? He said he would be honored, and Véronique was amused. She thought it would be fun for the girls to meet him. And she imagined that seeing his boat would be entertaining for them, too. She knew he had several, and it would be nice to see him. She texted back that they would be delighted, and he answered that his tender would pick them up at eight o'clock at the dock at Eden Roc. She told the girls about it when they got back from swimming.

"Nikolai who?" Juliette asked with a puzzled expression. She had never heard of him, and couldn't imagine how her mother knew him. "You know how I hate boats, Mom. They always make me sick."

"I have a feeling his is big enough that you won't get seasick. Let's do it." She hadn't seen him since they'd had dinner on the terrace of his suite in Rome, when he'd nearly killed her with the Ferrari, which she hadn't mentioned to her daughters, nor the fact that she'd been slow to get out of the way.

"How do you know him?" Joy was curious. He didn't sound like the sort of person her mother knew. She was a quiet person and didn't hang around with jet-set billionaires.

"We met in Rome, on my way to Venice to do research on your father's painting." It sounded respectable, even though the explanation was incomplete. "He's Russian," she said, to prepare them for his larger-than-life persona. She just hoped he didn't try to seduce her daughters, but she doubted that he would.

"It sounds boring," Juliette said, not in the mood to have dinner on anyone's boat, or get seasick. And it was Joy's last night before she went back to L.A. She said she didn't want to spend it with a stranger, and Juliette agreed.

"I don't think he'll be boring," Véronique said mysteriously, "and if he is, I promise we'll come home early. Just trust me. I think it will be interesting for you to meet him. He's a very colorful character."

"Did you go out with him, Mom?" Joy questioned her further, not really serious about it, while Juliette rolled her eyes as though that were a ridiculous idea. They could even less have imagined that she'd been driving all over Italy with a British photographer, eleven years younger than she was, and was planning to meet him in Berlin as soon as they left.

"I had dinner with him," Véronique said demurely, referring to Nikolai. They had no reason to know about Aidan.

They left the cabana at six o'clock. The girls grudgingly agreed to have dinner on the yacht when their mother insisted, and they all went to their rooms to bathe and dress. Véronique lay down for a while and wondered what she should tell Aidan. She knew how jealous he had been of him, and annoyed when Nikolai texted her in Venice. She didn't want to upset him, and she decided to wait until the evening was over to tell him. She didn't want to lie to him either. And before they went out to meet the tender at the dock, she sent Aidan a quick text that said only "Going to dinner with the girls. Talk later. Love you, V." It was all he needed to know right now.

She had fallen asleep for half an hour and dressed in a hurry, and hadn't bothered to look out the window of her suite. She stopped in the girls' room to pick them up for dinner, and found Joy staring at an enormous yacht, anchored off the hotel. It was twice the size of any of the boats around it.

"I think it's a battleship, or maybe a cruise ship," she said with a look of amusement. It had an ominous appearance, its hull was painted black, and it was a huge motor yacht, with two large tenders tied to the stern. And from the distance, she could see a flock of sailors getting into one of them.

"I think that may be where we're having dinner," Véronique said quietly as Juliette stared at her.

"Are you joking? Who is this guy?"

"Some sort of Russian billionaire. I'm not sure what he does, but apparently he's very well known."

"He must be an arms dealer to have a boat that size," Joy commented as they followed their mother out of the room, and down the steps to the boat dock, where the tender was already waiting for them, with six uniformed sailors in attendance, and an officer to meet them. The crew was British, and looked very pleased to see the girls as they greeted the three women politely, and helped them into the high-speed wooden tender. The girls said not a word as they rode the short distance to the enormous yacht. Joy couldn't resist asking, and one of the boys in uniform told her it was 450 feet long, and currently one of the two largest private yachts in the world. He said it had a helipad and a swimming pool, and their owner was currently building a larger one. Joy nodded as she listened, and glanced at Juliette. They were both startled that their mother knew the owner of the boat. And even more so when they saw him.

Nikolai was waiting for them on deck, in white linen pants and an open white shirt, with a heavy gold chain around his neck, and a gold Rolex watch with diamonds on the face. He looked thrilled the moment he saw Véronique. He embraced her warmly, and greeted Joy and Juliette, as a stewardess handed all three of them flutes of champagne.

"Would you like a tour of the boat?" he asked them, and all three enthusiastically said yes. He led them up a staircase to the top deck, where there was an enormous sun deck with luxurious chairs, a bar, an outdoor movie screen for warm nights, and the helipad, which looked enormous and had one of his jet helicopters sitting on it.

A deck below they went to the wheelhouse, where the captain and three officers showed them around. The boat had a crew of fifty, many of whom were in evidence on deck, and admired the two girls as they walked by. And at every opportunity, Nikolai turned and smiled at Véronique as though they were old friends, which didn't go unnoticed by the girls. Véronique wasn't sure if they were horrified or impressed, but they were bowled over by the boat, which seemed nearly as big as an ocean liner.

They visited six guest cabins, two drawing rooms, a movie theater, an enormous gym with every possible kind of equipment, and a spa with two uniformed massage therapists on duty, as well as a hairdresser and manicurist, he said proudly. There was a library filled with books, a huge wood-paneled indoor dining room for bad weather, and an even larger outdoor one for warm nights, and an outdoor bar and sitting area on every floor, as well as a card room where Nikolai said he liked to play poker with his friends. And the last stop was the galley, where their meal was being prepared by three main chefs and four sous-chefs. It looked like a floating city, and when they went back to the main deck outside the largest living room, there was caviar waiting for them at one of the outdoor bars. Just being there was an overwhelming experience, and Véronique could see that both girls were vastly impressed. Their host was charming, pleasant, intelligent, and warmly hospitable. He was obviously very proud of his boat and delighted to show it off. There was a slightly rough-around-the-edges quality about him that was undeniable, but he was extremely nice, and welcoming to all of them.

He switched from champagne to vodka with the caviar, which the girls were happily devouring. Juliette showed no sign of being seasick. You could feel no motion of the boat whatsoever with its enormous stabilizers, he explained to them. He said that he had crossed the Atlantic with it several times, and had a larger boat he kept in the Caribbean, near St. Bart's. It was luxury and riches to such an extreme degree that it was hard to imagine, and Véronique couldn't help wondering how Aidan would have reacted to it. It seemed pointless to object, one could only stare in fascination. It was hard to fathom anyone having that much money. And the boat was beautiful, even if its opulence was excessive. It offered every comfort money could buy. And the art on the walls was worth millions. The decor was gaudy and he loved it.

Véronique thought it was exciting just seeing it. He had two Picassos on board, several Jackson Pollocks, and a massive Chagall in the main salon. The girls were speechless, particularly Juliette, with her background in art. Véronique almost laughed at the astonishment on their faces, as Nikolai led them to the dining table an hour later. The buffet set out for them was a feast, complete with lobsters and a suckling pig, which was delicious. And tonight there was no sign of his young female companion. He appeared to be alone, although Véronique suspected she was on the boat somewhere, since he had kept her in the bedroom waiting for him for hours, while he dined with Véronique on the terrace at the Hassler. He seemed to have no qualms about sequestering her. He was the kind of man who would always have a beautiful woman on his arm, as an accessory if nothing else.

"Did your mother tell you how I met her?" Nikolai asked the girls as they ate dinner, and they were fascinated.

"No, she didn't," Joy answered, with a meaningful glance at her mother. She was even more intrigued now that they had met him.

"I almost killed her in Rome, with my Ferrari," he said with a remorseful look at Véronique, who smiled her reassurance. "It was terrifying, and she was so nice about it. The traffic was terrible, and everyone drives too fast. I just missed running her over. We were staying at the same hotel, so I took her home, and called a doctor. And then we had dinner," he said proudly, as though dining with her had been an honor. "And now here we are, friends." He beamed at all three of them. "And you are on my boat. I promised her in Rome I would bring my boat for dinner. So I did." The steward was pouring a 1983 Château Margaux as he said it, which impressed Juliette even more.

"You never told us about it, Mom," Joy said reproachfully, about her near accident in Rome.

"I was fine." Véronique dismissed it. She hadn't wanted to worry them, and once she got to Venice, she had met Aidan and was too busy having fun with him to think about it anymore.

"She flew through the air like a butterfly," Nikolai said, remembering the hideous moment when he thought he had killed her, or at least injured her very badly. "Rome is a very dangerous city. How was Venice?" he asked Véronique then.

"Wonderful. I went to the monastery I mentioned to you about my painting. They're researching it now. I haven't heard anything yet. And then I went to Siena and Florence, which was fantastic. I love the Uffizi," she said, as her daughters stared at her.

"When did you do that?"

"After Venice," she answered innocently. "Before meeting you here."

"You never told us that either. We thought you went back to Paris."

"As long as I was in Italy, I thought I'd do a little sightseeing." She was vague as she said it, and the two girls exchanged a look, which Véronique ignored.

They were eating profiteroles and chocolate soufflé for dessert when Nikolai lit a cigar and turned to Véronique. "I have a project for you," he said, smiling at her. It was obvious to both her daughters how much he liked her. "I want you to paint my portrait. I'm commissioning you to do it. I will come to New York in the fall, and you can do it then." He didn't ask her if she wanted to, or had time. He assumed she would, and she laughed at the suggestion.

"You don't even know if you like my work. And I haven't done a portrait in a long time, not a serious one."

"She's very good," Joy interjected.

"I give you my confidence," Nikolai said to her, as he waved the cigar at her. It was obviously Cuban, and Véronique loved the smell—it reminded her of her father. She correctly guessed that it was a Cohiba. "I will tell you when I'm arriving."

"You might be very disappointed in my work." She was nervous about doing it, but Nikolai wasn't.

"I don't believe that. I am sure you are a great artist," he said, as the stewardess poured Château d'Yquem in their glasses, and the three women sipped it with pleasure.

Nikolai talked about his art collection then, and told the girls that he would be happy to receive them at his house in London, or on any of his boats, at any time. They sat at the table chatting for another hour, and then finally Véronique said that they should go back to the hotel—it had been a long day and Joy was leaving early the next morning. But all of them were sorry to leave him. He had been an extremely congenial host, and being on his yacht had been an unforgettable experience. He kissed all three of them as they left, and waved as the speedboat took them back to the dock. Véronique and her daughters felt like Cinderella after midnight when they got back to the hotel.

"Holy shit, Mom. What was that?" Joy said as they walked up the stairs to the lobby of the Eden Roc. She was grinning broadly. "Did he really almost kill you in Rome?"

"Not really. He missed me by quite a lot," she said, thinking, Thanks to Aidan. "But he was very nice about it. He had an amazing suite at the Hassler, and we had dinner on his terrace."

"That sounds pretty racy to me, Mom." Joy was looking at her with new eyes, and her mother laughed. It never dawned on them that she might know someone like him. And it was certainly a rarity in her life.

"It wasn't," she assured her. "He had a girlfriend there. A very pretty girl, younger than you."

"I'm not surprised," Juliette added. "I saw some very pretty young girl run into the hair salon while we were on the tour, but she had disappeared when we got there. I can't believe that boat. He must be the richest man in the world."

"Just one of them," Véronique said. It was a whole new breed of wealth that had materialized in recent years, and one saw it frequently in Europe. She had seen others like him in Paris. "It's hard to imagine. The boat was incredible, wasn't it?"

"I can't believe you didn't tell us you went to Florence," Joy commented.

"You girls are busy, and most of the time I don't do anything very exciting. Nikolai is an oddity for me, too. But I thought you'd enjoy seeing the boat. I'd heard about it. It was even bigger and more impressive than I expected."

"I don't get seasick on boats that size," Juliette said, as though she'd made an important discovery, and her mother and sister laughed. They'd had a lot of wine, and were all in good spirits.

Véronique said goodbye to Joy that night, since she was leaving early the next morning, and as soon as she got back to her room, Aidan called her. He had left her a message earlier, and she hadn't returned the call yet. He sounded worried.

"Where were you tonight?"

"Doing something crazy," she admitted.

"Like what?"

"Nikolai Petrovich was in the area with his boat, and he invited me and the girls for dinner. I thought they'd like to see it."

"What's he after?" Aidan almost growled at her, and it confirmed how jealous he had been before, but she didn't want to lie to him. It was a bad habit she didn't want to get into, even if he didn't like what she was doing, and she knew he wouldn't.

"Just showing off his boat. It was something new and different for the girls." She didn't tell him how fabulous it was or what a good time they'd had. She had just told him where she had been, and that was enough.

"He'll probably try to sleep with one of them," he said with a strong tone of disapproval.

"I hope not," she said lightly. "He's older than I am."

"Or maybe he'll try to sleep with you." He sounded panicked at the thought.

"Don't be silly. The girl he had with him in Rome was about twenty. So what did you do tonight?" she said, changing the subject, but she could tell his feathers were ruffled about their evening on the yacht.

"I missed you. I had dinner with my rep and started hanging my show. It's hard to get anything done here." He explained about his problems with the show then, and after they'd talked for a while, he relaxed. He mentioned that he'd had a very good offer from a gallery in New York to sell limited editions of some of his photographs, which was how he made his living between shows. He didn't make a fortune on his work yet, but enough to live on. His needs were modest, and eventually he hoped to increase his prices once his photographs were in museums. He was working toward that goal.

She told him then that Joy was leaving in the morning, and Juliette was going back to the château with a realtor to find out what it might sell for, so they could set a fair price if she bought out her sisters. "She seems to be very intent about it."

"And you're going to help her?"

"Yes, I am," she said softly, and he sounded pleased.

They talked for a while, and progressively relaxed with each other, and he was in better spirits when they hung up.

"And don't go off having dinner with that Russian again," he said sternly. "I'm sure he's dangerous, and probably an arms dealer or something." There was no way to know.

"He might be," she conceded, and she didn't tell him Nikolai had commissioned her for a portrait. It would have upset Aidan all over again, which wasn't her intention.

He promised to call her the next day, told her he loved her, and they hung up. After that Véronique walked onto her terrace and looked at the giant motor yacht still sitting in the water. It was all lit up like a floating city. She could still see it from her bed, as she lay there, thinking of the two men she had met that summer, Aidan and Nikolai, and how different they were. One flaunted his fortune in every way he could, the other said he was allergic to rich people and believed in simple values. She enjoyed Nikolai, but she was in love with Aidan. And as she thought of them, she fell asleep.

* * *

In the morning when she woke up, the yacht was gone. Nikolai had sent her a text, saying he was going back to Monaco to pick up friends, and to text him if she would like dinner on the boat again. She answered his text and thanked him for a wonderful evening.

She met up with Juliette in the cabana a little while later. She was making copious notes about the château, and was determined to meet with an architect before she left. And she didn't mention it to her mother, but she was going to visit Elisabeth and Sophie on her way to the château that afternoon. She wanted to see them again before she went back to New York. She had liked Sophie when they met, and her mother.

Véronique wished her luck when she left a little while later, and she spent the afternoon dozing, sunning, and reading a book. It was a perfect afternoon, and she was happy. Her visit with the girls had gone well. Joy seemed relaxed and excited about her acting career and her new manager. And Juliette was in love with the château. And when they left, she would go to Berlin to see Aidan, and they would pick up where they left off. All was well in her world.

* * *

Juliette had the driver stop at Elisabeth's office in Biot on her way to the château that afternoon. She was with a patient, and the nurse asked her to wait for a few minutes. Juliette glanced through a French magazine, and ten minutes later Elisabeth emerged from the exam room, surprised to see her, as Juliette stood up with a warm smile.

"I was on my way to the château, and I thought I'd just stop by to say hello." Elisabeth looked pleased and was touched by it. She was wearing her white lab coat and had a stethoscope around her neck.

"Are your mother and sister with you?" She wondered if they were waiting in the car. She was going to invite them in.

"My sister left for L.A. this morning, and my mother is at the hotel. I came alone, I have an appointment with a realtor to appraise the château. We need to know how much it's worth." Elisabeth nodded and thought it was a good idea.

"It needs a lot of repairs," she reminded her.

"I know. Is Sophie here?"

"She just went out a little while ago, to see friends in St. Paul de Vence. She liked very much meeting all of you yesterday," Elisabeth said kindly. "You were all very nice to her. She was afraid, and so was I, that the meeting would be difficult. Your mother was very elegant about it," she said openly. "It must have been painful for her."

"She liked you, too," Juliette said simply. "She

felt better after she met you. I think she was sad to see the château. It has a lot of memories for her."

Elisabeth nodded. It did for her, too. She had said nothing the day before, but Paul had taken her there several times when Véronique and the children were away. Sophie had been conceived there, which was not something she was proud of, and she wouldn't have mentioned it to Juliette, but it had been awkward going back there the day before with Véronique. She had been foolish in her youth, and they would all be happy when the place was sold. It was too full of their old ghosts and a past filled with regrets.

"I hope you sell it soon," Elisabeth said, as she walked Juliette back to the car. Juliette didn't tell her she was thinking of keeping it and buying it from her sisters. The idea was still too new. And she promised to come back soon and visit them again before she left.

"Say hello to Sophie," she said to Elisabeth, and the woman who had been her father's lover waved as they drove away.

The realtor was waiting for her when she got to the Château de Brize. He was a serious man who knew the region well, and everything that had sold recently. He warned her that the château would not bring a high price given its current state of disrepair. She said she understood, and they walked the property together for several hours and he examined everything, and explained it to her in English, alternating with French she understood. It was nearly six o'clock by the time they finished. They were both hot and tired, and he checked some notes he'd brought with him, and then they sat down on the front steps of the château. The caretaker had opened everything for them, and the realtor looked at her with a concerned expression.

"I don't want to disappoint you, or give you false hopes. Everything has to be repaired here. The wiring, the plumbing, the roof. Someone will have to put a great deal of money into it, to bring it back into a condition where it can be used. It will probably cost more to repair than to buy it. I don't think you can expect to get more than six hundred thousand dollars for it. Six hundred and fifty tops." That meant that offering them top dollar, her share was worth a hundred and fifty thousand dollars, and she would owe her three sisters just over four hundred and fifty thousand dollars in all, if they agreed. It was a lot to borrow from her mother, and she didn't know if Véronique would be willing. But she knew that her share of her mother's estate would be a great deal more than that. It would be an advance on her inheritance. And she was going to use the money her father had left her to start the repairs. And she could sell the shop in Brooklyn to add to that. As the realtor said, it was going to be an expensive project, but she could do it slowly over time, and even live there once it was in working order, when it was safe.

"Do you know a contractor in the area, and an architect?" Juliette asked him.

"I do. There's a good firm in St. Paul."

"I'd like to get an estimate of how much it might cost someone to do the repairs." He nodded, jotted down the name, and handed it to her. She looked at the note. Jean-Pierre Flarion. He'd given her the phone number and address. And then she thanked the realtor for his time, and paid him what they'd agreed to for the appraisal, which was a small fee.

"Would you like me to list it for you now?" he asked her hopefully.

"Not yet. I'll be in touch," she said, and then got back in the car to head back to the hotel, and as they drove through St. Paul, she had an idea. She called the architectural firm on her cell phone. It rang several times, and finally a harried voice picked it up.

"Oui?" Yes? She asked to speak to Mr. Flarion, and the voice said it was he. She explained that she had a château in the area, and she would like to consult someone about repairs and restoration.

"What château?" The voice sounded intrigued.

"The Château de Brize," she said clearly.

"It's been unoccupied for years. It's in terrible condition. You're thinking of buying it?"

"I own it," she said. "It was my father's. Would you be willing to come out and look at it tomorrow?"

"I might," he said, sounding interested. "Let me check something." He was back in a minute. "I can do it at ten o'clock tomorrow morning. After that I'm busy. And I have to go to meetings in Nice the rest of the week."

"Tomorrow at ten will be fine," she said, feeling a ripple of excitement run through her. She was actually doing this. She was meeting with an architect. It was happening. She wanted to scream, she was so excited as she thanked him and hung up.

She went to find her mother in her room as soon as she got back. Véronique could see from the look in her eyes that it had gone well.

"What did he say?" She smiled at Juliette.

"He said it's worth between six hundred and six hundred and fifty thousand dollars, which means it would cost me just over four hundered and fifty thousand to buy out the girls. Would you lend me that much, Mom?" She held her breath as Véronique thought about it and nodded.

"How will you pay for the repairs?"

"I can use the money Dad left me, and whatever I get for the sandwich shop if I sell it, after I pay you back what I owe you on that. It'll give me a start."

"I think I'll need to lend you some more for the repair work. We can add that to what you borrow to pay the girls. And you have to ask them how they feel about it, and if they're willing to accept what you offer them. But the price sounds fair." Véronique was businesslike as they made some notes together, and when Juliette went back to her room, she was floating on air. She was going to have a hotel!

They had dinner that night in a little Italian restaurant in Old Antibes. Véronique had walked past it several times with Aidan, it looked casual and friendly, and they wandered around for a while after dinner, and then went back to the Eden Roc.

Juliette could hardly wait for her meeting with the architect the next morning. She lay in bed that night for hours, unable to sleep. All she could think of was what she wanted to do with it. She already had most of it mapped out in her head. She could visualize the Château de Brize on the list of Relais and Châteaux. She was guessing it would take a year to do the repairs. And she fell asleep calculating how much the work might cost. She was nervous about what the architect would say. And that night, she dreamed about the château. There were horses in the stables, flowers in the gardens. They would grow their own vegetables, and she knew exactly how she wanted the kitchen. She would make all their baked goods and do the cooking. She woke up several times, afraid to miss the meeting. And finally, she fell into a heavy sleep, imagining that she was in her own room at the château.

Chapter 14

Jean-Pierre Flarion was waiting for her when she got to the château ten minutes late the next morning. She had overslept after tossing and turning for most of the night, worried she'd be late, and she had raced to get ready.

He was a tall, pleasant-looking man in his mid-thirties, and he had brought everything he needed with him, notepads, measuring tape, camera, computer. Juliette apologized profusely for being late when she got there, with her hair in a wild haze of blond curls, which she hadn't had time to brush properly. She'd worn blue jeans and running shoes, so she could explore everywhere with him, and didn't care if she got dirty. He had worn a blazer and jeans, and he looked startled when he saw her.

"I imagined someone much older," he said as they walked into the château. He seemed more interested in Juliette than in the building or the repairs. He spoke perfect English, which made it easy for her.

"I just inherited it from my father," she explained. "I own it with my sisters. I'm going to buy them out, and turn it into a hotel."

"That's an interesting idea," he said with a look of approval, as he took out an iPad and started making entries. "You'll have to hire someone to run it," he said practically.

"I can run it myself, and do the cooking," she said, and he nodded, impressed by her enthusiasm, which seemed boundless.

They went through each room methodically, while he measured and made notes. They discussed the leaks with the caretaker, and the condition of the roof.

"I don't know if I need an architect or a contractor," she said seriously.

"I do both. And you're right. You shouldn't change anything in the structure. You should keep it in its natural original state, but you have a lot of restoration work to do."

"I know," she said bravely, wondering if he'd be expensive. But at least he was local. She didn't want to bring down a fancy architect from Paris. Or even Nice. He was right there.

They examined every structure until lunchtime, and she was filthy by then, from the dust and dirt of many years. And they agreed that they had to do major work in the kitchen. But the furniture looked good to her. She'd have to have it all reupholstered and have new curtains made. But the rugs her mother had bought were still beautiful and of the period.

"You can get some wonderful things at local auctions," he told her.

And finally they had done as much as they could, and he said he needed to go back to his office to do some calculations to give her a rough estimate.

"I can have it for you by late afternoon."

"That's fine." She hated to tell him she was at the Eden Roc, so she gave him her cell number, and he said he'd call her on that. And then he startled her and asked her if she'd like to have lunch. She hesitated for a moment and then accepted. They had lunch at the restaurant in the square of St. Paul de Vence, and he had her try something called **socca,** which was local, very much like pizza, but made with chickpeas instead of tomato, cheese, and dough, and it smelled delicious as they took it out of a hot oven.

"Why would you want to burden yourself with a crumbling old château?" he asked her as they shared the **socca.** "Why not just sell it?"

"I fell in love with it when I saw it again two days ago. I feel like it's my destiny to have it. The minute I saw it, I knew I wanted to turn it into a hotel." She told him about her sandwich shop then, and how she had given up a career in art history to go to the Cordon Bleu, and how much she loved baking.

He told her that his family were all attorneys, and his father had wanted him to go to work for the family law firm in Draguignan, and he had refused, gone to school and become an architect, and moved to St. Paul de Vence, which he had always loved, and now he had his own firm. He seemed very proud of what he'd accomplished, and they spent two hours talking nonstop over lunch. He promised to call her later that afternoon, with his estimate, and she thanked him for lunch and left.

He was smiling when he went back to his office. He had never met anyone like her. She was full of energy and good ideas, and excitement about what she was doing. She seemed like the ultimate nurturer, and everything about her was womanly, from her face to her sensuous lips to her body. He had had to fight himself every moment to concentrate on what she was saying, he just wanted to look at her.

He felt like a schoolboy when he called her on her cell phone late that afternoon. She was sitting at the pool with her mother at the Eden Roc, talking about her meeting with him that morning. Juliette said that he seemed like he knew what he was doing.

The number he gave her as an estimate for the repair work sounded low to her.

"Are you sure?" She sounded suspicious. She didn't want him to draw her in and double it later.

"Is that too much?" He was worried.

"No, too low. I don't want bad surprises later."

"There's always a bit of flex once you start doing things. But I calculated it carefully, based on what we saw today. Would you feel better if I doubled it?" he asked, teasing her, and she laughed.

"No, I wouldn't. Okay, that sounds good to me."

"How soon do you want to start?" he asked her, and she thought about it.

"Yesterday. But it will probably take me a month or two to get squared away in New York. Or longer." She had to buy out her sisters, and sell her sandwich shop in Brooklyn, and she didn't know how long that would take. And it was mid-August now. "Let's say sometime in September, or the beginning of October. Will you have time for me then, or do you have a lot of other projects?"

"I'll have time for you," he said. "Just let me know when you're ready to start." Just as she had felt when she saw the château again, that it was her destiny, he felt the same way about her.

"Thank you," she said with a sigh of relief. She turned to her mother after she hung up. "I have an architect. I'm all set. Now all I have to do is buy out the girls, sell my shop, and I'll be on my way." Véronique smiled at the look in her daughter's eyes. She had never seen her this happy and alive. Juliette knew exactly what she wanted to do.

"When are you going back?" Véronique asked her.

Juliette thought about it for a minute before she answered. She had wanted to see Sophie again, but she didn't want to waste another day. "Tomorrow," she said firmly. "I'll ask the concierge to get me a flight out of Nice. What about you, Mom? Will you stay here for a while?" She knew her mother had nothing else to do and was in no hurry to go back to Paris or New York.

"No, I think I'll leave tomorrow, too," she said quietly. "It won't be fun here without you." She didn't tell her that she wasn't going to Paris but would go to Berlin instead. She was just as excited about seeing Aidan as Juliette was about the château, but she didn't say anything. She couldn't wait to see him and help him set up his show. She texted him as soon as Juliette dove into the pool. And he was thrilled to hear that she'd be in Berlin soon.

Chapter 15

Véronique flew straight to Berlin, without stopping in Paris, five hours after Juliette left. At the airport, Aidan was just outside security, waiting for her, with a big grin on his face. They had been apart for only a few days, but it felt like an eternity to both of them. They held hands leaving the airport, and walked to the Austin-Healey in the garage. Just seeing it felt like coming home to her. And Aidan looked as if he'd been working hard. He was wearing a faded T-shirt and torn jeans. He'd been framing photographs himself and hanging the show.

She brought him up to date on everything as they drove toward Berlin on the new motorway that had been built for the airport. She told him that Juliette had met with an architect the day before, and was going home to sell her shop in Brooklyn.

"And you're helping her?" he confirmed. Véronique nodded with a smile. It was sweet of him to defend her daughter's interests, without even knowing her.

"I'm sure her sisters won't mind, and they'll be happy to get the money out of it quickly, especially Joy and Sophie." She knew they could all use the money for their projects, Timmie for her shelter, Joy for her life and career in L.A., and Sophie for her studies and to help with her support. From what she could see, encouraging her daughters to make it on their own had worked, and she was proud of them.

They left the motorway as they reached the city, and Aidan drove into the Mitte district. He pointed out landmarks to her, and showed her where the Berlin Wall and Checkpoint Charlie had been. She'd never been to Berlin, and was looking forward to discovering it with him. They were staying at a small bed and breakfast near Brunnenstrasse, where his gallery was and other avant garde locations, like Curators Without Borders, started by Sarah Belden, an art dealer from New York. There was graffiti everywhere, and the buildings were gray and spare. Aidan had already warned her that their hotel was barely more than a hole in the wall, but it was close to the gallery and easy for him. A glimpse of the Cipriani and Hôtel du Cap had given him a strong indication that her lifestyle was far grander than his, but he had guessed that anyway, from her manners, her demeanor, and the way she dressed. Even when she wore simple clothes, he could see that they were expensive, and she always looked chic. He was sure that she lived well in Paris and New York, he just didn't know to what degree. But he wasn't going to show off for her. He wanted to share his real life with Véronique, and this was it.

They stopped at the small hotel to drop off her things, and she laughed when she saw that it was even worse than he had said. There was a student with pierces and tattoos and a shaved head behind the desk—he had to search for Aidan's key, and finally found it in a drawer. The place looked disheveled, as did the guests, but when they got to the simple room, it was clean. There were only the bare basics, and a tiny bathroom, and she said she didn't care. They left her bag and went out, and walked the short distance to the gallery arm in arm. There were shops, restaurants, and galleries all along the street, edgy-looking people, and a mixture of old and new.

"I'm so glad you came." Aidan beamed at her, proud to be with her. She was a beautiful woman, and all he could see was her. He had eyes for no one else. And when she saw the gallery, she was far more impressed than she'd been with the hotel. It was big, and spare, the floors were concrete, the ceilings were high with painted beams, and the walls were smooth and bare, with excellent lighting to show off the work. There was a girl at the desk, and three young people hanging photographs where he had told them to. Two walls were already covered with his impressive, troubling photographs. As he had said when he met her, he photographed the tragedies and ills of the world. His work was haunting and a sad view of life: A man who had been severely beaten. Prostitutes and drug addicts, derelicts and heartbreaking children. Troubled people who had the sorrows of the world in their eyes.

"We all turn away from scenes like that," he explained as she looked at the images. "I want people to see it. You can't run away from life because it's ugly or sad." It was a harsh view of the world, and was far more disturbing than the work of Diane Arbus or Nan Goldin, who had photographed freaks and drug addicts as well. Aidan's view of life was far more raw and even more upsetting. There was an aching beauty to it, as Véronique stood gazing at what was on the walls. She wondered how much of it would sell. It wasn't the kind of work she would have wanted to wake up to and see in the morning, and yet socially the statement had to be made, and he was brave about expressing it. He didn't shrink away from the ugliness of a gutter scene, or a ghetto, and his photograph of a crying child in India standing beside its dead mother brought tears to her eyes. It was powerful, and a reflection of who he was as a person. He was the champion of the poor and downtrodden, the voice of people who had none. It was easy to see, looking at his photographs, why he was so contemptuous of people with money or who had an easy life. Véronique felt there was room for both in the world. Aidan was more politically and socially extreme, which was loudly expressed in his work.

"They're beautiful," Véronique said with admiration, and he was thrilled.

"Sometimes I worry that they're a little too harsh. I don't want to scare people away, but most of the time that's how I feel."

He introduced her to Karl, the gallery owner, a young man in his early thirties, covered in tattoos with bolts in his ears. He shook her hand very politely, and she noticed that he had a "von" in his name, so he was an aristocrat, in a very modern world. From his appearance, no one would have guessed it. The people working in the gallery looked as extreme as she'd been told the Berlin art scene had become. It was far more intense and aggressive than the art world in Paris, which had remained more bohemian in a familiar way, and less avant-garde. But this was exciting and felt different and new to her. It was also energizing being there with him, and a whole new universe for Véronique, who had a passion for art, but of a different kind. But Aidan liked other forms of art, too, and had been as thrilled to be at the Uffizi in Florence as she was. And at the time, historically, he had pointed out to her what they were doing during the Renaissance was considered "avant-garde," too. It was an interesting way to think about it, and had amused her when he said it, but there was truth to it.

Anyone who created was ahead of their time, whenever it was, and often shocking in the moment, whether it was the first nudes, the concept that the earth was round, or what Aidan was doing today. She loved how open his mind was artistically, and how innovative and daring he was. Looking at his work inspired her, to get back to work again herself, with her painting. It made her think of Nikolai, and the portrait he wanted to commission. She wondered if he'd actually call her. She thought he would be fun to paint. He had such a strong personality reflected in his looks and expressions.

Aidan took her to lunch at a beer garden, where they ate sausages and drank tall glasses of dark beer. And after lunch, they visited several other galleries, to give her an idea of what was happening in the local art scene. It was all very avant-garde, and although it wasn't her usual sphere of interest, she liked seeing it and what other artists were doing. It gave them much to talk about, the direction of art today, the motivations of the artists, their vision as compared to hers, how one generation of artists led to another, with sometimes shocking differences. It was exciting for him to be with someone as passionate about art as she was, in whatever form. And she was very open to new ideas, which Aidan liked, although her own painting style was far more traditional and took no risks. His was all about sticking his neck out and daring to be real, as he perceived it.

Finally, they went back to his gallery. Johnny Gardner, his rep, was there. He was younger than Aidan with spiked black hair and talked about Aidan's work to Véronique with great seriousness. She liked meeting him, and he left a few minutes later to meet an artist who had a studio up the street. And then Aidan got to work framing, and she helped him in minor ways, and they watched the preparators hang his show. Aidan stopped them every five minutes to change something, switch two pieces, or move one by a few inches. He was a perfectionist about his work and how it was shown. And Véronique loved being part of it. The excitement about the show was tangible in the gallery.

They stayed until eleven o'clock that night, then sent out for dinner, Cajun food from Zagreus Projekt, and the food was very good, as they hung two more walls while they ate. And then they went back to his hotel and fell into bed, exhausted. Even if he was intense about his work and the show, he loved having Véronique there.

When she woke up the next morning, he began caressing her. They were lying in bed naked, and she was still half asleep as they started to make love.

"What a nice way to wake up," she said sleepily afterward, rolling over to look at him, and he kissed her.

"Thank you for helping me last night. You have a good eye," he complimented her.

"So do you, and you do great work."

They showered together and went back to the gallery a little while later. It took them two more days to hang the show. There were several nooks and clever spaces that gave them additional walls and expanded the show. And then he was ready, as ready as he would ever be. He changed three pieces before leaving to go to the hotel to dress for the opening. There was a huge amount of his work in the show, and he was hoping for great reviews.

Aidan wore a black shirt and black jeans for the opening, and Véronique was wearing black leather pants and a black sweater she had bought when she took a few hours to go shopping on Oranienburger Strasse.

"You are gorgeous," he said admiringly, and kissed her as they left the hotel, and walked back to the gallery. He was excited about the show, and so was she, for him. The most important art critic in Berlin had promised to be there, and as soon as they walked in, Karl, the gallery owner, told him he'd had a call from a museum in Spain that wanted to acquire some of his work, and there was another one in Hamburg that was inquiring, too. It was an important show for him, and he was happy to share it with her.

People began arriving very quickly, there were hors d'oeuvres and music, and an interesting crowd, many art lovers. Other artists and collectors had come from Italy, Spain, and England, and the critic Aidan hoped would come did, and loved the show.

Aidan was the star of the evening, and his work was much discussed and praised. And at one point, as Véronique looked around, she realized that most of the people in the room were in their twenties and thirties, nowhere close to her age. It suddenly made her feel very old, and she wondered if she looked ridiculous in her black leather jeans. She had worn her hair down at Aidan's request. It reminded her of the British expression "mutton dressed as lamb," referring to old people trying to appear too young, and she hoped she wasn't.

She was very different from the people surrounding Aidan. She wasn't edgy, she just loved him and was excited to be there, but the evening was a sharp reminder that their two worlds were extremely different. She was having a good time, but this wasn't her scene, and she wondered how he would fare in hers. He could fit in if he wanted to, but he had lots of sharp edges and strong opinions and wasn't likely to change any of that for someone else. And she respected that about him. She wondered if he could even be happy in her world, with his distrust of people with money, and contempt for traditions that made no sense to him. Everything had to be honest and stark and seem real to him, or he wouldn't tolerate it. As he said, he was hated bullshit and couldn't stand it.

And no question, there were times when her world was less than honest, and pretense and artifice ruled the day. Few people could afford to be as direct as he was. He had nothing to lose and no one to please except himself. Véronique had been adapting to other people and situations all her life, often at her own expense, which Aidan didn't like. He thought she should be harsher with people, and more blunt, which she insisted to him wasn't her style. In his opinion, the right message for people who offended you in some way, or were rude, dishonest, or inconsiderate, or used you, was "Sod off." He had already suggested more than once that she say that to one of her daughters, when appropriate. The idea had made her laugh. They would have keeled over in a dead faint if she did.

Véronique was always unfailingly polite, and her good manners and breeding showed in everything she did, which Aidan accused of being a lie, and he hated liars. To Aidan, if someone did you wrong, you kicked their ass and stomped off. Even his work had that feeling to it. It got right in your face and grabbed you by the throat. He had a gentle heart, but there was an element of porcupine to him, too. He bristled whenever he was upset. Véronique was softer and smoother, and together, in an odd way, they complemented each other. She softened him, and he gave her courage to be stronger, something she had wanted to do for a long time, but in a nice way, and more gently than Aidan suggested. "You can't be gentle with assholes," he had told her in one of their late-night discussions. "They don't get it. You have to be as tough as they are, or they'll walk all over you forever." In some ways, Paul had. And even her children did at times. They took her for granted, and it bothered Aidan sometimes when he listened to her on the phone with them; and he would scold her for being too meek with them when she got off.

Juliette called her while they were at the gallery that night to tell her that she had put the sandwich shop on the market. She had discussed it with Arnold, and come up with what seemed like a fair price for her business, and she wanted to tell her mother about it, and was surprised by all the noise in the background. It made it hard to talk to her mother, and she sounded busy.

"Where are you?" Juliette was annoyed. The girls expected her to be available when they wanted her, but not to bother them when they were otherwise occupied. She was supposed to be a mother on call, with no plans or needs of her own, and they were always surprised when she had other things to do, as though she lived in a locked room until they called, when she was expected to spring to attention.

"I'm at a gallery opening," Véronique said, straining to hear. She was standing too close to the music, but didn't want to go outside. She could tell that Aidan wanted her with him, and this was his big night. She didn't tell Juliette that she was in Berlin, not in Paris. She didn't need to know. It would have led to other questions she didn't want to answer, like "with whom?" and "why?"

Juliette repeated what she had just said so her mother could hear her better, and went on as though Véronique had nothing else to do. It was often the style of their exchanges. "I'm busy, Mom," ended a conversation immediately, Véronique being busy meant nothing.

"I talked to Timmie," Juliette continued. "She's willing to sell to me at the price you and I talked about. She wants the money to add to what Dad gave her for the shelter, and she's starting to look at houses on the West Side, but it could take her a while to find one. I called Joy, but we keep playing phone tag. She got the job on that soap, and she's working every day for the next few weeks. I think she's sleeping with her new manager," Juliette said as an aside, continuing the conversation they had about him in the South of France. "She sent me a text the other night that she was having dinner with him about the cosmetics campaign he's having her audition for. She said she'd call me when she got home, and she never did. Maybe she thought it was too late to call in New York, but I get a funny feeling about him, like she's hiding something." The three sisters knew each other well, and so did Véronique. She had had the same feeling, too, that Joy had something up her sleeve with her new manager.

"I hope he's for real, and not taking advantage of her," Véronique said, sounding worried.

"He's very well known, and he represents some big people," Juliette reassured her. "I googled him when she told me about him. And she's right. He's **very** good looking. So what do you think?" Juliette asked her, as the music in the gallery got louder. They were playing jazz, and it reverberated off the concrete floors and walls.

"About what?" Véronique shouted in the noise of the crowd. "Joy's manager?" She didn't know what to think. It was too soon, and she had no information about him.

"No. About the price I'm asking for the shop. Is it enough?" Juliette was focused on the château project again, and what she had to do to make it happen.

"I don't know. What did Arnold say?" Véronique said, feeling pulled in different directions and sounding distracted.

"He said it sounded right to him, for the equipment, and my clientele."

"Then I'm sure it's fine. I'll call you tomorrow," Véronique said. It was impossible to pursue the conversation here and now, and she didn't want to.

"I'm busy tomorrow. I need to go to my storage space in Yonkers and inventory some spare equipment I have. I want to sell that, too."

"Fine," Véronique said, as Aidan waved her toward him, and she nodded. "I love you. Talk to you soon." She ended the call then and went to find Aidan. He wanted to introduce her to an important German publisher, who was interested in doing a book of his work. He was a very interesting man, and he and Véronique had a serious conversation that lasted for quite a while. They were mutually very impressed. And it was nearly midnight when the crowd began to thin out. Aidan was thrilled with the turnout and the evening, and everyone he had hoped for had been there. The gallery owner had done a good job luring them in, and the work had been very well received. Johnny Gardner, his rep, was ecstatic about the show, too.

The reviews were great the next day, which wasn't always the case with work like his, which shocked and offended as much as it pleased. But the critics had "gotten" it, and seven of the works had sold at high prices. Aidan was delighted. He was being hailed as one of the most important young photographers on the art scene. And what he wanted now was to be in more museums.

They talked about it at lunch at the Paris Bar the next day, and Véronique gave him good advice. He had already come to respect her wisdom and good head for business. When he complimented her about it, she laughed and said it was in her genes, because of her grandfather's art business years before. Listening to her made him feel more every day that it had been destiny taking a hand in it from the moment he first saw her at the Fontana di Trevi, and again in Venice. And he said it to her several times. He was convinced they had been fated to meet, as part of their karma.

"You didn't mind being with the oldest woman in

the room?" she asked him with a cautious look. It had occurred to her several times. Some of the girls at the opening were younger than her daughters, and he could have been with any of them. It was a very youthful scene, and Véronique looked different from everyone there, whereas Aidan fit right in, even with the salt-and-pepper hair. It was definitely his milieu, not hers, and although she had enjoyed herself, she had felt it.

"Don't be stupid," he scolded her, sounding very British. "You were the most beautiful woman there, by a long shot. Who cares how old you are? I don't, why should you? And I saw all the men watching you, half of the room wanted to meet you. And my German publisher wanted your phone number. I wouldn't give it to him. I saw you first." He smiled at her.

"Thank you for that." She had liked talking to the publisher, but had no interest in pursuing it further. She was totally happy with Aidan, and it amused her again to realize that he was jealous and somewhat possessive. It was flattering and told her that he cared. "That whole scene is a lot edgier than I am." Even if she had been wearing black leather jeans, her shoes were Chanel. Almost everyone else there was wearing flip-flops or sneakers. Most of them looked as though they had dressed out of secondhand shops. She didn't have the knack to pull that off, and didn't want to. Aidan had worn black cowboy boots that he had found at a vintage shop in London, and that had been well battered by whoever wore them before him. It was a look that she just didn't have. She was chic and well put together whatever she wore, and sophisticated in a way they weren't.

"I was proud to be with you," Aidan said quietly. "That's all that matters, and if I wanted to be with a girl with a vulture tattooed on her chest, a snake around her neck, and pierces all over her face, wearing a torn T-shirt, I would be. There are lots of girls like that. There's only one you." He smiled at her, and she could see that he meant it, and she was relieved. She had admitted to him that she had felt out of place for the first part of the evening, and then relaxed and forgot about it, as she talked to more people and had interesting conversations with them all. It was a very international crowd and everyone spoke English.

For the next two days, they explored Berlin. They went to the Museum of Photography, one of the Berlin State museums, and the Museum for Contemporary Art at the Hamburger Bahnhof, a former train station. They drove around the city, went to the Botanical Garden, and window-shopped on the Kurfürstendamm. And Véronique insisted that she wanted to go to the Jewish Museum, which had a Holocaust Tower, and honored the Jews who had died in the Holocaust. It was an overwhelming experience, as she looked at photographs and exhibits, and they listened to the tour. They were both deeply moved. They were silent when they walked back out into the sunshine. The experience had been haunting, and Véronique couldn't shake off the mood. They talked about it for the next two hours as they walked around, and then went back to the hotel, and lay down for a while to rest before going out to dinner. It had been a very full few days since she'd arrived. And she had loved every minute of it. Suddenly her life was more interesting than it had been in years.

She thought about it, lying on the bed, as Aidan dozed off, and her cell phone rang. It was Timmie.

Véronique answered in a whisper, not wanting to wake Aidan. "Where are you?" Timmie asked her. "At the movies? Why are you whispering?"

"I'm just around other people," Véronique lied. She seemed to be doing that more and more often. But there was no way to explain Aidan, and certainly not that he was asleep next to her. Suddenly Véronique had a secret life. It was a first for her. That had never happened. "What's up?" Timmie had on her most serious voice and sounded as though someone had died. Véronique had instantly picked it up, she knew her children well.

"We all got a letter today, and you will, too. Bertie is suing us, and the estate. He wants a quarter of everything, including the château, and he wants to bar Sophie Marnier from getting anything, since Dad never acknowledged her in his lifetime."

"That doesn't matter," Véronique said calmly.

"You can make bequests to anyone you want. You can leave it all to your dog if you want, in the States. In France, you have to leave your children two-thirds of everything, but not in the United States. So he can't take anything away from Sophie." She wondered if Bertie had a chance of prevailing with the others, she wasn't sure, but Paul had made it perfectly clear why he had cut Bertie out, which seemed reasonable and fair, in view of everything Paul had given him before.

"I can't say I'm surprised," Véronique said with a sigh. "But I'm sad to hear it. It's a headache none of you need, nor I. What does Arnold say about it?"

"That he probably won't win, or even go to court. But he could cost us a lot in legal fees. He says Bertie doesn't want to go all the way on this, he just wants to bully us into giving him a settlement. And we're not going to. I talked to Joy and Juliette this morning, and they feel the same way I do—screw him. He's a shit and an asshole, and he always was. He's been trying to rip us off since we were kids and he stole our allowances. He can go to hell." Well, that was clear, as Véronique listened, and she didn't disagree, although she wouldn't have said it as harshly.

She still felt sorry for him, but she was appalled by his behavior. It seemed to get worse over the years, and there was a real tone of desperation to it now. She suspected that he must be deep in debt. His father occasionally had been, too, with bad investments he made, but had always gotten out of it honorably. Financially at least, Paul had been an honest man. Bertie wasn't.

"He wants to depose us. What a pain in the ass," Timmie added, sounding livid. "And Arnold says he can't handle it for us, since he's not a litigator. He'll oversee it, but he's hiring a litigator for the case, so the meter starts running now. Just what we didn't need. I'll e-mail you the letter. Ours came in the mail, so yours probably did, too. It probably went to New York." Véronique could easily imagine what it said and wasn't anxious to see it. "I have to meet the litigator tomorrow. Juliette has some kind of meeting she says she can't change with a restaurant broker, and Joy is on that soap every day and out at night. I can never reach her. She must be sleeping with her hot new manager," Timmie said in an irritated tone, and Véronique smiled. Joy had definitely sounded smitten with him.

"We seem to be unanimous on that. Let's hope he's a nice guy and a decent manager, and not just bilking her for money."

"Joy's too smart for that. She never loses money to guys." Unlike Juliette, they both knew, but didn't say. "So I have to go to the meeting alone. I swear, I hate Bertie's guts."

"He's certainly not a good guy," Véronique said sadly, "but he's still your half-brother. Hopefully he'll see the light one of these days." Véronique never gave up hope. Timmie had years before, and so had Paul. Véronique had continued to try to influence him positively, to no avail. And now he was suing them all. By now, Véronique was discouraged by it, too.

"He won't see the light in this lifetime, Mom. He's a crook and a petty thief." Véronique couldn't disagree, but still found it depressing. "One of these days he'll wind up in jail, where he belongs. Dad thought so, too."

"Thank God his father won't be here to see it if that happens. It would have broken his heart."

"He knew what Bertie is. That's why he left him out of the will. Anyway, I just wanted to let you know what's happening here. When are you coming home? We need you here, Mom." Timmie sounded young and vulnerable as she said it, which was unlike her. She was usually so tough and strong, and seemed so invincible. But their father's death had shaken them all. It was as though part of the foundation they relied on had crumbled, and now they all felt unstable and unsure of themselves. It reminded Véronique of how she had felt when her father died, which was why she had married Paul within the year. At any age, losing a parent puts one face to face with mortality, of those you love and yourself. Paul was an enormous loss, no matter how inadequate he was as a parent.

"I'll be home soon," Véronique said vaguely. She

had no plans, and she wanted to be with Aidan, but she sighed as she hung up. Aidan had woken up and heard the last of the conversation.

"Something wrong?" He was worried for her, when he saw the troubled look on her face.

"Yes. No. Predictable, but upsetting anyway. My stepson is suing all of us and the estate, because his father left him out of the will. I knew it would happen. He's not a good person, sad to say." Aidan smiled at her, and kissed her.

"You know my answer to guys like that—'Sod off.' " She laughed at what he said, but she knew he meant it.

"Easier said than done. I've spent twenty years trying to keep the family united, despite the divorce, and children of two marriages, but Paul's will ended that fantasy. He cut out his own son, and included a love child no one knew existed. So much for my fantasy. But even so, if he's suing us, we have to deal with it and go through all the motions, even go to court if he insists. I think it's just a ploy for blackmail, but the American legal system is set up for this, and even encourages people like him to sue. He'll have a field day before it's over."

"Can he win?" Aidan asked her.

"I doubt it. And the girls won't settle with him. Only the lawyers will win. It will cost a fortune to defend, and he's probably using a contingency lawyer, which will cost him nothing unless he wins."

"Sick system," Aidan said with a disgusted look.

She looked at him mournfully then. "The girls want me to come home. I hate to leave you again so soon."

"Then don't. They're adults. Let them work it out for themselves." He looked disappointed that she wanted to leave.

"I can't tell them to 'sod off,' Aidan," she said gently. "They're my kids. And he's suing me, too. I should probably go back to New York, meet with the lawyers, and see what's going on. They're hiring a litigator, and I should meet him. I can come back to Europe afterward." She didn't invite him to New York, as she preferred to be with him where her daughters wouldn't intrude on them, or discover him, yet. They could work that out later, but this wasn't the right time with everyone still upset over Paul, and now Bertie. And the idea of their mother having a man in her life would be shocking and new to them. She had no illusions about that. "Will you come to Paris when I get back?" They could have a wonderful time there. He nodded but looked like an abandoned child. It was a sweet side of him that she loved, where none of the porcupine quills he occasionally exhibited were in sight. And she sensed that he had abandonment issues because of his mother's death when he was so young, although he never mentioned it again after he first told her. It was a painful subject.

"What about going to London with me now?" he asked her with a pleading look. "You could leave from there." She thought about it for a minute and nodded, and he looked pleased. He wanted to show her his studio, his apartment, and his world there. Until now they had only traveled together, and he wanted to introduce her to his daily life. She would have liked to do the same, but didn't know how. Except in Paris, when she was alone. New York would be much harder, because of the girls. And she had more freedom in Paris to do whatever she wanted. Her maternal leash was shorter in New York, which he didn't understand, having no kids of his own. Aidan could do whatever he wanted. And he thought she was babying the girls by going back.

"They're grown women, let them work it out," he repeated as they packed. They had decided to skip dinner at the Borchardt, and drive back to London that night. He had finished in Berlin.

"That's my job, Aidan. You're a mother forever, even when they're grown up." His parents clearly hadn't felt that way. And the concept was foreign to him.

"They need to stand on their own." He was adamant about it in the school of "sod off," which had become a joke between them. But most of the time he meant it. It just wasn't Véronique's style.

Aidan called Karl, thanked him for the terrific show, and told him he was leaving, and Karl promised to be in touch over further sales, museum inquiries, or whatever came up. And his rep had gone back to New York the morning after the show. They drove nearly to Antwerp that night in the now-familiar Austin-Healey. They stayed at a small inn, and got up early the next morning to press on.

And on the drive to London the next day, Véronique took a turn at the wheel and loved it. They reached the English Channel near Calais at Coquelles and put the Austin on the train for the thirty-five-minute crossing, going through the "Chunnel." They had breakfast on the train and finished just as they reached Folkestone, and they went back to the car. It took them another two hours to reach London, and they went to Notting Hill. He lived in a loft there filled with camera equipment and treasures he had collected on his travels. As they walked in, Véronique saw that it looked decidedly like the home of a bachelor, with sweaters tossed on the couch, no food in the fridge, and the bed still unmade from when he had left. He said he had a cleaning woman who came from time to time, but he had forgotten to call her. But despite the disorder, it had a warm, cozy feeling, and a potbellied stove in one corner. He confessed that the place was freezing in winter, but he didn't mind. And she liked the neighborhood when they went out together to buy groceries. He was out of everything, including coffee, and they bought fish and chips, which they agreed were awful but which they both loved. They spread it out on newspaper to absorb the grease and dusted it with vinegar and salt.

"Mmmm . . . it's so good," Véronique said with a grimace, and he snapped a picture of her while he laughed. Being with her made every place he was better, and he told her in bed that night how much he would miss her. She had agreed to spend two days in London with him, and after that she thought she should leave. She had heard from Juliette and Joy by then, too, and they were as upset as Timmie about the lawsuit Bertie was threatening to bring against them. And she'd had a frantic call from Elisabeth Marnier, who was also panicked about it. Véronique reassured her that it would probably come to nothing, and that Sophie's position was secure, since her father had acknowledged her as his daughter in the will. It was just a vehicle Bertie was using to try and get money, and Véronique didn't think he'd be successful. She promised to keep Elisabeth informed from New York, and told her not to worry. Elisabeth felt better after talking to Véronique, which seemed ironic to both of them. In the end, Paul had left them to take care of each other and his children, and he had skipped out. It was so like him.

Véronique spent the next two days totally focused on being with Aidan. They went to the Tate Modern, and the Victoria and Albert Museum, and all his favorite galleries. They lay in his bed, after

Véronique helped him clean the apartment and change the sheets. They cooked dinner together one night, and on the last night he took her out. She wanted to take him to Harry's Bar, where she was still a member, to compare it to the one in Venice, but it was much more formal in London, and a club, and neither of them wanted to get dressed up. They just wanted to relax with each other, do fun things, and make love. She felt as though they were storing up their time together for the lonely days ahead. She knew she would miss him a lot, and he said the same. Neither of them could imagine a time now when the other hadn't been in their life. This seemed so normal and natural that her own home and her daughters seemed like strangers to her. Wherever Aidan was felt like home to her now.

The morning she left, she stuck a Post-it on his bathroom mirror, reminding him that she loved him, for him to find later. And they could hardly tear themselves away from each other at the airport.

"I'll be back soon. I promise," she said as they kissed. He already looked bereft. "I'll meet you in Paris as soon as I can." It was the next stop in their discovery of each other's worlds. And like Venice, Florence, and Berlin, London had been a success. She felt totally at ease with him, and enjoyed his apartment. She hoped he would like her place on the Île St. Louis as much. But he had already said he loved Paris, so she wasn't worried.

He made her promise to call as soon as she

landed, and they kissed one last time as people walked around them, and then she finally went through security and waved until they couldn't see each other any longer. And with a heavy heart at the thought of leaving him, Véronique boarded the plane to New York.

Chapter 16

When Timmie walked into Arnold Sands's office to meet the litigator he had hired for them, she didn't know what to expect. She knew his name was Brian McCarthy, he'd gone to Harvard, and he had an incredible reputation for winning almost every case. Arnold didn't think Bertie's case would be a hard one to beat. He admitted that hiring Brian McCarthy to do the job might be overkill, but he said that Brian representing them would terrify Bertie's lawyer, and might even get him to drop the suit. He had Brian as a bulldog, and Timmie liked the idea of him terrorizing Bertie and his contingency lawyer. In her opinion, they deserved it, and she wanted to unleash the wrath of the gods on them, and the vengeance of all four sisters. From everything Arnold said, it sounded like Brian McCarthy was the man to do the job.

He was already waiting in Arnold's office when Timmie arrived. Arnold gave her a warm hug and introduced Brian, who looked nothing like Timmie had expected. She had expected him to look somewhat like Arnold. Instead he looked like a quarterback for the Green Bay Packers, or an offensive tackle, or a tree. He stood six feet six, with shoulders that could have filled the doorway. He had a handsome face, but a fiery look in his eyes, as though bar fights weren't unfamiliar to him, and he had green eyes like hers, and bright red hair. He looked Irish to the core. Arnold had neglected to tell her that he'd been captain of the football team at Harvard, and had turned down a career in the NFL to practice law. He had a warm smile, but he looked tough as nails, and she was a little taken aback, if nothing else because of his size. He was huge. Timmie was a tall girl at six feet, but she felt like a midget next to him. And he weighed easily 250 pounds. He wasn't fat, he was solid. And he began speaking right away, about what he thought of her brother's lawsuit, and how he had behaved. Timmie just sat there and smiled, amused.

"Something funny?" he asked her, seeming puzzled. He was quick, tough, direct, and pulled no punches.

"Sorry, I was just thinking that my brother is going to faint when he sees you, and squeal like a little pig." She loved the idea, and Brian grinned. Although Arnold had warned him that Timmie could be difficult, he saw no sign of it so far. She was supposedly a strong-headed woman, but Brian could handle that. She didn't scare him.

"My little brother is taller than I am, and plays for the Lakers, if you want me to bring him, too," Brian quipped, and they all laughed. "I'm sorry, I just have no respect for guys like your half-brother, who screw up, and then try to extort money out of everyone else. From everything Arnold tells me, your father was right to leave him out of the will. He's had plenty of chances till now. He doesn't need to try and blackmail it out of his sisters." Brian was aware, too, that an illegitimate child of their father's had surfaced in the will, and Arnold had told him it was an enormous shock, but seemed to be resolving peacefully. Véronique had called him from Cap d'Antibes, and said the meeting with the Marniers had gone well, and they were as nice as the detective had said. They wanted no trouble and were grateful for anything they'd get. The Parker women had been fortunate with that. It was Bertie who was the thorn in their side now.

"How do we get him to give up and get lost?" Timmie asked, wishing Bertie would just disappear into the mists. Brian didn't think he would. This was a crapshoot for him, and worth it, if they caved and paid him off, which he said immediately he hoped they wouldn't do.

"Don't worry, there isn't a chance in hell of that," Timmie reassured him with a stubborn look.

"Good, then we'll tell him that, convince him that you mean it, and remind his lawyer that he doesn't have a leg to stand on. And beat the shit out of him in court if he doesn't give up. And I don't think he will. It's not in the nature of a guy like that, he has nothing to lose and everything to gain. I don't think he'll want to take this all the way to trial, but he'll want to give all of you a big headache in the meantime—depositions, discovery, forensic accounting of the estate, whatever they can pull—which will cost you money, and annoy the hell out of you, and is designed to make you cough up money to get rid of him."

"We won't," Timmie said, and looked as though she meant it. He believed her.

"What about your sisters? Will they want to settle?" Brian wanted to know more. And she was a good place to start. He could already see that Timmie meant business, and was smart. She was beautiful, too, but that was beside the point. This was business.

"My sister Joy won't. She agrees with me, and she hates Bertie, too. Maybe not as much as I do, but she's on the same page. So is Juliette, but she's the family softie and bleeding heart."

"I thought you were the social worker," he said with a wry smile.

"Yeah, and the meanest kid on the block," she said proudly. "I'd beat the shit out of him myself if I could." Since he had been blunt with her, she didn't hesitate to do the same with him. He was a whole other breed from Arnold, who was genteel, polite, and a gentleman to the core. Brian McCarthy was a street fighter, and it showed.

"Well, allow me to beat the shit out of him for you," Brian said, pretending to be gallant, when in fact he was just tough.

"Where do we start?" Timmie said, looking Brian in the eye.

"We respond to the suit for each of you. What about your mother? How does she feel about this?"

"She's disappointed in him. She raised Bertie since he was eight. She was the last one to give up her illusions about him, even after our father. She won't give him anything now. She knows he's a crook, although she hates to admit it." Brian nodded.

"They've asked for discovery, so we give them what they want. All your father's papers, financial statements, everything that involves accounting, and the same for all of you, and your mother. He's just doing it to annoy us, but we have to comply."

"Are you serious? Why can't we just ignore him, if this will never go to court?"

"Because we have a legal obligation to give them what they ask for. They have a right to discovery, to see what they can find in your financial records," the litigator explained.

"Well, I'm not doing it," she said stubbornly. He watched her eyes intently. She was as tough as Arnold had warned him.

"You have to, Miss Parker. Do you have something to hide?" he asked her bluntly, and she looked incensed.

"No. I don't have time. I take care of people who are dying on the streets and need a place to sleep. I can't waste my time for some asshole who wants to rip me off."

"He may want to rip you off, but right now the law is on his side, and he has a right to ask us to produce all financial records for all six of you, including your father's estate."

"Let the others do it. I can't," she said, blowing him off, and he looked stunned.

"I don't think you understand. This isn't a lottery. You **all** have to produce your financial records."

"I get that. I won't." She held her ground. Brian looked at Arnold in dismay, who looked embarrassed and tried to explain it to Timmie again, in gentler terms.

"I'm not stupid. I understand. I told you. I **don't** have the time. I'm not shortchanging my clients to spend weeks digging through financial records I may not even have anymore and don't know where they are."

"Well, look for them," Brian said in a stern voice, and she shook her head. "Then I can't represent you," he said simply, and stood up. "You have a good case, but I'm not going to waste my time dealing with clients who won't cooperate with the most basic principles of a lawsuit." He turned to Arnold with fire in his eyes. "Count me out. I'm not your man."

"You're just making a point of this because you're a man," Timmie said in a querulous tone, and Brian looked at her in a rage.

"You're kidding, right? You're accusing me of being sexist, because I expect you to help me comply with discovery. What are you? Some kind of militant feminist? Hire a woman then, but she's still going to expect the same things I am. This is the law, not a war between the sexes."

Timmie's issues about men had come out in spades, and she wouldn't back down. "Men always have to prove the point that they make the rules and can tell you what to do. Or they bullshit you into it." Like her father, but she didn't say it. "Or they lie to you, or sleep with your best friend." Brian felt sorry for her as he listened—clearly she had other issues than her half-brother's lawsuit, and he suddenly saw that her blazing green eyes were not just angry, they were hurt. He lowered his voice when he addressed her again.

"I'll tell you what. I won't sleep with your best friend. I will never lie to you, because I never lie no matter how much you might hate what I say. And when it's a point of law, you'll do what you have to, or a minimum at least so you don't make me look bad or get me disbarred. When something is my opinion or advice, you can argue with me and do what you want. When it's a point of law, we play by the rules. How does that sound to you?" Her eyes met his fearlessly for a long moment, and then she nodded.

"Okay. I can live with it." He wasn't sure he could, but he had agreed. And he owed Arnold a favor, so he was trying to hang in, for his sake. "Are we done?" she said, standing up. "I have to get to work. I can't waste my time on this bullshit of my brother's all day." Brian wanted to say he couldn't either, but he didn't say a word as they shook hands and she left the room. Brian turned to Arnold when she did.

"Holy God. How did you get me into this? I should be charging you double for this case," he said, and Arnold smiled. "I damn near strangled her. I hope her sisters aren't as bad as this."

"Timmie's not 'bad,'" Arnold said compassionately, although he hadn't been happy with the meeting either, and how she had behaved. "She has issues with her father. He was never there for any of them. He was a very selfish man, and she's still angry about it. I think she's had some difficult relationships, the usual romantic disappointments."

"No wonder. What does she do, bite them in the neck, or just rip their heads off? That is one hell of an angry woman."

"Her sisters are very sweet, the two I know. I've watched them all grow up. And their mother is an angel. You won't have any trouble with her. I don't know about the girl in France, but they met her last week, and I hear it went very well. She's supposed to be a nice girl. Timmie is the only challenge you'll have."

"When I was a baby public defender, I had a guy who killed thirty-one people in a drive-by shooting. He was a hell of a lot nicer than she is. That woman needs a muzzle and a leash."

"She'll calm down," Arnold tried to reassure him, but he wasn't sure she would. Brian left his office then and made an appointment with Juliette for the following week. He wanted to meet them all, so he knew who he was dealing with. Timmie had been a hard place to start, but he wasn't planning to take any guff from her or let her run the show. That wasn't his style, and he could hold his own with tougher clients than her.

Timmie had been equally unnerved by the meeting on her way to work that day. She wasn't used to lawyers threatening her or ordering her around. Brian McCarthy seemed like a chauvinist to her, and he had the misfortune of being a much larger version of her ex-fiancé, who had cheated on her. She had seen the resemblance immediately, except for the red hair. And he had played football at Harvard, too, though he wasn't the captain of the team, and he was younger. He had been her age. Timmie had read on the Internet that Brian was thirty-nine and a full partner of his firm. His credentials were excellent, but she was determined not to take any shit from him or anyone else.

She said as much to her mother when she called her about the meeting the night Véronique came home. It was midnight, she was unpacking, and thinking about Aidan. She missed him terribly. She had called him when she landed, as promised, which only made her miss him more.

Timmie didn't ask her how the flight was or welcome her home. She went straight into a diatribe about the meeting with Brian McCarthy.

"I don't like him," she said, furious again.

"Why not?" Véronique asked, trying to focus on it, not on Aidan, which was all she had on her mind, and she was tired from the flight back to New York. Timmie hadn't thought of that.

"He's a bulldog and a sexist, and I'm not going to let him push me around."

"Did he try?" Véronique was surprised. He didn't sound like the kind of man Arnold would hire, but she could hear how upset Timmie was. Just talking about him made her livid.

"We have to produce all our financial records for 'discovery.' I don't have time for that, in Bertie's bullshit case to rip us off."

"I expected that," Véronique said calmly. "We all have to do it."

"You don't work, Mom. I do," she said with a sharp edge to her voice that her mother didn't like.

"You still have to comply, Timmie," Véronique said firmly. "Was that your battle with the litigator?"

"I didn't like his tone or his style. He looks like a frat boy in a suit." And so had her ex-fiancé.

"Arnold says he's an excellent litigator," Véronique said, sounding tired. She really didn't want to get into Timmie's battles with the lawyer because she thought he was a sexist and looked like a frat boy. They needed a litigator for the case, and Arnold said he was the best person for the job.

"Just stay away from him and do what you have to," Véronique advised her, and after a few more minutes of grousing, Timmie hung up, clearly in a bad mood. To her mother, it sounded like she was overreacting, and it did when Timmie complained to Juliette, too.

It depressed Véronique to be home. And it was five in the morning in London, so she couldn't call Aidan again. Back in her New York apartment, she suddenly felt as though the time she had spent with him was unreal. Maybe it was only a crazy summer romance and nothing more. Rome, Venice, Siena, Florence, Antibes, Berlin, London. They had covered the map of Europe, but where would they go from here? He was going to visit her in Paris, and she had promised to go back to London. But then what? Maybe he had been right in the beginning, that lives like theirs couldn't mix. They had many things in common, except their backgrounds and their age. How much did it matter? She no longer knew.

She went to sleep feeling tired and discouraged, and lonelier than she'd felt in a month. It was as though none of it had ever happened and he was just a dream. And Timmie's angry call about the litigator was hardly a warm welcome home. As usual, Timmie had forgotten to ask her mother how she was or what she'd been doing. It was no wonder she told them nothing about her life, Véronique thought as she drifted off to sleep. More often than not, her relationship with her children was a one-way street, with all the love and effort flowing from her to them.

Chapter 17

Véronique had Arnold draw up the papers for the money she was advancing Juliette from her own estate, against her share. He had the other girls sign off on it, so they couldn't claim later that they were opposed to it, or didn't know. And as soon as she received the funds from her mother, Juliette paid both her sisters the agreed-upon amount. And the same amount was wired to an account set up for Sophie Marnier in Nice, and she was thrilled. The other two girls were equally pleased. And Sophie was now off the hook for the château, and delighted to be.

Juliette had received some additional money from her mother that she needed for repairs, and was waiting for the sale of her sandwich shop to complete the rest. Timmie had added her money to what she planned to spend on a house to start her shelter, and she was still looking for the right one. And Joy put it with the money from her father to further her acting career, and support herself between jobs.

Joy had admitted that she was dating Ron, her new manager, and was crazy about him. He was helping her with her career, but beyond that she said he was incredibly nice to her, and they were seeing each other almost every night. And for once, she and the man in her life were in the same city, and not on separate continents on tour, which Véronique thought was a hopeful sign. At twenty-six, she was having her first serious relationship that seemed to work, although it was still very new. Véronique was hoping to meet him, but Joy said they had no plans to come to New York. Some things hadn't changed. Joy still kept her distance and was more independent than both her sisters. And her whole life was in L.A., not New York. But she sounded warmer than usual, happier, and more relaxed.

And Juliette was meeting with restaurant brokers to try and settle the sandwich shop. She'd had a couple of nibbles and no bites yet. She had called Jean-Pierre Flarion several times on Skype to keep him interested in the project, and he told her not to worry. He would be available when she was ready to move ahead. He was formal and polite with her, and very professional. She could hardly wait to start work on the château. All she had to do now was sell her business.

Véronique organized a meeting with Brian McCarthy and Timmie and Juliette to discuss the lawsuit, and Timmie got in a fight with him again. Bertie had asked for depositions, and his lawyer had made a formal request, still to annoy them, and Timmie again said she had no time. And she was looking for a building for her shelter. Véronique couldn't believe how rude she was to him and how stubborn. Brian got red in the face, and remained calm, but Véronique apologized to him after Timmie left. And by then, Véronique had guessed what the problem was. He was the image of Timmie's ex-fiancé, who had cheated on her, only bigger, and Timmie couldn't separate the two in her head. And she was hostile and distrustful of men anyway.

Véronique mentioned the similarity between the two men, when she spoke to Timmie on the phone that night, after pointing out how rude she'd been, and Timmie got angry at her, too.

"Don't be ridiculous." She denied it too heatedly to be honest. "They don't look anything alike. That's psychotic."

"Yes, they do," Véronique said firmly. "There's no point making this more difficult for all of us. We hired the man to handle the suit for us. Let him. You don't have to like him, just let him do his job." Timmie had sounded like a shrew at the meeting, and Juliette had rolled her eyes at their mother. When Timmie got a bee in her bonnet, or disliked someone, she was a witch. But so far Brian hadn't quit, which Véronique thought was a miracle, after what she'd seen that day. But he was clearly not enjoying the case.

She spoke to Aidan several times a day, and he was as lonely and unhappy as she was. She felt like she'd been in New York for a hundred years after two weeks.

"When am I going to see you?" he said mournfully. There was a heat wave in London, and he was sitting in his loft in his underwear, in no mood to do anything. He sounded depressed, and so did she. She was tired of the battles with the estate, and Timmie's war on their litigator. She felt swamped by what she was doing in New York.

"I don't know," Véronique said miserably.

"They're not children, for God's sake," he complained. "Why can't you just leave?"

"I'm trying to help them with the estate, and we have to set up depositions. Timmie hates the litigator, so she's declared war on him. It's all small stuff but it adds up to a giant mess."

"It adds up to our not being together," he said unhappily. "I miss you." Aidan was frustrated and impatient and annoyed by how much time she dedicated to her children, when they seemed to spend none with her. The inequity had struck him from the beginning, and she didn't seem to see it, or even mind. She was used to the lopsided relationship she had with them.

"I miss you, too. I should be able to leave for

Paris in a couple of weeks," she promised. But then what? She couldn't see beyond the next trip. How would they ever have more than that? He had a career in London, she had obligations in New York, and an extended life in Paris and three daughters, who had been her whole life for twenty-nine years. And the question of who fit into whose life, with her and Aidan, wasn't clear yet. "Let's just take this step by step," she tried to say reasonably. Aidan's porcupine quills were showing again. And she was trying to keep him calm, and reassure him, while taking care of what she needed to do in New York.

It was another two weeks of legal calls, meetings with Brian about the lawsuit, and talking to Arnold about the resolution of Paul's estate, when she had a quick dinner with Juliette and Timmie at the end of September. Juliette was exhausted from trying to sell the sandwich shop, unsuccessfully so far, and Timmie was looking at buildings in all her spare time, and hadn't found the right one yet. Juliette said she was going to Cape Cod for a weekend to take a break. And Timmie had been invited to the Jersey shore to stay with someone she worked with. And Véronique suddenly realized she was sticking around for nothing. They had no time to see her, had their own lives and plans, and she was there in New York, in case someone needed her. There was no reason to, he was right, they weren't children. She couldn't wait to call Aidan when he woke up.

"I'm done. For now anyway. What are you doing this weekend? I don't know what I'm here for. Let's go to Paris. Do you have time?"

"Do I have time? I've been waiting for you for a month. Get your ass over here. When can you come?"

She thought for a second. "Tomorrow. I'll get organized in the daytime, and take the red-eye. Shall I meet you in Paris?"

"I'll be there!" he said, elated. He had begun to feel as though she didn't exist, and their love affair even less. And she felt that way, too. She had realized that night after talking to her girls that part of her mothering was a habit, and it wasn't as necessary as she liked to think. They liked knowing she was around if they had a problem. But the rest of the time, she was obsolete.

Véronique was excited, too, as she got ready to leave the next day. The girls didn't call her, and she hadn't told them yet that she was leaving. She texted them both at the end of the day: "Going to Paris for a few weeks, love Mom." They were used to it and didn't seem to care, and she had handled a lot of the legal details for them since she'd been back. She texted Brian, too, with her French contact numbers, in case he needed to reach her about the lawsuit. And she got on the plane that night with a broad grin. She could hardly wait to see Aidan. He was arriving an hour before she would, and was going to wait at the airport for her, so they could go into the city together. She was excited about showing him her apartment on the Île St. Louis. It was the perfect counterpart to his loft, unlike her large, serious Fifth Avenue apartment in New York, which was much more daunting, and not as much fun. Paris was where she relaxed, and she was excited to do so with him.

The plane arrived on time, and she was the second person off, and hurried toward customs. She hadn't requested assistance from the airline this time. She wanted to be alone with him when they met. They had been apart for almost four weeks, and it felt like a lifetime.

She saw him the minute she came through the doors from customs at Charles de Gaulle Airport. He was wearing jeans and a black leather jacket as he swept her up in his arms immediately and kissed her. They couldn't move for a few minutes and kept standing there and kissing. And then finally they walked out of the terminal and hailed a cab. She had brought only one suitcase, as she had a full wardrobe in Paris, and Aidan only had a small bag and his camera. He was looking forward to taking pictures in Paris, particularly of her.

"My God, it's so good to see you," he said, smiling at her. "I was beginning to think you were never coming back, and I had imagined you." He looked relieved.

"Me, too." She couldn't even remember what she'd done for all those weeks, but she'd been busy, mostly with Paul's estate. And Bertie's lawsuit had been time-consuming, with all the material he wanted for discovery, from all of them, and her, too.

The drive into the city took half an hour, and the cab stopped along the Seine on the Quai de Béthune, as the Bateaux Mouches drifted by. Aidan instantly lifted his camera and took a shot, and then followed her into the ancient building. As they walked up the stairs, Véronique mentioned that they were crooked because the building was so old. It was a prime location, and she had waited years to find it.

And when they walked into her apartment, the floors had a gentle slope, too, and the view was beautiful and typically Parisian as they looked across the river at the Left Bank.

They set their bags down, and he put his arms around her and held her, smelling her hair, feeling her cheek on his, and just inhaling the beauty of her.

"Would it be rude to ask this soon where the bedroom is?" he asked, grinning at her, and she laughed. She pointed with a smile and a mischievous look, and he carried her into her bedroom and deposited her gently on the bed, sat down next to her, and kissed her. And a moment later, their clothes were on the floor and their bodies wrapped around each other, and all the loneliness and worry of the last few weeks vanished with their lovemaking. It was the perfect homecoming for both of them, and a long time before they lay back, relaxed in her comfortable bed, as he glanced around the room. It was homey and cozy, and very feminine in pale blue silk, but he liked it. She walked around with him then and showed him the living room, her study, the dining room and kitchen, and two small guest rooms where the girls stayed when they came to Paris. And he could see that she loved it, the apartment was perfect for her, and he felt totally at ease there, too.

They sat in her ancient bathtub afterward, planning what they were going to do. She wanted to show him all her favorite places, and he had a few of his own to share with her. They went out for a walk, and had lunch at a restaurant in the Place du Palais Bourbon, and then walked along the Seine for a while, and eventually bought wine and cheese, salami and pâté for that night, to eat in her kitchen, with a fresh baguette. Suddenly everything about her apartment and their life together felt incredibly romantic. And the lights on the Bateaux Mouches lit the Seine as they drifted by that night, while they sat on the couch and ate dinner, and wound up making love again. He couldn't keep his hands off her, and she lay there, looking at him, wondering how she had gotten so lucky. And they slept soundly in her bed that night, as though they had always lived together. Their relationship had a feeling of always been.

Their second day in Paris was even better. They walked to the Grand Palais to see an exhibit, spent some time in the Louvre, walked through the Tuileries, and sat on a bench talking for a long time. It was like every city they'd been in that summer, perfect for them, and their discoveries about each other. And that night they had dinner at Le Voltaire, her favorite bistro in Paris. The food was incredible, and they walked home afterward, looking at Notre Dame all lit up.

"What are you thinking?" he asked her, as they walked along hand in hand.

"How happy I am with you. You're so good to me, Aidan." She was just as good to him, and he was wise enough to know it.

"I told you. It was destiny. We were meant to meet each other. I was meant to meet you in Rome, and save you from a speeding Ferrari, driven by a mad Russian. Actually, I think the kiss under the Bridge of Sighs did it," he said, smiling at her. It had certainly been an unforgettable summer, and they had moved into fall together. They walked back to her apartment, and sat in her study for a while, talking, and then went to bed.

The next morning she got a call from the guardian at her parents' house on the Left Bank. They were having a problem with the roof, and he wanted her to look at it and decide whether they should redo the roof, or patch it and wait another year. About once a year, something like that came up, and she told Aidan over breakfast of café au lait and croissants that she needed to go there.

"You still have your parents' house?" He looked surprised. She had told him but he'd forgotten, and it sounded strange to him, since he knew her father had been dead for thirty years.

"I never had the heart to sell it. I grew up there, and Paul and I stayed there when we were first married. We used it when the children were small. And after the divorce, I stopped using it. Too many sad memories. I thought about staying there when I came to Paris, a few years ago, but then I found this apartment and it's easier and more fun. And the girls like it here better."

"Why don't you sell the house then, if no one uses it?" He looked mystified. There were so many ghosts in her life, and relics of a distant past, too many of which seemed to be painful for her.

"It's too special to sell," Véronique said simply. "My mother inherited it from my grandfather. She left it to my father, for me one day. And I suppose I've been saving it for my girls. I guess they'll sell it. I don't have the heart to. It's a seventeenth-century house on the Left Bank. It's older than the château." She smiled wryly. "And in much better shape. I'm a better proprietor than Paul." She still spent considerable money every year to maintain it. She'd had offers to buy it several times over the years, mostly from wealthy Arabs, and once from an American, but she had no desire to sell it, and doubted she ever would. "Do you want to see it?" she asked him, as they finished breakfast.

"Sure." He was curious about it. It sounded like an interesting old relic to him.

They walked there after breakfast. It was near the Invalides, Napoleon's tomb, on the rue de Varenne. They walked past the Rodin Museum and Matignon and continued down the street. She took out a key, and opened one of the heavy doors, and stepped over the high threshold into an elegant courtyard. The house was a quadrangle, with a part of the house on each side of the square. There was a wing for the guardian, large stables for the carriages, and ahead of them a spectacular house in immaculate condition.

Aidan stopped to look at her as she rang the bell at the guardian's lodge, and the man greeted her warmly when he appeared. She introduced him to Aidan, and they walked toward the main part of the house, and up a short flight of white marble steps that were spotless. Aidan felt as though they were visiting someone, not touring an empty house. And she always felt that way, too. She remembered her parents too well here, and even Paul and her own children.

She took Aidan's hand in her own then, and as soon as Luc, the guardian, opened the door, she led Aidan into the front hall, with original seventeenth-century wood floors, exquisite moldings and boiseries, and a huge chandelier overhead that was covered to protect it. Everything was immaculate and in perfect condition. There were crystal sconces and enormously high ceilings, which had been painted with clouds and angels. She led him through three small sitting rooms into a large living room, looking out at a perfectly manicured garden, filled with flowers and trees in neat designs. There was a formal dining room, where her parents had given grand dinners, and even a ballroom that looked like Versailles.

Upstairs she took him into countless beautiful bedrooms, including her parents', their elegant dressing rooms, and the room she had stayed in as a child. There was a remarkable library still filled with books. And all the furniture was carefully covered. The only thing missing from the walls were the paintings, which she had long since sold or taken to New York, most of which had originally been purchased by her grandfather. There were also seventeenth-century murals, which were still intact, and some of the walls were upholstered in fabrics. It was easily one of the most beautiful houses in Paris.

Aidan hadn't said a word since they entered, and as they sat in her mother's private sitting room, looking at the garden below, she glanced at him and saw how stunned he was.

"It's beautiful, isn't it? Now you can see why I

don't sell the house. I just can't." She was still deeply attached to it, and everything it represented in her life, her childhood, her parents, her marriage, even though she hadn't stayed there in years. And being there, he had understood several things that hadn't been clear to him before, but were now.

"It's a museum," Aidan said in a hushed voice, as Luc waited discreetly for them downstairs. "I can't even imagine living here as a child, or as an adult." The shabby cottage he had grown up in had flashed instantly into his mind. The contrast underscored all the differences between them, like lightning striking his head. He felt dizzy, he was so overwhelmed.

"It's a very special house," Véronique said simply. She didn't say it to brag, she looked at it as home. And it told him who she was. He was floored. She was so modest and unassuming that he had never suspected something like this. And it was equally obvious that she could afford to keep it. Every inch of the house was meticulously maintained. She led him back downstairs then and they went back to the courtyard, as Luc pointed to the roof, explained the problem to her, of rusting gutters and tiles that were coming loose on the mansard. He was afraid of leaks that winter, which they had always avoided until now. But he admitted that it would be an expensive job to replace the roof instead of doing minor repairs. She listened and then nodded.

"I think you should do the full job now," she said firmly. She didn't want to risk the house.

"I thought you'd say that, and I agree," Luc said, nodding. "But I wanted you to decide. It's a lot of money," he told her regretfully.

"So would be repairing the house." He knew that, too, but tried to save her money wherever he could.

Véronique walked Aidan into the garden then, with its fragrant flowers and perfectly arranged flower beds. There was an old swing that her children had used. And with a last glance around, they crossed the courtyard. She thanked Luc, and a few minutes later they left. Aidan looked like he was about to faint. She thought he had fallen in love with the house, and she was pleased. He stood rooted to the sidewalk on the rue de Varenne, and stared at her like someone he'd never met.

"Who are you?" he said, with a panicked expression.

"What do you mean?" She didn't understand his question. It made no sense to her.

"Just that. Who are you that you grew up in a house like that, and can afford to hang on to it forever? Do you know what I grew up in, Véronique? A shack that should have been condemned, with a tiny bedroom for my parents, and a bed on the living room floor for me, and half the time we had nothing to eat because my father drank our grocery money. Our whole house was smaller than one of your bathrooms. What the hell are you doing with me?"

"I love you. I'm sad you grew up that way," she said with pain in her eyes. "I hate all the bad things that happened to you . . . your father . . . your mother dying . . . not just that you were poor. Sad things happened to me, too. It's not about the house. I love the house, and I was lucky to live here, but that doesn't change the fact that we love each other, Aidan." She sounded certain as she said it.

"I don't belong in your world," he said with a grim expression as they started walking down the street. He looked agonized.

"You're not in love with a world, you're in love with a woman, and I'm in love with you. I don't care what you do and don't have."

"I don't want anything from you. Do you understand that?" He stopped walking and was shouting at her and didn't even know it as people stared.

"I know that," she said quietly.

"All this time I thought your ex-husband had the money, and he'd been generous with you. It's your money, isn't it? It was all you . . . this house . . . the château. . . . Was he rich, too?" Aidan was overwrought, and she knew she couldn't do anything to calm him down. "Why didn't you tell me?"

"I thought it would be rude to say I had the money. And to answer your question, he had nothing. And I didn't care. In fact, it became clear later on that that was why he married me. It didn't matter. I loved him, we had three children. Having money doesn't make me who I am."

"Oh, yes it does!" he bellowed at her. "It's a whole lifetime of living like this, of having everything and not knowing how poor people live."

"Why are you punishing me for that? I'm responsible about what I have. I give money to help people. Why is it my fault that my family had money? Why are you blaming me?"

"You should have told me," he snarled at her as they started walking again. "It would never work between us. How could it? And your kids would think I'm after your money."

"They'd figure out eventually that you're not. And I'm not giving up our future for them. They have their lives, I have a right to mine. You're a good person, Aidan. I love you. It's not fair to punish me because I own that house or lived there as a child. Can I only be a good person if I slept on the floor and starved? Why? Do you think you have an exclusive on goodness because you were deprived, and I'm a bad person because my family had money? What does that have to do with us?"

"You can't understand anything about me," he said angrily.

"Then you shouldn't have pushed me out of the way of the Ferrari if I wasn't worth saving, or followed me around Venice. We have a right to this if we want it. It's not about rich people and poor people. It's about two people who love each other, and I don't give a damn if you grew up rich or poor, except that I'm sorry it was painful for you, and I don't care what you have now."

"Of course not. You're rich. Why should you care? You're everything I've hated all my life."

"And what if you were wrong? What if there are bad poor people and good rich people? Now, wouldn't that be a surprise." He didn't answer as he stormed along, and she kept up with him. They were all the way back to her place before he spoke again. He stood outside her apartment building and looked down at her miserably.

"Do you want me to leave?" he offered.

"Of course not. I'm not the one with the problem here. You are. For God's sake, Aidan, grow up. Okay, so I have money. So what? And if you can't love me in spite of that, sod off." He looked at her in amazement then and burst out laughing.

"I can't believe you said that to me. Oh my God! You did it! You told me to sod off." He couldn't stop grinning.

"I'm sorry, but you deserved it." She looked embarrassed.

"Maybe I did. But you've got to admit, it's a hell of a shock to fall in love with a woman and think she's a little rich, and then find out you have a house like that, gave your husband a château, and God knows what else you have and could buy all of Paris if you wanted to."

"Not exactly."

"Well, I wasn't ready for this. And you're so goddamn discreet, I never knew. Other than the hotels you stay at, but so do a lot of people with, I suspect, less money than you."

"That's how it's supposed to be. Discreet. Do you want me to act like Nikolai and wear a gold and diamond watch and have a five-hundred-foot boat?"

"God forbid. And why are you so tough on your kids and make them all work for a living as if none of you had a dime?"

"Because I don't want them to be lazy or spoiled. Whatever they get later is something else. For now, I want them all to have jobs and work hard and live on what they make."

"Do they know about all this?" He waved vaguely toward the house on the other side of the river.

"Of course."

"And that it's your money and not their father's?"

She nodded. "I don't make an issue of it, but they figured it out a long time ago. He was very spoiled."

Aidan was shaking his head as they walked up the crooked stairs, and he collapsed on the couch in her small sitting room. Although comfortable and charming, this was a far cry from the house he had just seen. She was definitely low key about her wealth and didn't show off, even if she lived well.

"I have to think about this," he said, trying to calm down. "I never thought I'd get involved with someone like you. I've never had this problem before. It certainly makes an ass of all my theories for all these years." She nodded at that, and he walked out to the kitchen to get a bottle of wine and poured himself a glass. "You're hard on my nerves," he complained.

"You're not so easy on mine either," she said, looking at him, with all the love she felt for him in her eyes. "I love you, Aidan. For richer or poorer, better or worse. I don't care what either of us has."

"Obviously. It's up to me to say that. I need to think about it. I'll let you know how I feel," he said. Then he leaned over and kissed her hard on the mouth, and before either of them knew what had hit them, they were in her bed and making love more passionately than ever before. There was a frenzy and desperation to it, and they were both out of breath when it was over, and she looked over at him with a small smile.

"Wow . . . you make love to me even better now that you know how rich I am," she teased him, and he grinned.

"Oh, sod off," he said, and kissed her again.

Chapter 18

Véronique and Aidan spent two weeks together in Paris, and after the initial shock of his discoveries about her fortune, he slowly calmed down. It took him a few days, but he started developing a sense of humor about it, which she thought was a good sign. It had been a stunning discovery for him, but the truth was that it changed nothing between them, as Véronique had pointed out to him.

They were devastated to leave each other when they left Paris, but Bertie's lawyer wanted to depose her, she had some things to do, and she needed to get back to New York. She promised to come back in a few weeks. It seemed like an eternity to both of them. Their time together had been idyllic. They went for long walks in the Bois de Boulogne and Bagatelle, went to exhibits they wanted to see, dug through the auction rooms at the Hôtel Drouot, which she introduced him to and he loved. They cooked dinner, went to restaurants, talked for hours, or made love and took naps. He even read poetry to her one night, after they found a book he had always loved at a bookstall along the Seine. There was nothing about any of their time together that didn't work, in spite of the difference in their ages and their backgrounds. It just didn't matter.

They left from Charles de Gaulle at the same time, and he walked her to her gate and kissed her, and waved as she went down the walkway to the plane. He felt as though he had lost his best friend when she left. And he called her on her cell before her plane took off. All he wanted was for her to come back soon, and she promised she would.

He had work to do in London, preparing for another gallery show. And she was busy the moment she got to New York.

On her second day back, Juliette called her. She had sold her sandwich shop and was ecstatic. Now she could leave for France. She was determined to leave in a week. In the end it took her two weeks. Joy and Ron flew in for a meeting with a cosmetics company that wanted Joy to be their face in a national ad campaign for a year that Ron had set up. It was a very big deal, and they were both excited about it. It was looking like a sure thing, and if she got it, they were going to pay her a fortune. And it would catch everyone's attention and further her career.

Joy arrived the night before Juliette left for France. It was a rare opportunity for the three sisters to have dinner together, and they invited Véronique to join them. And Ron had agreed somewhat nervously to have a drink with Véronique to meet her before the girls' dinner. Ron came to the apartment with Joy, and his eyes nearly fell out of his head when he saw her mother's art.

"Holy shit, are those real?" he whispered before Véronique walked in, and Joy nodded, with a grin.

"Most of them were my great-grandfather's," she whispered back. "He was an art dealer." Ron didn't even want to think about the fortune the paintings alone represented, as Véronique walked into the room in slacks and a simple sweater, looking strikingly like Joy. She smiled at the tall handsome man standing next to her daughter. He gazed adoringly at Joy, and then anxiously at her mother. He suddenly felt like an awkward kid in the elegant room as he met Véronique.

"I'm so happy to meet you," Véronique said warmly, and offered him a drink. He wanted a vodka on the rocks but didn't think he should. He hesitated. "How about champagne?" She asked for his help opening a bottle of Cristal in the kitchen. She poured them each a glass and they went back to the living room to sit down. She praised him for how much he was helping Joy with her career, and Joy looked touched—her mother was doing everything she could to put Ron at ease—and slowly he relaxed. He could tell she was a nice woman, with her daughter's best interests at heart. She admitted to having been unhappy about Joy's acting career for several years but said she had finally come around, and was impressed by what he'd done to help.

"And this is only the beginning," he said, smiling at Joy. "She's going to be a big star one day. I'd love to see her get a part where she can use her singing talent, too. And this ad campaign will be great exposure for her. The whole country will see her face for a year." Véronique liked hearing that he respected her singing talent, too, and agreed that Joy had a fabulous voice.

They chatted for an hour and finished the bottle of champagne. Ron had three glasses and had fallen in love with Véronique by the time they had to leave for dinner, and he kissed her on both cheeks when he left them on the street. And Véronique wished him luck at the meeting the next day. He waved as their cab drove away. Véronique turned to Joy with a broad smile.

"I love him. He's smart, honest, his ideas for you are terrific, and he's crazy about you." She was immensely pleased. Joy beamed at her mother.

"He's such a good person, Mom," she said in a voice choked with emotion as her mother hugged her.

"So are you. I'm so proud of you," Véronique said, and meant it.

"Thank you," Joy said with tears in her eyes, and held her mother's hand all the way downtown to the restaurant. It was a rare close moment between them, and Véronique hoped it would be the first of many.

Juliette and Timmie were meeting them at Balthazar in SoHo to celebrate Juliette's departure. Juliette was excited when she arrived for their girls' dinner. She had spoken to Jean-Pierre Flarion half a dozen times to tell him she was coming and wanted to decide what part of the project to tackle first. And she was planning to see Elisabeth and Sophie, on a weekend Sophie would be home from Grenoble.

And Timmie thought she might have found a home for the shelter, and was happy about that. And Joy and Véronique looked like they had a secret. Véronique told them after they ordered that she had just met Ron and loved him. Timmie had met him the night before and liked him, too. "He's a keeper," Véronique confirmed, as Joy agreed.

"You all have great projects under way," Véronique said admiringly. "I think I'm going to go back to painting," she added, and Timmie was surprised.

"Why? You haven't painted in years. Why now?" She acted as though Véronique had said she was going to become a belly dancer in a Moroccan soukh.

"Why not? I have lots of time on my hands. And I saw so much art in Italy this summer, it inspired me." She was excited about it, but they weren't.

"It just seems silly to start a career at your age," Timmie continued. "You don't need to. And if you take portrait commissions, you'll be tied down, and people will be telling you what to do."

"That's true. But I think I'd enjoy it." They all stared at her blankly as she said it. They were ecstatic about what they were doing, and so was she for them, but the idea that she also wanted to be excited about something seemed silly to them. "What do you think I ought to do?"

"Travel a little, relax, see friends," Timmie answered, and Joy added to it. It sounded incredibly boring to Véronique as Timmie outlined the life she should live at only fifty-two.

"Be there for us when we need you," she added. It was honest, and they had never been quite as candid about it, that she should do nothing but wait to hear from them if they needed her. A mother eternally on call, with nothing else to do.

"You guys don't need me very often," she pointed out. "And I need to do more than that. I've been trying to decide for several years what to do, now that you've grown up. And in his will even Daddy thought I should go back to painting. Actually, Nikolai asked me to do a portrait of him the next time he's in New York."

"Watch out for him," Joy warned her, laughing. "He seemed like he had the hots for you when we were on the boat."

"I don't think he does," Véronique said, smiling at them. "But he'd be fun to paint. He has a very expressive face."

"And a very **im**pressive boat," Joy added. They had talked about it for weeks after.

"Thank God you don't need to worry about that, Mom," Juliette said kindly. "You don't need to get married again, or even go out with anyone. You're totally self-sufficient." She meant well, but Véronique found what she said depressing.

"I wouldn't go out with, or marry, someone because I 'needed' to financially. I'd go out with someone, or be with them, because I love them." They looked instantly uncomfortable when she said it.

"Well, you don't need to," Timmie said, dismissing the idea, but Véronique decided to pursue it.

"What if I wanted to? If I fell in love with someone," Véronique said, and all three women stared at her again.

"Like Nikolai?" Joy was shocked.

"No, not Nikolai. Someone. Anyone. What would you all think?"

"We'd think you were crazy," Timmie said instantly. "Why would you want the headache, at your age? Besides, there are no decent guys out there for women your age. They're all married." She had managed to crush all hope in one fell swoop. "There aren't even any decent guys at my age, let alone yours. Besides, Mom, you're better off the way you are, and you have us." The blinding insensitivity of what she'd said took Véronique's breath away. But it was a revelation as well.

"I have you, but you all have busy lives, as it

should be. How often do we talk to each other? Not very often. Once a week? Every ten days? You all want to have partners in your life—why wouldn't I?" They wanted her available to them when they needed her, but not to be bothered with her the rest of the time. And they didn't mind at all that she was alone. In fact, it suited them better.

They looked at her as though she had momentarily lost her mind, and then Joy changed the subject, and they talked about Ron and her meeting for the ad campaign the next day. Juliette rhapsodized about the château. And Timmie talked about her homeless shelter. But the idea of Véronique having a life, or a project, or going back to painting, or meeting a man, was of total indifference to them, and seemed absurd. She was supposed to be chained to a wall, waiting for them, for the rest of her life. It made her realize that to them, she wasn't really a person, she was a thing. An object for their convenience. A service bureau. She was still thinking about it at home that night after dinner. It had depressed her hearing their point of view. Her happiness and well-being were of absolutely no interest to them. And she told Aidan about their conversation when he called.

"Children are an ungrateful lot," he said. "That's why I've never wanted any. I'm sure it doesn't even occur to them that you want someone in your life, don't want to be alone forever, and could be happy with a man."

"They act like I'm a hundred years old," she said, hurt by how insensitive and self-centered they were. She was constantly worried about their happiness, and they never gave a thought to hers.

"No," Aidan said sensibly, "they think you're their mother, who's ageless and timeless, superhuman, and who has no needs of her own. They think they can pull you out of the closet whenever they need you to comfort them or clean up a mess, and then shove you back in when they're finished with you. Kind of like a Hoover," he said, and she laughed at the image of a vacuum cleaner.

"Exactly like that," she agreed. "It was an awful feeling listening to them. They don't care about me at all. It never dawns on them how I feel. They think I'm a machine. They don't even want me to paint, they think it's pointless, why bother?"

"Well, I want you to paint. I think you should go back to doing portraits."

"I've been thinking about it," she said, but didn't mention Nikolai. And she had no idea if he'd actually call her to pursue the commission.

"When are you coming back?" he asked plaintively.

"I don't know yet. Timmie and I have our depositions in the lawsuit." They had taken Juliette's a few days before, before she left for France, and she said it had been a nonevent and the questions were boring. And they were going to do Joy's in L.A., at Brian's request. "As soon as we're finished with the depositions, I can figure out when I'm coming back."

"Soon, please," he said with a wistful voice. He hadn't mentioned his qualms about her fortune since a week before she'd left Paris. She was hoping he would forget about it, or get used to it in time.

After they hung up, she thought about her daughters and what they had said. She didn't see how she could even mention the subject of Aidan if they thought she was so over the hill that she shouldn't be dating, and should stay alone for the rest of her life. What was she supposed to do with that? . . . **oh and by the way . . .** I **have a lover who's eleven years younger than I am, and we never get out of bed. . . .** She couldn't even imagine introducing him to them after what they'd said. And she hated keeping him a secret. But they had expressed very clearly to her that they had no interest in her life, and didn't even think she needed a life, an activity, or a man. Just travel and friends, and them. She knew they loved her, but they never thought about what would be good for her, only for themselves. In that they were not unlike their father, who had only considered himself and what he wanted, all his life. It made for a relationship with them that was entirely a one-way street, which was precisely what she didn't want, but what they had. And they would have been totally horrified if they'd known that she and Aidan were in love. It made her sad to realize that they didn't know her at all, and didn't want to. And they liked knowing she was alone, which made her more accessible for them. It made her even more grateful to have Aidan. She would have been miserable without him if she only had her children. Aidan said that was the nature of all children, but she wasn't so sure.

Véronique's deposition in the lawsuit from Bertie was uneventful, although it took forever. It was five hours, with a brief break for lunch. It took place in Brian McCarthy's offices, in his conference room. Arnold was there to lend moral support she didn't need, and she was very impressed by Brian, and thought he was a very good attorney. He objected in the right places and had instructed her carefully beforehand what not to answer, and how not to fall for Bertie's lawyer's tricks. She was well prepared. They asked her a great many financial questions, and as she told Aidan later, it was boring.

And Timmie's should have been as well. Brian briefed her about what not to say and what to look out for, but Timmie had arrived with an attitude about being there and how inconvenient it was for her. She was busy at work, and had to cancel an appointment with her realtor to see the house again that she liked to make an offer on it. She had asked Brian to change the day of the deposition, and when he couldn't, she was angry at him. And she argued with him about the questions he told her to deflect.

Bertie's lawyer was much harder on her than he

had been on Véronique, and not nearly as polite. And Bertie sat glaring at her evilly throughout. By an hour into it, Timmie was seething, as Bertie's lawyer goaded her. And she complained to Brian that he wasn't objecting fast enough. By the end of the deposition, Brian was livid, Timmie was enraged, and Bertie's lawyer looked pleased. And as soon as they left, Timmie gave Brian a piece of her mind about what he hadn't done, should have done, and said that the whole deposition had been a waste of her time. And he was so furious, he stormed out without saying a word, and she did the same after that.

She was back in her office, looking like she was going to kill someone, when he called. She couldn't believe he had the nerve to call her after the lousy job he'd done.

"I want to make a deal with you," he said, when she answered her office phone. She recognized his voice immediately, and was tempted to hang up. Arnold had already called her and asked her to back down before Brian quit. They needed him for the case, he was the best in the city, and she couldn't ride roughshod over him. And now Brian was calling her himself.

"What deal?" she said tersely.

"I don't know what your issue is with me, if you don't like me personally, are taking it out on me that your half-brother is an asshole, or just hate men.

Or maybe you have some issues with your father. If you do, I'm really sorry. But either we work this out, or I'm done. I would like to see if we can have dinner like two civilized adults, see if we can come to some kind of peaceful resolution here. And if you still hate me as much after dinner, I'll resign from the case. I can't do your family justice the way this is going, and I don't need the aggravation, and neither do you. So what do you say? Dinner? Restaurant of your choice. How about Twenty-one?" It was one of the best restaurants in town, and a favorite of hers.

"What do you care if I like you?" she growled into the phone, startled by his offer. She had actually been enjoying hating him. It gave her a place to vent.

"I'm a nice guy. I don't deserve this. And I don't need the case. I took it as a favor to Arnold. But it's a piss-ant case, no one's going to get decent money out of it, and your half-brother is a jerk. We all know that. As far as I'm concerned, I've already expunged the favor I owed Arnold. It's already been more of a pain in the ass than I need. But I think it's too bad that little shit is rattling sabers at you with his sleazy lawyer. I'd like to help you, but only if we're a team. No team, no case, and I'm out." He'd been very direct with her, and in spite of herself she was impressed.

"I'm sorry. I guess I got carried away today. It's

just such a waste of time, and it blew my whole day. My clients need me, and I had some other things to do." She had a client who'd just been admitted to a mental hospital after a suicide attempt and Timmie had wanted to visit her.

"So did I. And depositions are like that. They waste everyone's time. Your mother's was even longer than yours."

"She has nothing else to do," she said dismissively, which he didn't think was nice. Timmie was just a very tough woman, and seemed to be mad at the world.

"So are we on for dinner?" It was a decent offer, and she couldn't imagine why he'd want to have dinner with her after what she said. She hesitated, and then figured why not.

"Okay. Twenty-one. When?" She didn't bother to say thank you.

"How about tomorrow night?"

She was free. "Fine."

"And I quit at the end of dinner if you like. You decide."

"That's pretty brave of you," she said sounding a little softer.

"I'm a brave man. I've been through worse. I'm not afraid to get fired. Even after I pick up the check." He laughed.

"I'll tell you what, if I still hate you, I'll pay for dinner," she offered.

"That's not the deal," he reminded her. "I pay for

dinner, you tell me if you want me to quit. Easy peasy."

"I don't hate you," she said, embarrassed. "I just get pissed. I hate wasting my time. And I do hate Bertie."

"He deserves it. I don't. Either way this is a win-win, and we can be friends. If you keep me on, we're a team. If you want me to quit, it'll save us the energy of a war, and we can be friends. I don't actually care if I get fired. It's a good deal." And also a very creative suggestion. She was impressed. "Do you want me to pick you up? Where do you live?"

"Downtown. I'll take a cab." He didn't tell her that he lived downtown, too, in Tribeca. She sounded definite about wanting to get there under her own steam.

She didn't mention his invitation to anyone. And the next day she was at Twenty-one at seven-thirty, as agreed. He was waiting at the bar, and drinking a bullshot. It looked good, and she ordered one, too. She'd had a long day, she'd visited her client in the psych ward, and had learned that morning that one of her favorite clients had killed himself the night before. They'd gotten him off the streets a dozen times, and he always bounced back. This time they had found him good housing, and he was so lonely for the streets that he hanged himself. She dealt with tragedies like it all the time. But she really liked the man who died. She thought about canceling dinner, but decided to come anyway. The bullshot helped, a little.

"Tough day?" Brian asked her. He could see it in her eyes.

"Very." She smiled at him, and decided she'd tell him about it when they sat down to dinner.

"I don't know how you do what you do. My job is bad enough. My mother is a psychiatrist—she deals with teen suicide as her specialty. It would kill me. And she's actually a very upbeat person."

"How did she get into that?"

"She had a twin sister who committed suicide when they were fifteen. This is her way of giving back. What about you? Why the homeless?"

"I did an internship at a homeless shelter when I was in grad school, and I got hooked."

"Where did you go to school?" he asked, curious about her, still trying to figure out why she was such an angry person, as they went to their table and sat down.

"Princeton undergrad, and I got my MSW at Columbia. I know you went to Harvard," she said admiringly, starting to relax a little. He was obviously a bright guy.

"God knows how. I had shit grades till law school, and then I did okay. All I wanted to do was play sports. Being at school was the price I had to pay to play football. It took me years to figure out that there were other things in life, like girls, and jobs where you don't get stomped to death and can use your brain, like the law maybe. I've always been a jock," he confessed. He had the body for it.

"Still?" She looked surprised.

"Not really. I gave up my knees to college football. Now I ski, play tennis, fool around. No time."

"I know that one. I used to have a life. Now I work eighty or ninety hours a week. It keeps me out of trouble."

"That sounds a little tough," he said sympathetically.

"So is being homeless." And then she told him about the shelter she wanted to start, with the bequest from her father, and the house she was looking at on the West Side. "I think I want to do it for women and girls," she said cautiously, "but I'm not sure. They just don't survive on the streets. It's too rough physically. I can keep some of the guys going, but I watch the women go down the tubes every day." He nodded. She clearly had a heart, but there was so much barbed wire around it. He was surprised to find he liked her in spite of himself.

They had a nice dinner, and she relaxed progressively as they talked about art, music, the things they liked to do in their spare time, when they had any. It sounded like he worked as hard as she did. And after a few glasses of wine, he admitted that he had broken up with a girlfriend the year before. They had lived together for five years.

"What happened?" Timmie asked him.

"She married my best friend from college. Apparently, he's more fun than I am, and doesn't work as hard. He's a chiropractor for the New York Mets. He gave me free passes, and I kept giving them to her. So there you have it. We all have our little stories. Now I'm solo again, which is just as well. I don't have time to date."

"Me neither," Timmie said firmly, and then unwound a little. "I broke an engagement two years ago. He cheated on me, and the guy before him cheated with my best friend. I figured I'd quit while I was ahead. Two strikes, I'm out."

"Nah," he said, looking at her kindly, "you just need to fire the players and get new ones. You've got to clean up the team sometimes, not give up the game. We all make mistakes." He smiled at her, as he realized how pretty she was when she wasn't angry. She was a beautiful woman, although he'd been blown away by her mother, whom he thought was a knockout, and incredibly nice. It was hard to believe they were related, but he didn't say that to Timmie.

"I haven't had a date in two years," Timmie admitted, "and I don't want one."

"That doesn't make sense, at your age," he said, looking at her, but it explained her anger. She was wounded, and hadn't healed. "You've got to get back in the game." He paid the check and smiled at her. "So what'll it be? Do I quit?" She smiled back at him.

"I had a nice time," she said, looking softer than she had all night.

"Me, too. That's beside the point. Am I fired?"

"Maybe not," she said sheepishly.

"Good, because either way I'd like to ask you out to dinner again. We can bitch about how hard we work, and whine about our nonexistent love lives because of the cheaters in our past." He made a face then. "Come to think of it, that sounds awful. Let's just have a good time and find something else to talk about."

"Thank you for dinner," she said as they left the table and walked outside.

"Thank you for not firing me. Do you want a lift? I live in Tribeca." She nodded, and in the taxi they talked about the Mets and their prospects for next year. He was good company and easy to be with. And he was right. He was a nice guy. Timmie thought so, too. He dropped her off in the West Village, and kept the cab waiting for a few minutes so he could talk to her. "Do you have a dog?" he asked, and she looked puzzled and shook her head.

"No. Why?"

"Neither do I. That's too bad. We could walk our dogs together." She laughed at what he'd said. She had really enjoyed the evening with him.

She smiled at him. "I had fun."

"So did I. I was sure you'd fire me after dinner." He grinned at her and walked her to her door, and then he got back in the cab and waved. It was the nicest evening she'd had in years. She was still smiling to herself as she walked upstairs, and so was he when the cab dropped him off in Tribeca. The evening had been a home run for them both.

Chapter 19

When Juliette landed at the Nice airport, she rented a car and drove to St. Paul de Vence. She had booked a room at thc hotel there and wanted to look for a small house, where she could live until the château was habitable, which wouldn't be for a while. The realtor who had appraised the château for her was already looking for her, and she stopped at Elisabeth's office on the way to the hotel. Sophie was just getting out of the car with groceries and looked pleased to see her.

"You're back!" She acted as if they were old friends, and Juliette hugged her warmly. She felt a strange bond to her, as though she were another link to their father, a legacy he had left her.

"I'm glad you're home for the weekend. I wanted to see you."

"I try to come home when I can to see my mother."

They walked into the small house, and Elisabeth was pleased to see Juliette, and convinced her to stay for dinner. She was making pot au feu, which Juliette loved. And Sophie said her mother made the best **hachis Parmentier** and **confit de canard** in the village. **Hachis Parmentier** was mashed potatoes with leftover ground meat, or duck, and was great on winter nights.

They chatted over dinner, and Juliette finally left them and drove to the hotel. She was so tired by then, from the flight and the excitement, that she fell into bed and was asleep instantly. But the three women had had a lovely evening. And Sophie had proudly said that she had a new wardrobe for school with some of the money Juliette had paid for her share of the château. And Juliette noticed they had new curtains. It gave them a few niceties they didn't have before and security they hadn't had.

And the next morning Juliette called Jean-Pierre and went to his office to look at the plans he'd been working on. He had designed a whole new kitchen for her, that he swore wouldn't be expensive to install. They were going to get the cabinets from IKEA and use old barn wood for the floor. He sat back and smiled at her, after she'd looked everything over and approved.

"I was afraid you'd change your mind," he admitted.

"Of course not." She was surprised that he'd think that. "I just had to get organized and sell my bakery. I got a decent price for it," she said, relieved. "And I sold some old equipment I had in storage." She had gathered every penny she could for the work on the château.

They had lunch together, and ate **socca** again, and then drove to the château to go over their plans. He said he could get started in a week. And two days later the realtor called her about a little cottage he had found her in Biot that she could rent for very little until she moved into the château. She and Jean-Pierre looked at it together, and he approved. It was only a few miles from where he lived, and he said it was a good area where she would be safe.

And on Sunday night, before Sophie left for Grenoble, she took him to dinner at the Marniers, and Elisabeth made her famous **hachis Parmentier.** Jean-Pierre had three helpings and Juliette had two, and she gave Sophie a hug when they left, and told her to stay in touch. They promised to text and e-mail.

"I like your friends," Jean-Pierre said as he drove her home.

She hesitated for a moment and then looked at him shyly. "They're not friends. She's my sister, or half-sister. Her mother and my father were . . ." She hesitated, and he nodded that he understood. "I didn't find out until after he died. I like them, too."

"It's nice that you can visit with them like that." Juliette nodded. She thought so, too. "It happens a lot here," he commented. "It always has. The king's court was full of love children, and people who were really the son or daughter of someone else. French people are complicated," he said with a smile. "But your father wasn't French."

"My mother is half French. Her mother was French. And her grandparents."

"Then you're French," he said with a warm look. "We have strong genes." And she had certainly felt the pull to come and live in France, she wasn't sure why. But he was glad she had. He dropped her off at the cottage and told her he would see her the next day. He was excited to work on the château and help her turn it into a hotel, and he could tell how much it meant to her. It still felt like destiny to him that she had come to St. Paul de Vence.

Joy had her audition with the ad agency for the cosmetics company the day Juliette left for France, and Joy called her mother afterward to tell her it had gone well. She was hoping to get the campaign, and Ron thought she would. She had looked gorgeous at the interview. She sounded very excited about it, and they were leaving for L.A. that night.

"Well, let me know what happens," Véronique told her. She could see that Ron was helping her with her career and how supportive he was. Joy seemed much more confident than before, and he wouldn't let her waste her time on things he thought wouldn't bear fruit. Her agent was much more willing to have her try out for everything. Ron wanted her to pick and choose. And if she got the national ad campaign, it would be a turning point in her career and fantastic publicity. Véronique couldn't help thinking that Paul had given each of them a way of achieving their dreams, even those they didn't know they had, like Juliette turning the château into a hotel.

She still felt sorry for Bertie and how angry he was, and she hoped he'd get over it and make something of his life. The girls all seemed to be headed in the right direction, in ways that were meaningful to them.

She was sad knowing that both Joy and Juliette had left New York, but she didn't say anything to Aidan about it. She knew he already thought she was too attached to her kids, given how old they were. And they were visibly less attached to her, which was normal at their ages. She was still somewhat hurt that they didn't think she should bother painting anymore, after all these years. And that they didn't think she deserved to have a man in her life. But she had Aidan, whether they knew it or not, so it didn't matter.

And the next morning Nikolai called her. He was in New York and said he wanted to see her.

"When do we start?" he asked her, in his deep voice and heavy accent.

"Start what?" She knew he couldn't have romance

in mind. She was way too old for him, given who he went out with, and the girl she'd seen banished to the bedroom in Rome.

"Your commission. My portrait."

"You're serious?" She was shocked.

"Of course. I commissioned you on the boat, when you and your daughters came for dinner."

"Nikolai, I haven't painted in years. You might hate it."

"I trust you. When do we start?" he repeated. She didn't even have art supplies anymore. "I have time tomorrow. I'm in New York for four days." She was thinking frantically while he talked.

"We can get started. I'll take some photographs and videos, and I can finish it afterward." Four days might be enough to lay in the groundwork, and then she could work on it in her own time. "Okay. I'll get organized. Tomorrow at ten?"

"Perfect. And then we have lunch. Yes?"

"Yes." She sounded breathless. She couldn't believe she had actually said yes to doing a portrait of Nikolai. What if she had lost her touch?

She raced out to the art store, bought the oil paints she needed, a canvas she thought might be the right size, and an easel, turpentine, and brushes, all the tools of a trade she had abandoned years before. She felt rusty and nervous, and foolish as she got it all together, took it home, and set it up in her kitchen, where she thought there was the best light, and then dragged a comfortable chair in for him to sit in.

She didn't say a word about it to Aidan that night, because it was Nikolai, although she was excited to do it, and Aidan could hear it in her voice.

"You're up to mischief. I can tell," he accused her good-humoredly, but he was relieved that she wasn't down about her daughters leaving town. She had no plans to see either for a long time, and he knew that Timmie wasn't particularly attentive or warm. He didn't like how solitary Véronique was when she wasn't with him.

"I'm just playing around with some art supplies," she said vaguely. "I got them this morning."

"It's about time. Well, get started." He was busy working on his next show, so he was occupied, too.

She followed his advice, feeling slightly guilty about not telling Aidan the whole truth, and Nikolai arrived at ten o'clock sharp the next morning. She gave him coffee and settled him in the chair in her kitchen after he gave her a bear hug. And she was surprised by how well it went as she sketched, and took some photographs and a video of him, and told him to move around freely as they talked so she could see all the angles of his face and find the one she liked best. And they had agreed that it would be a three-quarter portrait, and he liked the size. He said it was just what he wanted. And she was astounded at how quickly her nervousness dispelled and she got absorbed in the work. She was sketching the underlay, and made some rough sketches on a pad, which she showed him when they stopped.

"Very good," he said, nodding his approval, and then he told her he had made a reservation at La Grenouille for lunch, which was one of the most elegant restaurants in New York.

She scrubbed her hands and changed quickly into a chic black Chanel suit when she finished sketching. His car was waiting downstairs. They sped down Fifth Avenue to Fifty-second Street between Fifth and Madison, and she had a delightful lunch with him, while chatting and talking about art, and his portrait and his remarkable boat. He was flying to another of his boats shortly, which he kept in the South Pacific. But he said it was smaller than the one she'd been on. He was remarkably easy company and fun to talk to, and after lunch, she went home and worked on the sketches again, and refined what she'd done that morning. They were off to a good start.

He came back the next morning, and she still hadn't told Aidan about it, only that she was painting and enjoying it, but she didn't want to upset him and tell him it was a portrait of Nikolai. They worked for three hours that day, two hours on the third day, and on the last day he only had an hour to spend with her, but she took another video and more photographs, and she was satisfied that she had all she needed. She didn't need more of his time.

"You tell me when you're finished, and I'll tell you where to send it. Hundred thousand dollars?" he asked her, pulling out his checkbook, and she objected immediately.

"No, no. Ten. Five. Don't be silly. And don't pay me anything now. See if you like it first. I'll send you photographs of it when I'm finished."

"Ten thousand is not enough," he said sternly. "You are a fine artist, not street artist," he said, and she laughed.

"We'll figure it out later," she said kindly. "You may hate it."

"I don't think so," he said, looking at her sketches before he left. "I like very much."

"Thank you, Nikolai." He hugged her again and was gone, and for the next three days, she worked furiously on it, while the memory of the portrait sittings was fresh in her mind, and then she found that she didn't have an ochre color she needed for the base. She had forgotten it because it had been so long since she'd painted.

She went back to the art supply store a little while later and bought that and another color she had always liked to warm skin tones, and she added a few more brushes. She was thinking about his portrait as she stepped off the curb to hail a cab to go home. Out of the corner of her eye, she saw something whiz toward her at full speed, and before she knew what had happened, a bicycle messenger had hit her, and she went flying and crashed to the sidewalk, as her package sailed through the air. Someone screamed when they saw her get hit. The cab she had hailed screeched to a stop, and the driver jumped out to help her. Someone else picked up her handbag and her package and set them down next to her, as Véronique lay on the ground and looked at the messenger and cabdriver in confusion. She was aware of tremendous pain in her left shoulder, but she didn't know where it was coming from, and she couldn't move when she tried to sit up. The cabdriver could see that she was hurt and told someone in the gathering crowd of onlookers to call 911. The messenger looked panicked.

"I didn't see you step off the curb," he said, but her head was spinning, and she couldn't focus on him, as the cabdriver told her not to try to get up. She couldn't have anyway. Her whole left side felt like it was broken in a million pieces, and then she heard sirens, and felt herself being lifted onto a stretcher, and the sirens were even louder as they sped through the streets, and a paramedic took her blood pressure and put an oxygen mask on her face.

"You're going to be okay," he said gently, but he had already noticed her arm at an odd angle, and her foot, and he knew there were broken bones. Véronique was mortally embarrassed when she threw up.

They took her to Lenox Hill Hospital, and

checked her into the emergency room. The paramedics stayed to fill out the paperwork, and a nurse asked her a long list of questions about her insurance, her age, if she wore dentures or glasses, her religious preference, if she had any allergies, and was she on medication.

"I think I hurt my hand," she said with a groan, "or my neck. Everything hurts." They put a warm blanket on her and told her a doctor would see her very soon. They didn't want to give her anything for the pain until he did, and she just lay there in agony, wondering how it had happened. She hadn't seen the boy who hit her until he did. She felt stupid and sick and was in terrible pain.

"Is there anyone you'd like us to call?" the nurse asked her, and she would have liked to call Aidan, but she didn't want to scare him. She thought of Timmie, but she didn't want to upset her at work, and how bad could it be? She wasn't dying, she was just hurting. She thought maybe she'd sprained her wrist.

She tried to doze so she didn't throw up again, and a doctor came in and woke her up, asked her what had happened, and then examined her. They X-rayed her entire left side, and then he told her the bad news.

"Well, it could have been a lot worse," he said philosophically. "He could have knocked you into the street, and you'd have been hit by a car, or hit your head on the sidewalk. You've got a broken ankle and a broken wrist. I think we can get by without pins. They're both clean breaks. We're going to put you out for a little while, and put casts on you. You should be okay in about five weeks. Do you live alone?" She nodded, feeling groggy from the shock and the pain. "Then I think we'll keep you here for a couple of days. You'll need to be on crutches, which will be hard with the wrist." She had fallen hard to the pavement but she was right-handed, so she could still manage, and maybe even paint.

They took her up to the orthopedic OR shortly after, ran an IV into her arm, and gave her something to make her sleep, and when she woke up, she was in the recovery room and a nurse in blue pajamas was calling her name, and offering her ice chips.

"How do you feel?" the nurse asked her.

"Kind of woozy," Véronique answered, trying to go back to sleep, but they wanted her to wake up, and the nurse said she could give her something for the pain when she was a little more awake, and then they would take her to a room. She had given them her insurance card in the ER when they asked for it, and they said she could have a private room.

They wheeled her into it two hours later, gave her pain medication, and she lay there feeling stupid and out of it. She kept thinking it must have been her fault, like the Ferrari in Rome, but she knew this was different. She didn't have a choice. The bicycle had hit her before she could even figure out what it was. And she wanted to finish Nikolai's painting, not lie around in a hospital, in pain. She wasn't fully awake until eight o'clock that night, and her wrist and ankle hurt like hell, but she didn't want to be all doped up. And she finally decided that she'd better call Timmie and let her know what happened. Her phone went straight to voice mail, which usually meant she was working, and Véronique didn't want to leave a message that she was in the hospital and worry her. And she didn't want to text, so she just let it go, and decided to call her in the morning.

They offered her more pain medication, and she slept for a few hours after that, and woke up at four in the morning in agony again. They helped her hobble to the bathroom, which was complicated and painful, and harder to manage than she'd expected with one foot and one hand. And she lay in bed afterward, exhausted by the effort, and realized that it was nine in the morning in London, and she could call Aidan. She waited another hour, trying to be brave, and finally got her cell phone out of her purse and called him. He sounded like he was in a busy place when he answered.

"Hi, darling. What are you up to? I'm at the train station, taking some pictures. Can I call you back?" he said cheerfully, and her voice was a croak when she said yes, and that stopped him. "You sound awful. Are you sick? Where are you?" She was trying not to cry then, but it hurt so damn much.

"I had this stupid accident," she said, and her tongue felt three sizes too big in her mouth and like it had sandpaper on it, from the drugs.

"What kind of accident?" he said immediately, his mind racing back to the Ferrari.

"It's nothing . . . it was just so dumb . . . I didn't see it . . . I was hailing a cab at the art store, and a bicycle hit me. I never saw it coming." She sounded vague and like she was having trouble talking, and he was instantly panicked.

"Are you okay? What happened?" But he already knew she wasn't okay from her voice.

"I broke my wrist and my ankle. But they're clean breaks so I'm fine. It could have been worse." And then she didn't mean to, but she started crying. "It's nothing, but it just hurts so damn much. . . . I'll be fine tomorrow." He doubted that that would be the case from the way she sounded, and two broken bones sounded like a lot to him.

"Are you at home?"

"No. They kept me at the hospital." He was less worried about her there, the way she sounded, but he didn't like her being alone.

"Did you call the girls?"

"Joy and Juliette left. They're in France and L.A. I called Timmie, but she's on voice mail, and I didn't want to scare her with a message that I'm in the hospital. I feel so stupid," she said.

"You're not stupid, although you've come down a notch. It's a lot less classy than being hit by a Ferrari," he teased her, and she laughed and felt better just hearing him. "I want you to call Timmie. Tell her to get her ass over there first thing in the morning."

"I'll call her in the morning. I don't want to call her at four a.m."

"Promise me you'll call her. And make them give you something to sleep. Call me when you wake up. Oh, and what hospital are you in?"

"Lenox Hill. I love you," she said, so happy to talk to him.

"I love you, too. Now try and get some sleep." She felt better after talking to him. Things didn't seem as out of control, and she took some more pain medication and slept for a few more hours, and tried Timmie again first thing in the morning. She was still on voice mail, and Véronique left her a message to call her without mentioning the accident, so as not to frighten her. Véronique always felt that she had to be strong for her kids, even though they were no longer children, and could have been helpful to her. But she almost never asked them for help. She couldn't remember the last time she had. She was determined to be self-sufficient and never burden them.

One of the nurses came in a little while later and showed her how to use the crutches, which was tricky since she couldn't use her hand easily, and she couldn't put weight on her left leg. She was exhausted and dizzy when she got back into bed. And

Timmie still hadn't called her back, when Aidan called her in her room.

"How are you feeling?" he asked, deeply concerned about her, but she sounded better and less out of it than the night before.

"I'm okay. The stupid thing really hurts, and it's hard to do the crutches with a broken wrist, but I'll manage." So far she couldn't even go to the bathroom alone, but she didn't tell him that. Standing on one foot, and trying to pull up her underwear with one hand was a juggling act, but she'd have to learn to do it. She made it seem funny when she described it to him, but in reality it wasn't.

"Did you speak to Timmie yet?" He sounded tense.

"No, she's probably busy. She'll see that I called, and she'll call me back."

"For chrissake, will you call her and leave her a message that you're in the hospital? At least she'll come over and help you. Swear to me you'll call her." They talked for a few minutes, and he promised to call in a few hours. She was exhausted, and still in considerable pain.

Timmie saw the two missed calls from her mother and got her message, but she'd been dealing with a crisis since the night before. One of her female clients had been badly beaten by her crack-addicted boyfriend. She'd called Timmie from the street, and Timmie had gone to meet her, taken her to the hospital herself and then called the police. And she'd gone to the shelter where they'd been staying, and got her children taken into foster care. It had taken her till that afternoon, and by then she had clients backed up at her office and rushed in to see them. She wanted to go back to the hospital to see her client, who was still in critical condition and hovering near death. And she had an important staff meeting at six o'clock, to talk about funding, and she had to be there for that. As head of her department, she had to run the meeting. It was one of those days when she felt torn in a hundred directions, and everything she had to do was crucial in some way. She knew she wouldn't have time to call her mother back that day, and sent her a text instead. "Too busy to call. Talk to you tomorrow. Big meeting tonight. Sorry." There was no way to explain the rest by text, and she knew her mother would just want to chat and catch up.

When Véronique saw her text, she didn't want to bug her. There was nothing Timmie could do anyway, and if she had a big meeting that night, she couldn't come over, so there was no point bothering her.

Véronique dozed for a few hours, and then Aidan called again.

"Did she call?"

"She sent me a text. She's busy, and she has a big meeting tonight. I don't want to harass her. I'm okay here." The crunch was going to be when they sent her home, and she hadn't figured that out yet.

She had called Carmina and told her where she was, but Carmina couldn't stay with Véronique, she had children and no one to leave them with at night. She suggested that Véronique get a nurse, but she didn't want one. It was just her ankle and her wrist, she hadn't broken a leg or had open heart surgery, so she didn't want to make a fuss.

"I don't give a fuck about her big meeting. Tell her you're in the hospital," he insisted. "This is what you have kids for. Otherwise why bother?" He had a point. And at his insistence, she finally sent Timmie a text.

"Had stupid accident yesterday. Broke left wrist and ankle. Talk to you soon, love, M." She didn't want to beg for her attention, or pressure her, but at least she had the pertinent information.

This time Timmie responded fairly quickly. "Thank God only your left wrist. Totally swamped today. Will call you tomorrow, love T." Timmie had groaned when she read her mother's text. That was all she needed right now, a complaining invalid to deal with. She'd been dealing with one major crisis after another all day, some of them life-threatening for her clients, and a broken wrist and ankle wasn't going to kill her mother. She wondered if she'd fallen down the stairs somewhere. But whatever it was, she couldn't deal with it right now.

When Aidan called again, Véronique told him, and he was livid. "What's wrong with her? And don't the others ever call you except if they want something? Whenever we're together, they call constantly, wanting your advice about something or your help."

"There's no point calling Joy in L.A. or Juliette in France. They can't do anything to help me anyway. And I'm a grown-up, I'm supposed to be able to take care of myself."

"Some job you're doing of it. One minute you're being run down by a Ferrari, the next by a bicycle. I can't leave you alone for five minutes. And I'm fucking furious at your daughter. With a broken ankle and wrist, she should have called. I don't care how busy she is, that's bullshit."

Véronique wasn't thrilled with it either, but she was realistic. Timmie was not the nurturing kind to come over and nurse her mother. And she dealt with high-pressure situations at work. Juliette would have come immediately, but she was three thousand miles away. And upsetting her over the phone served no purpose. Véronique needed someone to help pull her underpants up, and help put her clothes on—she didn't need sympathy over the phone, although she loved talking to Aidan. But she was the nurturer in the family, her children never had been. They'd never been called on to do that, for her or anyone else, since none of them were married or had kids. They hadn't nursed their father either after the stroke.

"What are you going to do when you go home?" Aidan asked, sounding worried.

"I'll figure it out. I didn't lose an arm or a leg, and I'll only have the casts for five weeks."

"Five weeks? What the hell are you going to do?"

"Hop around on one foot, and use my right hand."

"Would Timmie stay with you? At least she could help you after work."

"I can ask, but I doubt she'll do it. She's busy." Aidan didn't comment, and she sounded tired after a while, and uncomfortable, and he told her to go to sleep.

She spent the rest of the day dozing and watching TV, and the doctor postponed sending her home the next day until she was steadier on her crutches. He thought another day would do it.

Aidan didn't call her that night, and neither did Timmie. And Véronique took a sleeping pill and didn't wake up until Timmie called her at seven o'clock the next morning. She was already in her office, and had been there since six. She couldn't sleep. Her client in the hospital had died at midnight, and the nursing staff had called her to let her know. She felt sick when they told her about it and she was ravaged when she called her mother, but sounded almost normal, just tired.

"Sorry I didn't call you, Mom. It was a zoo here yesterday. So how the hell did it happen?" She tried to focus on her mother's minor accident and not her client's tragic death the night before. Her client had been twenty-three years old and had three kids, whose lives would be ruined now, too, with their mother dead and father in jail. He had been arrested the day before, and would be charged with murder now, so he was gone. Their kids would remain in foster care or a state institution.

"I got hit by a bicycle messenger," Véronique said, feeling stupid all over again.

"Christ, you're lucky he didn't kill you. I know this sounds awful, but I just can't come over today. There's too much going on here." And she wanted to visit her dead client's kids in foster care. "Is Carmina taking care of you?" Timmie sounded faintly patronizing as she said it. The crises she dealt with were so much bigger and more dire.

Véronique sounded sheepish. "I'm at Lenox Hill, learning to use crutches."

"Well, at least you're safe there. I'll come over tomorrow, I promise." Timmie sounded relieved that she was in the hospital. She was safe and alive and didn't need her help to get around.

"I think I'm going home tomorrow," Véronique answered.

"Good. I'll come over this weekend for sure."

Véronique nodded, and was angry at herself when tears filled her eyes. Somehow she had thought that if Timmie knew she was in the hospital, she'd come over. But she was too busy. It made Véronique feel as though no one cared about her, as she lay in bed and stared out the window after they hung up. She wanted to go home now, even if she killed herself in her bathroom. Being in the hospital was worse.

There were tears rolling down her cheeks as a doctor walked into the room, wearing a surgical cap and mask and dark blue surgical pajamas. She assumed he must have just gotten out of surgery, when he came over to the bed to examine her, and Véronique waited to see what he'd say. So far the only thing anyone ever asked her was if she'd been to the bathroom and how she was doing on her crutches. She was feeling sorry for herself when the doctor announced that he was sorry, but they had decided to amputate the arm and leg. Her eyes flew open wide then, and she stared at the doctor and started to laugh in amazement.

"Oh, you shit! I almost believed you." He had pulled the mask down by then, and was kissing her. It was Aidan. "What are you doing here? I love you, thank you for coming!" She had never been as happy to see anyone in her life.

"It was the thing you mentioned about not being able to pull your own underpants up that actually caught my attention. I thought it was only fair that I come over to help you, although I'm much better at pulling them down than up," he said as he took off the surgical cap and stepped out of the pajamas. She was laughing and was thrilled that he was there. "And since your wretched children don't take care of you properly, I thought I would. I would have worn a nurse's costume, but I look like bloody hell in drag." He sat down in the chair next to her, and the loving look that passed between them was worth everything she had just been through. "When can you go home?"

"Tomorrow. But I have to practice on the crutches."

He shared her breakfast with her when it came, and she told him to go to the apartment and settle in. Carmina would be there, and she gave him her keys so he'd have them. She told him to stay in her bedroom. And he left a little while later to clean up after the plane. She called Carmina and told her he was coming, and offered no further explanation.

He called her when he got to the apartment. "All right, I'm not freaking out this time. But I just thought I'd ask. The Renoir and Degas, and all these lovely little pictures you have around the place, I assume they're real and were your grandfather's. Correct?"

"Yes," she said in a small voice, hoping he wouldn't panic again. "Is that okay?"

"No, it's dreadful, and I think you should sell them. Woman, this place is a museum. I still have no idea what you're doing with me. And by the way," he said sternly, "what the hell is that portrait doing in your kitchen?" She realized that the painting she had started of Nikolai had been sitting there when she went to the art store.

"It's a commission. He offered to pay me a hundred thousand dollars."

"Take it," Aidan said, but didn't sound pleased about it. He was still jealous of him.

"I bargained him down to five or ten," she said, laughing, and slightly embarrassed that she hadn't told Aidan sooner.

"You're a real businesswoman. I should be angry at you for not telling me, but since you're an invalid, I'll give you a pass this time. Just don't do it again."

"I won't. But he's harmless. It's just a commission."

"I certainly hope so. If it was more than that, I'd have to kill him." He was joking, but she could hear that he was upset, more about the portrait than her art collection. The house he'd seen in Paris had prepared him. "I like your Paris apartment better, by the way," he added, "it's more human scale and cheerier. This is a bit serious for me. The art is fabulous though." He had taken a tour of her paintings while Carmina watched him with suspicion, afraid he would turn out to be an art thief. She had no idea who he was, but Véronique had given him carte blanche, and he had put his bag down in her bedroom, which said a lot. "I'll be back in a while. Can I bring you anything?" he offered.

"Just you. I'll need clothes to go home in tomorrow. They cut my jeans off when I came in. But we can figure that out tonight."

"I'll be back shortly," he promised, and half an

hour later he was in her hospital room again with a big bouquet of flowers and a huge teddy bear balloon to cheer her up. He had bought the balloon at the hospital gift shop, and it was holding a blue banner that said "It's a Boy!", which made her laugh when she saw it.

"Thank you so much for coming," she said again, and they kissed for a long moment, and a nurse walked in and smiled.

"Well, you're looking a lot happier today," she commented as Véronique beamed. "How are you doing on those crutches?" She hadn't tried them again, and Aidan and the nurse tried to help her get the hang of it, but with the cast on her wrist, and her wrist hurting, it wasn't easy. The nurse suggested she take a wheelchair home, too, which would be safer if she went out.

"I feel a hundred years old," Véronique said, frustrated and annoyed, but she was better than he had feared. She had sounded awful on the phone.

He spent the day with her, and eventually jet lag caught up with him. He lay down next to her on the bed when she made room for him, and he went to sleep while she read a magazine the nurse had brought her. He was sleeping peacefully with his head on her shoulder at six o'clock, when Timmie walked into the room and stared at them. Timmie appeared almost as tired and worn out as her mother. They both had dark circles under their eyes.

"**Who** is that?" Timmie asked, with an outraged expression.

"A friend from London. He flew over to see me," Véronique said, trying to sound calmer than she felt. She felt like a kid who had been caught by her mother, kissing her boyfriend.

"What's he doing in your bed?" Timmie was shocked. She had no idea who he was or why he was sound asleep on her mother's bed.

"He's sleeping. He just got in."

"What the hell is this?" Timmie asked as Aidan woke up and stared at her. He figured out immediately who she was, from the fierce look on her face, and he sat up next to her mother.

"I'm Aidan Smith," he said calmly, "and I came over to take care of your mother, since no one else showed up to do it." He got off Véronique's bed then, stood to his full height, and extended a hand to her as he crossed the room. "I assume you must be Timmie. Rotten luck, this accident," he said coolly. Timmie shook his hand but withdrew hers quickly. She wasn't prepared for Aidan's calm demeanor. Trapped in the bed, Véronique was mildly embarrassed.

"What is going on here?" Timmie asked, sounding like a police sergeant. "Is there something I should know?" She glared at her mother with accusing eyes.

"I don't think so," Aidan answered coolly. "Unless you'd like to explain why you were too busy to see your mother. Your mother was actually fine with it. I, however, found it somewhat distressing. I daresay, she'd have come to the hospital for you." Timmie was so shocked by what he said that she didn't answer for a minute, and the three of them just stared at each other. "I don't have children," he went on, "but if I did, and I were in the hospital with broken bones, I would want them to visit me."

"I had a client crisis. She died in fact, and I had to deal with the hospital, the police, and her children in foster care." Timmie sounded hostile as she said it, and furious at what Aidan said. "And I had an important meeting last night," she added sternly, but he had taken the wind out of her sails. And whoever he was, he was clearly not frightened of her. And it was easy to see that he obviously had a close relationship with her mother. She wondered what she had been up to recently. "You seem to have a life we know nothing about, Mother," Timmie said angrily, and as she said it, she remembered their recent conversation about their mother questioning them about how they would feel if she had a man in her life. Clearly, it had been a loaded question and not as innocent as it appeared. "What have you been doing?" Timmie asked her pointedly.

"Aidan and I have been spending time together since this summer," she said simply. "We met in Rome." She didn't list all the other cities where they'd been, or Timmie would have fainted on the spot, and she looked like she was going to split a gut as it was.

"Is this serious?" Timmie asked her. It wasn't the time or place Véronique would have chosen to answer the question, but she had no choice now. And she didn't want to betray Aidan by denying it. He had come through for her, and she felt she owed it to him to be honest with her daughter.

"It seems to be," Véronique said quietly.

"Nice of you to tell us," Timmie said with fire in her eyes, and she turned around and walked out of the room.

Véronique and Aidan looked at each other, as he stood next to the bed. He could see that Véronique was upset.

"Are you okay?"

"I think I am," she said quietly, as he sat down next to her. "She wouldn't have liked it whenever I told her. I think they like it better when I'm alone. It's easier for them." And they didn't have an audience when they treated her badly or ignored her. Timmie clearly hadn't liked Aidan calling her on not coming to visit sooner. It hadn't been loving or attentive of her, but Véronique knew that was Timmie, and she'd obviously had a crisis to deal with, for her client, which hadn't gone well.

Véronique sent her a text a little while later. "Sorry that was awkward. Thank you for coming to visit. I love you." It was all she wanted to say at the moment.

Timmie called both her sisters the moment she got home. As soon as they each answered the phone, she said, "Mom had an accident, and she has a boyfriend." The difference between Joy and Juliette was evidenced by their reactions. Juliette immediately asked what kind of accident, in a worried tone. And Joy said just as quickly, "Who's the boyfriend?" She told both of them what had happened, and about meeting Aidan at the hospital. Juliette was upset that their mother hadn't called her.

"She probably didn't want to worry you," Timmie said practically. And she told them that Aidan looked younger than their mother, and they seemed to be serious about each other. "He was asleep on her bed when I walked in," she told Joy, "and he gave me shit for not coming sooner."

"You didn't go to see her right away?" Joy asked her, sounding shocked.

"I couldn't. I was too busy yesterday and today. One of my clients got beaten to death by her boyfriend and I had to deal with her kids. And I had to run a staff meeting last night." Timmie sounded faintly embarrassed as she justified it, but at least she hadn't been getting her hair done. She had been dealing with a tragic situation, which her mother was not.

"So how did he get into it?" Joy asked with interest. She would never have suspected it of their mother.

"He flew over from London, to take care of her, he said. I don't know where she's been hiding him, but he's here now, and he doesn't look like he's going anywhere soon."

"He must think we're awful"—Juliette sounded mortified—"with none of us with her. Is she okay?"

"I don't know. I guess so. She has two casts on. I never got to talk to her. I was so pissed off, I walked out."

They had both asked where she was, and Timmie told them Lenox Hill. And both girls called her after talking to Timmie. Neither of them mentioned Aidan, and Véronique smiled at him after she hung up. Both girls had been very sympathetic.

"The jungle drums are beating," she said with amusement.

"Did they say anything about me?" he asked her.

"Not a word."

"I'm sorry I locked horns with Timmie in the first five minutes, but I didn't like her attitude."

"Maybe it's good for her. It wasn't right of her not to come sooner," Véronique conceded. "I'm so glad you're here, though." And then she looked apologetic. "I'm not going to be much fun with these stupid casts on." She could still barely hobble across the room after practicing that day.

"We'll manage," he said with a wicked look.

"That's not what I meant," she laughed at him, and then she lay back against her pillows and grinned.

"Well, welcome to the family, Aidan. You've met Timmie. Now you have to meet the other two."

"I can hardly wait," he said, as he lay on the bed with her again. "It should be interesting, but I'm much more intrigued by their mother."

All three girls had a lot to think about after what Timmie had told them. It was something they never thought they'd have to deal with, a man in their mother's life. And a younger man.

Timmie told Brian about it when they had dinner in her neighborhood that night. It was their second date.

"Does it really surprise you?" He seemed startled that it would. "She's a beautiful woman." And she hardly looked older than her daughters.

"Yes, it does," Timmie admitted. "She's been alone forever. My father always had lots of women. But my mother never had anyone. A few dates here and there, but nothing serious since my father. And she was very devoted to him."

"It sounds like she's due for someone in her life," he said sensibly. "I hope he's a nice guy. She deserves one," he said kindly, and Timmie didn't say a word.

Chapter 20

Timmie went to visit her mother on Sunday afternoon, after calling first. And Aidan opened the door to the apartment. She was chilly with him when she walked in and ignored him after that. They had gotten off on the wrong foot. And she didn't stay long. Véronique was hobbling around on her crutches, and she was still in pain. And Joy and Juliette had called her. But all of them were busy. Joy was learning her lines for the soap she was still on, and they were still waiting to hear about the cosmetics campaign. And Juliette was working on the château with Jean-Pierre. They had had a near disaster on Friday when a plumber doing some welding work had caused a small fire, but fortunately they had put it out before it did too much damage. Still it had unnerved them both, and he was helping her clean up the mess over the weekend. And Elisabeth Marnier had come to help them.

Timmie had made her offer on the house for her shelter, and was waiting for an answer. She told her mother about it when she came to visit, and she looked excited. Aidan left them alone while they talked. And then he came back to walk Timmie out when she left. She gave him an icy look, didn't answer him when he said goodbye, and closed the door sharply behind her.

"She loves me," he said to Véronique with a wry smile. "She's just afraid to show it." She hoped that the two would make peace soon, but Timmie had made no comments about him. She didn't dare. But she was being more careful with her mother, and more respectful. Both Brian's and Aidan's comments had gotten to Timmie. Véronique's accident had shaken them all. It could have been a lot worse.

Véronique and Aidan had played cards and watched movies all weekend, so when Timmie left, he went out for a while with his camera, and was happy when he came back. He said he had gotten some great shots in the park, and he made them a delicious pasta dinner, and afterward he did some work on his computer. He had brought some of his work with him, so he could stay with her in New York as long as she needed him, and after she got her casts off, he wanted her to come to London, and she said she would. It would be December by then. It seemed like a lifetime away as she hobbled around on her crutches.

And on Monday, she got back to work on Nikolai's portrait. Aidan growled every time he walked past it, but he admitted, as she added to it, that it was very good. She was doing a great job, and studying the photographs and videos to help her bring life to it, and learn his expressions. She was meticulous in her work.

She was working on it a week after the accident when Arnold called her, and asked if she'd read the morning paper. She hadn't.

"Bertie was arrested yesterday," he informed her in a somber voice, "for securities fraud. He's going to have much bigger problems now than the estate. If he's convicted, he's going to go to prison. I'm glad Paul didn't live to see it. It would have broken his heart." But they both knew it wouldn't have surprised him. He had always predicted it could happen, and feared it would.

Véronique called Timmie immediately to tell her, and surprisingly Timmie picked up the phone. Brian had already called her. Véronique had assumed he would drop the lawsuit, but Timmie said that Brian thought he might still press for a settlement to pay for his criminal attorney, who would be costly and would not work on contingency.

"Are you on better terms with Brian now?" her mother asked her. Timmie had sounded quite mild about him.

"Actually I am," Timmie said, seeming almost giddy. "He took me out to dinner twice. The first time he told me he'd quit if I still hated him at the end of dinner. We went to Twenty-one, and had a good time, so he didn't quit." Véronique was amazed, and thought it had been a clever tactic. But she knew that Timmie was still on the warpath with Aidan, and Véronique hoped she'd get over it soon. It was hard to fault him, whatever they thought. He was being wonderful to her.

She called Joy and Juliette after that to tell them about Bertie, and neither of them was surprised. He had been rotten and dishonest for too long. It was bound to happen. Véronique commented afterward to Aidan that both girls sounded happy.

"I have a feeling that Juliette is involved with her architect in St. Paul de Vence," she told him. And Joy was happy with Ron. "Timmie just told me she's going out with the litigator." Everybody's life was on track at the moment. Except Bertie, who was headed for prison.

And over the next five weeks, while Aidan kept Véronique company, Timmie remained chilly but civil with him when she visited her mother. Her offer on the house had been accepted, and her shelter project could get under way. And eventually, Véronique got more skillful with her crutches.

Véronique had been worried about Thanksgiving, and the ongoing tension between Aidan and Timmie, but the holiday turned into a nonevent, which kept things simple. Juliette and Joy didn't come home. Timmie volunteered at a crisis center. And Aidan and Véronique were alone. Aidan cooked a chicken, and Véronique made traditional stuffing and everything that went with it, and they shared a quiet, cozy Thanksgiving with each other.

She finished Nikolai's portrait the week before they took off her casts. Even Aidan admitted that it was terrific. She e-mailed Nikolai jpegs of it, and he was thrilled and said it was splendid, and asked her to ship it to London. She sent it to him as a gift, and refused payment for it. She told him it had been a pleasure to do it and had gotten her painting again.

And her casts were finally taken off at last, the day after she shipped the portrait. Aidan took her out to dinner to celebrate, and he asked her that night when they could leave for London. He had been in New York with her for exactly five weeks. He felt completely at home with her there, and even Carmina had come to love him. But he needed to get back to London and work on his show. He had done as much as he could in New York, and had been incredibly patient about it.

"We can go as soon as you want after Christmas, or you can go now and I'll join you right after the holiday," Véronique said gratefully. He'd been wonderful to her. "I need to be here for Christmas but nobody needs me here after that. The girls are all over the place. Timmie's busy. I'm all yours at the end of December," she said with a peaceful look. "Or we can go now, and I'll fly back for Christmas, and come back to Europe right after."

"Music to my ears," he said. And they agreed to go three days later so he could catch up on work. And Véronique planned to return to New York for Christmas with her daughters, which seemed right to her and fair to Aidan.

She had dinner with Timmie before she left, who told her all about the house she'd bought. She was on budget so far. She had just given the foundation where she worked three months' notice, and she admitted that she was seeing a lot of Brian.

"What about you and Aidan?" she asked, looking worried. She still didn't like him, after their unpleasant beginning. But Véronique thought that all three girls were subtly nicer to her now that they knew he existed. Joy and Juliette called her a little more often, and Timmie was less aggressive, and a little more attentive to her mother.

"It seems to work. Very well, in fact," Véronique said quietly. "I think you'd like him if you got to know him, and give him a chance."

"It's weird that he's practically the same age as the man I'm going out with," Timmie said in a plaintive tone. Aidan was two years older than Brian.

"It's not weird. It just is. Our age doesn't seem to matter to either of us," Véronique said simply, with no apology to her daughter. "It works. We're different. We have our own ideas, he lets me be who I am. And he likes me. I'm happy with him." She didn't know how else to describe it. Her relationship with Aidan was easy. And even Timmie had admitted to her sisters that he didn't seem to be after their mother's money. They had all looked at his work online, and he was respected in his field. And Véronique had never been happier. Even her daughters couldn't deny it.

"When are you coming back?" Timmie asked her.

"I'll be home for Christmas," and as she said it Timmie looked sheepish.

"I won't be here, Mom," Timmie said, looking apologetic. "Brian just invited me to Boston. And I'd like to go." Véronique was startled and called Joy and Juliette that night to ask the same question. Joy was going to Saint Barts with Ron over the holidays, but hadn't told her mother yet. And Juliette hated to disappoint her mother, but she wanted to stay in France. So all of her daughters would be away for Christmas, and Véronique could spend it in London or Paris with Aidan. She told him the next morning at breakfast the day before they left.

"If you're expecting me to complain, don't," he said, beaming at her. "How long can you stay in Europe?"

"Maybe a couple of months." She smiled at him. Her girls were all busy and it made her more grateful than ever that he was in her life. She had a real opportunity to build a life with him now, and take time for herself. It was time.

* * *

Aidan and Véronique flew to London, and it felt great to be in his loft again. They were planning to stay there for ten days, so he could catch up, and then go to Paris for Christmas and New Year's and stay at her apartment for a while. And he had set up a corner for her in his apartment to paint if she wanted to. She planned to go to St. Paul de Vence with Aidan for a weekend so she could see Juliette's progress on the château, and meet Jean-Pierre. Apparently romance was blossoming at a rapid rate there, too.

They'd been back in London for a week, settling in, when Véronique got a call on her cell phone from Brother Tommaso in Venice right before Christmas. He said that he had an interesting provenance to discuss with her, but first he wanted her to send the painting. He promised to call her again as soon as he had seen it. She called Arnold immediately, and asked him to send it to Venice.

"What was that about?" Aidan asked her when she hung up.

"I don't know. Brother Tommaso said he has an interesting provenance to tell me about. He wants to see the painting now, so I had Arnold ship it to him. I can hardly wait for him to tell us."

* * *

They spent Christmas at Véronique's apartment in Paris, just the two of them, and went to Christmas mass at Notre Dame. And New Year's Eve with Juliette in St. Paul de Vence, with Jean-Pierre. Véronique and Aidan both loved him, and the château was coming along faster than Véronique expected. And they spent January at her apartment in Paris. Brother Tommaso called them again in mid-January, and he asked Véronique to come to Venice. The painting had arrived safely, and he had examined it carefully. Aidan said it was like waiting to find out if they'd won the lottery, but he'd caught up on his work, and was willing to accompany her to Venice. They flew down on a Friday afternoon, and arrived at the monastery at four o'clock, as the brothers were going into the chapel for their evening service. It was a sunny winter day, and Venice looked more beautiful than ever.

Brother Tommaso was waiting for them in the library where he had first met them, and the Bellini was standing on an easel. He got up from his desk immediately to greet them, and say how happy he was to see them.

"I have had a wonderful time researching your painting," he told Véronique, and then picked up a pointer and moved it, showing them important details that he had used to ascertain its veracity once he saw it.

Aidan couldn't stand the suspense any longer and asked him, "Is it a real Bellini?"

Brother Tommaso looked at them both seriously, and gave them an answer they didn't expect. "Is it a Jacopo Bellini? No, it's not." Véronique's heart sank a little as he said it, but she wasn't surprised. She had always doubted its veracity, and she'd been right. "I researched it carefully since I last saw you, determined to attribute it to Bellini the father, Jacopo, and I simply could not do it. But my research led me to a very interesting painting that belonged to the first Earl of Dudley at the end of the nineteenth century.

"The painting was last exhibited publicly in 1955, and then surfaced again fifty-five years later to be sold at auction in 2010. The painting is called **The Madonna and Child in a Landscape,** and it was painted by Giovanni Bellini, Jacopo's son. Once I traced that painting, I was absolutely certain that your painting is the work of Giovanni, and not his father as I first thought. So you have a Giovanni Bellini, my dear, not a Jacopo. I have no question of it."

Both Aidan and Véronique looked impressed by how thorough he had been and the end result. And then he added, almost as an afterthought, "Perhaps that it is a painting by Giovanni Bellini and not his father will be good news for you as well. Jacopo's work sells for somewhere between twenty and a hundred thousand dollars in today's art market. The painting by Giovanni Bellini that I mentioned sold for over five million dollars at Sotheby's in 2010.

And your painting is a rare treasure and might sell for even more." They both looked stunned by what he said.

"And the provenance is almost as remarkable as the artist," he continued. "I found a record of it in some very old art books that we had in the library. First only a description of it, and then later it surfaced in two different editions. It was purchased by a French family here in Venice, at the turn of the century, and they took it to France with them. The one thing I do not know is how it found its way back here, when you bought it. But it had a long journey in between, and not always a happy one. The family that bought it were French bankers, by the name of Berger-Cohen, and it hung in their Paris home for many years. It passed to one of their children, their oldest son, I believe, in 1918. And it was in his possession until 1940.

"In 1940, we lost track of the piece completely. It simply disappeared. But we were able to trace the family to their sad fate. All of the Berger-Cohens were sent to labor camps in Germany during the Occupation of Paris, and to the best of our knowledge, none survived. They had a very extensive art collection, and pieces of it have surfaced in various places over the years. In Germany, in England, one in France, several in South America. All but a few have been placed in museums, because of their importance.

"And now this one has appeared. Somehow, it

found its way back to Venice and you bought it. We can only believe that it was taken with the rest of the Berger-Cohens' collection by the Nazis when they sent them away. Clearly, the dealer who sold it to you so many years ago had no idea what a treasure he had in his possession, given how little you paid for it. And now, my dear," he said, looking at Véronique, "you have a great, great treasure in your collection. You must cherish it and take good care of it. It truly belongs in a museum." The three of them stood looking at it in respectful silence for a long moment, and then Véronique turned to Brother Tommaso.

"But what about the Berger-Cohens? They all died in the camps?"

"I believe so. The painting obviously fell into German hands when they were taken. Sometimes it is easier to trace a work of art than a person. But from what I read, they all disappeared." He looked respectful as he said it, and Véronique was pensive. It was such a sad story, and she felt guilty now owning a painting that had come to them in such an unhappy way. She thanked Brother Tommaso profusely for his research, and wrote a very handsome check to the monastery, and another to his private intention, for him and not the charity, and he kissed her on both cheeks. She asked him if he would keep the painting until she could arrange for shipment back to New York, and they left the monastery with the documents he had given her.

She didn't say anything to Aidan as they walked back to the hotel. They were staying at the Danieli in the city this time.

"What are you thinking?" Aidan asked her, as they walked away from San Gregorio. He had expected her to be overjoyed and she wasn't. She was strangely silent, and he sensed something heavy on her mind.

"I was thinking about the Berger-Cohens, and what happened to them." The painting made the Holocaust even more real than the museum in Berlin. Aidan nodded, and he could see how upset she was. "Maybe we could see if there is a member of the family still alive in Paris."

"That was seventy-five years ago," Aidan said gently. "Even if one of them did survive and returned from the camps, they'd be dead by now." She nodded, and they walked back to the hotel in somber silence. And she was very quiet that night. They went to their favorite trattoria, but it was less lively at this time of year and Véronique looked distracted and sad.

And she was still strangely silent when they left Venice the next day. The painting had turned out to be worth a fortune, but she didn't seem to care. She felt no better than one of the Nazis who had taken it. And she told Aidan that she felt as though, owning it, there was blood on her hands.

"They're all gone now," he told her reasonably. "You might as well enjoy it. It's a beautiful painting, like the ones your grandfather left you. And your ex-husband wanted you to have it, as a gift to you."

"None of my grandfather's paintings were stolen from people who went to labor camps," she said sadly, and he didn't argue with her. He could see there was no point. And she quietly went to work on her computer when they got back to her apartment in Paris. She sat there all afternoon and all night, and came to bed long after he was asleep.

And she went back to work on it the next morning and for several days. Four days later, she had culled three names from the lists she'd pored over. There were thousands of Cohens in Paris, and just as many Bergers. She had found three Berger-Cohens in Paris. She showed the list to Aidan, and called them that afternoon.

The first one was a young woman who said her family was from Alsace and had never lived in Paris. The second one was a young man who said he was a student, and he explained that his parents were Paxed by French law and were never married. His mother was named Berger and his father Cohen, and they had combined the name for him. And at the third number, a young woman answered. She said that her name was Henriette Villier, that François Berger-Cohen was actually her grandfather, and they lived with him in his home, to take care of him, and the phone was listed in his name. She answered the questions as though she thought Véronique was a telemarketer, and seemed surprised when Véronique asked if she might come to see them, as soon as possible.

"Is something wrong?" the young woman asked, sounding scared.

"No. I believe that I may have something that belonged to your grandfather, or his family, a long time ago, and I would like to discuss it with him."

"That's not possible," the young woman said firmly. "His entire family died during the war. He was the only survivor, and all of their possessions were taken—their home and everything they had."

"I know," Véronique said softly. "Will he talk to me?"

"He is eighty-eight years old, and he's not well. He was a boy then. His mind is clear, but he may not remember the item you believe you've found," his granddaughter explained.

"I'll bring him a photograph," Véronique said. She had one on her computer, and could have Aidan print it for her. "May I come tomorrow?" she asked doggedly.

"I have to pick my little boy up from school," Henriette said with a sigh. "Come at five o'clock. But please don't upset him. That was a very sad time for him. He doesn't like to talk about it."

"I promise, I'll do my best not to upset him. I think he will want this, if it belonged to his family, to his parents." They hung up, and she turned to Aidan with a look of wonder in her eyes. "I think

I've found him, one of them. He's eighty-eight years old. So he would have been thirteen then."

"What are you going to do?" Aidan looked worried. She had acted as though she were possessed for the past four days, since they'd been to Venice, and she had heard the story of the provenance from Brother Tommaso.

"I'm going to see him tomorrow. Will you come with me?" He nodded. He couldn't have done anything else. And he knew he had to go with her. Destiny was beckoning again.

Chapter 21

Véronique was anxious all day, waiting for five o'clock to come. They left her apartment at four-thirty and drove to the address in the fifteenth arrondissement, and parked the car across the street. When they got there, they saw that it was a small battered house. It looked as though it had been dignified once, but it had a beaten-down quality to it, and it needed paint and repairs. And the street was not a handsome one.

Aidan stood next to Véronique as she rang the bell. A woman in her early thirties answered the door, wearing a navy skirt and heavy sweater with a little boy standing next to her. There were cooking smells from within, and an aura of genteel poverty as they walked in. There was chipped yellowed linoleum in the front hall, with an old, worn rug over it, and a wheelchair next to the stairs.

Véronique introduced herself and Aidan as they entered. The woman put the little boy in front of the television and turned it on, and with a hesitant look, she took them both upstairs, as though she were afraid this was some kind of scam. Véronique had been so insistent that she had given in—she hoped she wasn't wrong. Some instinct had led her to allow Véronique to come and she sounded sincere and determined on the phone.

Véronique was carrying the photograph of the Bellini in a manila envelope. Her hands were cold, and she was shaking as she followed the woman up the stairs with Aidan right behind her. And Véronique had spoken to Henriette in French.

They walked down a long hall with threadbare carpeting, and the woman opened the door into a small bedroom, where an old man was sitting in a chair with a walker beside him. He was reading, and he looked up as they came in. He was wearing an old outdated suit that had seen better days. But he was clean and neat, and his eyes were clear as he looked at them.

"Pappy, these people have come to see you. They want to talk to you," his granddaughter said, as Véronique smiled at him. He looked at her as though she might be familiar to him, and then imperceptibly he shook his head.

"I don't know you," he said clearly.

"No, monsieur, you don't," Véronique said quietly. "I would like to tell you a story about something I own, and ask you about it." He nodded. He rarely had visitors and welcomed the interruption. He glanced at Aidan, and then nodded at his granddaughter. He was willing. The woman pulled up two narrow chairs for Véronique and Aidan, and she sat down on the bed. There were several small ordinary paintings on the walls, and he had a view of the garden.

Véronique told him of buying a painting in Venice on her honeymoon many years ago. "I gave it away, to my husband in a divorce, and recently the painting came back into my possession. And I have always had questions about it as to its authenticity. It appeared to be a Bellini, or might have been a good copy." He looked at her intently as she explained. "I took it several months ago to a monastery in Venice, wanting to know more about it, and its provenance, and whether it's really a Bellini. If it was, I wanted to leave it to my children. We visited the monastery again last week, and they have traced the painting.

"It belonged to a family in Paris from around 1900, a family by the name of Berger-Cohen. In 1918 it passed to the eldest son of the original owner. And in 1940, the painting disappeared, at the same time the family . . ." She couldn't go on for a minute, and tears filled the old man's eyes. "The family disappeared as well," she said in a choked voice. "The monks believed that none of the family survived, but they didn't know that for sure. I found you via the Internet. I came here to find out if you are part of that family." The old man couldn't speak for a moment as he looked at her and tears ran down his cheeks.

"I was thirteen years old, and after school I went home with one of my friends. I came home late, and my whole family was gone. All of them, four sisters, my parents, my older brother. My sisters were younger than I. They took everyone. Neighbors hid me for a time, but the Nazis found me anyway. I had to go out at night to forage for food, the people who hid me didn't have enough food for me, too. I was sent to a different camp than my parents. None of them survived. I discovered it after the war, the Red Cross helped me.

"I was liberated from the camp I was in by the Americans when I was eighteen. I met my wife there. She was only seventeen then. And we were married a short time later. We came back to Paris. We worked very hard. She had lost all of her family, too. We waited a long time to have children. And this is my granddaughter Henriette. She takes care of me. Her father, my son, lives in Lyon. Our house, that my family was taken from, was in the sixteenth arrondissement. We have never found any of our possessions. I became a teacher, and my wife was a nurse, a very fine woman. She died three years ago."

He pulled his sleeve up as he said it, and showed Véronique and Aidan the faded number tattooed on his arm. It brought it all alive for her, and she nearly felt sick. She could imagine him being sent to the death camp as a boy, and meeting a young girl there, and somehow surviving and finding their way together afterward.

She took the photograph out of the envelope then, and handed it to him. He was silent for a long time, lost in another world.

"It belonged to my grandfather. He left it to my father. It was in our dining room. My mother loved it." He smiled then. "I always thought it was silly, with all those angels." He looked at Véronique, and then at Aidan. "Yes, I remember the painting." His eyes were two limpid pools of grief.

"I was hoping you would, although boys of thirteen don't always notice paintings. All I wanted to know is if it is indeed your family who owned it. I would like to return the painting to you. It belongs with your family, not mine. You are the rightful owner, it was stolen from you. I won't steal it from you again. It is worth a great deal of money now, many million euros. You may want to sell it, for the benefit to you and your family now. If you like, I can introduce you to people who can sell it for you, or you can sell it at auction. It will cause a great deal of excitement in the art world, particularly as it has been authenticated now by a reliable source. I will have it shipped to you if you like, or sent to a dealer directly. You and your family should talk about it and decide what you want to do."

"You want to give it to me?" For a moment he looked confused. It had been an emotional meeting for him, and his granddaughter was sitting on the bed looking stunned. As she realized it wasn't a scam, she wondered if they were angels fallen from heaven. She was crying, too. And so was Véronique, and Aidan's eyes were damp as she touched the old man's hand.

"It belongs to you. Just as it did to your father and grandfather. You are the rightful owner of this painting, with the 'silly angels.'" She smiled through her tears, and so did he.

"Why are you doing this for me?" His voice was shaking.

"Because it's right. It is justice, finally, just a tiny little bit of it, after all these years." It was going to change their lives, although he didn't know it yet. Véronique guessed that it would fetch at least five million dollars or more on the art market, from some extraordinary collector, just like the Giovanni Bellini that had sold at Sotheby's in 2010, as Brother Tommaso had said. It was a very, very rare painting with a fascinating history. "You can have your granddaughter call me, whenever you're ready, and tell me where to send it. It is in Venice with the monks now. They will ship it to you for me."

"My mother would be happy," he said in a quavering voice, and then he kissed Véronique on the cheek. "Thank you. Thank you for giving us back something that belonged to us. All these years, all we had, my wife, and I, were memories."

"And now you have dreams. You can do whatever

you like." She smiled at him, and she and Aidan stood up. They had worn him out, and he had a lot to think about. He pressed Aidan's hand, and she could see that there were tears in his eyes, too. Véronique leaned down and kissed the old man's cheek then. "Goodbye, Mr. Berger-Cohen. Take good care of yourself."

"Goodbye," he said, sounding weak now, "and thank you. My family will be very happy." Happier than he knew or could imagine. That kind of money was hard to visualize, in the context of the life he'd lived since he was a boy, got deported, and lost everything, his family as well. Véronique smiled and left the room, and they followed his granddaughter down the stairs to the front door. Véronique gave her all her contact information on a piece of paper.

"Let me know when you decide what you want to do. It should be sold very prestigiously. I'll be happy to help you do that." The woman looked at her in astonishment.

"I don't know how to thank you," she said in a shaking voice.

"You don't have to. It belongs to him," Véronique said softly, and she and Aidan walked out into the cool air and across the street to the car. Neither of them said anything for a few minutes, and then he stopped her and looked at her.

"I can't believe you just did that." He was thunderstruck by what had just happened.

"It was the right thing to do," she said simply. "It belongs to him, not to me."

"Do you realize what it's worth?" She nodded, and smiled at him. She felt light as air and happier than she'd ever been. "You know, for a rich girl, you are a very, very good person," he said, smiling at her, as he slipped behind the wheel of the car. He pulled Véronique close to him. He had never loved anyone more in his life.

She stood looking out the window at the moonlit Seine that night, thinking of François Berger-Cohen, and of Paul, who had started it with his odd will. He had done more for all of them after his death than he had for anyone in his lifetime. He had given Timmie her homeless shelter. Juliette had the château to turn into a hotel. Joy was on her way with her acting career, with a solid manager and good parts to look forward to. Sophie had been recognized and united with her sisters, and she and her mother had a small nest egg. Bertie had finally been called to order and stopped. François Berger-Cohen had his painting back, and a fortune for his remaining years and his family, as some small compensation for what they'd been through. She was painting again. And each of them had met the person they were meant to, as a result of his gifts. She had met Aidan while pursuing the provenance of the painting he had always insisted was real, and he'd been right. Timmie had Brian, and they were perfectly suited to each other. He was a match for her feisty ways. Juliette had met Jean-Pierre while rebuilding the château, and Joy had a manager who was a good man and loved her. Paul had given each of them what they needed and wanted, and all of their dreams. He had known exactly what each of them needed. His final gifts to them were greater than anything he could have given them while alive. He had created miracles from wherever he landed in heaven, not only for his children, but for her as well.

Aidan had come up behind her while she was looking out the window, and put his arms around her.

"What are you thinking?" he asked her, but he could guess.

"About everything. How well it all turned out." She leaned against him, and felt safe in his arms.

"You did a good day's work today," he said, and then kissed the top of her head. "Come to bed," he whispered, and when they climbed into her comfortable bed, he held her in his arms. He knew he would never forget the look in the old man's eyes when she told him she was giving him the painting, or in hers when she did. It had been an extraordinary gift, just like Paul's precious gifts to all of them.

About the Author

DANIELLE STEEL has been hailed as one of the world's most popular authors, with over 650 million copies of her novels sold. Her many international best sellers include **Undercover, Country, Prodigal Son, Pegasus, A Perfect Life, Power Play, Winners, First Sight, Until the End of Time,** and other highly acclaimed novels. She is also the author of **His Bright Light,** the story of her son Nick Traina's life and death; **A Gift of Hope,** a memoir of her work with the homeless; **Pure Joy,** about the dogs she and her family have loved; and the children's book **Pretty Minnie in Paris.**

daniellesteel.com
Facebook.com/DanielleSteelOfficial
@daniellesteel

LIKE WHAT YOU'VE READ?

If you enjoyed this large print edition of
PRECIOUS GIFTS,
here are a few of Danielle Steel's latest
bestsellers also available in large print.

Undercover
(paperback)
978-0-8041-9498-3
($28.00/$35.00C)

Country
(paperback)
978-0-8041-9463-1
($28.00/$34.00C)

Prodigal Son
(paperback)
978-0-8041-9462-4
($28.00/$34.00C)

Pegasus
(paperback)
978-0-8041-9459-4
($28.00/$32.00C)

Large print books are available wherever books are sold and at many local libraries.

All prices are subject to change. Check with your local retailer for current pricing and availability. For more information on these and other large print titles, visit www.randomhouse.com/largeprint.